The Crystal Needle

By Daniel Peyton

Copywrite © 2011 Daniel Peyton
All rights reserved.
All characters in this book are fictitious, and any resemblance to real persons, living or dead, is coincidental.

This book is dedicated to my mother for helping me smooth out the rough edges and to the EGA, who inspired me to write again. And to my lord and savior Jesus for providing a gift that fills my heart with joy each time I am able to practice it.

A thank you also for Louise Berry for also helping clean and smooth out the book.

The Crystal Needle

Prologue

" I wish to tell you a story. But first I must tell you that there are things in this world that you do not know of, namely, magic and witches. I am a stitching witch, as is my sister. Stitching witches are much like any other good witches, except we have the special talent of needle crafting. When a witch comes of age, she is given a mission in life. All missions are kind and important: We assist those who need our help. The mission my sister and I received was very special. We were to advance the craft of embroidery throughout the world. It became a complicated task, but it was one filled with joy. We were given two needles, one of pure obsidian and the other of pure clear crystal. These needles made our magic more powerful than we could have ever imagined.

We were young during the reign of the Pharaohs in Egypt long ago. Over centuries, we moved from Egypt to Greece to Rome, and further. Where civilization went, we followed. Our one objective was to help keep the art of embroidery alive. Though we are quite powerful, our mission included rules. We were not allowed to use our magic to make major changes to the world. We were unable to bring back life once it was spent. Third, true love is a gift that no magic can alter or create. Last, and most importantly, we were to remain humble and leave the major human affairs to the humans. With these rules and a clear objective we traveled throughout the western world for over three thousand years, finally settling in the new world.

What follows is what happened to my sister and me in the fulfillment of our mission. But the story also involves some very special people who helped me keep you safe so that you could hear this story"

Chapter 1: Your Average Family

The Hendersons were an average family. William Henderson, the father, had an addiction to football in the fall, home improvement in the summer, and working in general. He was a large man with a good figure for one in his late forties. William's mother and father taught him from early on you worked for your living, and though he was left with a large inheritance, he would continue working whenever and wherever he found the chance. Loud and friendly, William was as cuddly as a bear and never imposing. Few people who met Will ever found they didn't immediately like him.

The mother, Marla Henderson, who was a college graduate with an MBA, was a driven woman, but not so much so that she stepped on anyone to get what she wanted. Marla had a strict personality, one that got attention and obedience when necessary. She grew up with a father in the military and a mother who was always willing to follow her husband's career. So, after living in practically every state in the union and some other countries, Marla settled her mind on living in New England. Being the direct woman that she was, she got her way and the family was on its way to their new home in Massachusetts.

Last in the family was their only son, Joseph Henderson, who wasn't your average kid fresh out of high school. Tall and well built, Joseph was a stage performer who started dance lessons before he was out of elementary school. His father wanted his son to be a football star. Joe, on the other hand, was less than interested in organized sports. Just about the only reason he considered joining the football team was for the attention from the girls. Even with their attention he considered it too much of a sacrifice. Joe still practiced dance now and then, and every day he jogged and went through a strength regimen to keep himself in top shape. His only real hobby was stitching, something that neither of his parents are interested in.

As they traveled toward their new home, William was focused on the road, Joe was focused on a stitching project, and Marla was focused on learning about their new hometown.

" Listen, 'Featherville was founded in 1692 during the infamous Witch Trials of nearby Salem. Featherville has maintained several districts which display life as it would have been during its founding.' Hey, honey, you should explore all that. Wouldn't it be fun to get a job as a 'resident'? "

Joe, who wasn't paying much attention, rolled his eyes, " Mom, I don't care about historic New England. I don't see why we are here."

William frowned while looking in the rearview mirror of their minivan, his eyes staring at his son. "Sport, you know that we are coming to build a business. This place is ripe for bed and breakfasts."

" Yeah, just what they need in this economy, more useless wastes of money. Is this why you got an MBA mom, to open some rinky dink little hotel and cook breakfast for strangers?" Joe picked up a skein of thread and cut a length from it.

Marla Henderson turned in her car seat and looked at him, " Joe, don't get all huffy again. We are almost there and I don't want another fight out of you. You should feel lucky that we want you to be part of this. You could be shuffled off to college now that you've graduated from high school. We are giving you time to enjoy being away from school."

Joe, who was stitching on an oriental pattern, didn't even look up at his mother, " Sure, all I ever wanted was to leave Atlanta and go work for my parents in a bed and breakfast."

William started in now. " Well, what do you want to do? There are a lot of schools around New England. Hey, maybe you can get into a college with a good team…"

" Listen, dad, I am not going to play football. I didn't in high school and I'm not going to in college. But, school might be nice, if I had any idea what type of education I want." Joe changed thread colors to match the lotus blossoms he was working on.

" You don't have to worry about it too much right now, dear. You can stay with us for as long as you like. Besides, school costs a lot and you don't want to get started in the wrong direction. That can get so expensive," Marla added.

William let out a grumpy huff, " Yeah, if your mother had her way, you wouldn't go at all. "

" That's enough. We're here!" Marla, who always had the last word, shut her husband up.

They turned off of the highway and drove down the main street of Featherville, Massachusetts.

Compared to the bustling metropolis of Atlanta, this was nothing. This was not the biggest tourist attraction of the area so the streets were less than packed. The main street was kept up in the old English styles, with store fronts that looked centuries out of date. One could tell that it was only a façade, since the advertisements in the windows were for cell phones and free Wi-Fi café's, yet the lamp posts were archaic in appearance, as were the mailboxes, fire hydrants, and some of the costumed residents. Most of the residents took a moment to watch the new car driving down the street.

" Boy, they look thrilled." William waved at a couple crossing the street, who didn't wave back.

Joe looked around the shops, hoping to find a local stitching store. " Hey, I expected to find more witchcraft stuff, you know, with all the stories about this area."

Marla opened up the brochure she had received from the Featherville city council.

" No, it says 'Featherville was founded by refugees of the witch trials and as such, any reminders of that unfortunate event have been quelled, often by the locals.' "

William looked over toward his wife's book, causing the car to swerve slightly. " Salem? But, it's eighty miles away."

Marla looked at the book for an answer to that, but found none. " I guess they wanted to keep their distance."

Joe set down his stitching, " Well, where is this house we are going to work on?"

" Just around the corner." William had been up here several times and had searched Salem and other areas for the best price on a nice old house. He found Featherville by accident and thought it was a perfect location for a bed and breakfast. The price was incredible as well. So he already knew his way around while the others hadn't even been to Featherville yet.

They turned down a dirt road that was marked with an ancient sign, 'Needle Pointe.' This made Joe smile and was the first thing he liked about the area. Down another dirt road was a pair of almost identical houses. They were built in the late 1600's but had a marked Victorian flair. Each had windows that were set with slag glass, with a single round stained glass window at the eave of their roofs. The house on the left had a moon rising in the stained glass, whereas the house on the right had a sun setting in the stained glass. Each house was in dire need of repairs, a lot more than a good coat of paint. Behind the homes was a thicket of trees that bordered a large, dense forest.

" So, which pile of rubble is our new home?" Joseph frowned at the sight of the two buildings.

Marla rolled her eyes. " The one on the left. I didn't know both houses looked the same. Will, who owns the other house?"

" Somebody named Elsabethe; that is all the real estate agent knew. Apparently, both homes belonged to her and she sold this one some years ago to the city. They never used it and it was put back on the market." William slowly stopped the car and put it into park.

Marla quickly unfastened her seatbelt, " Lucky us, they put a very low price tag on it."

" Yeah, lucky us." Joe retorted from the back seat.

The family disembarked from the minivan and walked towards their new home/business. Marla was enchanted with the historic building and all the possibilities that would make it more attractive to tourists. William was on the phone with the movers, who had of course gotten lost. Joe was the last out of the van; holding his stitching in his hand he simply continued with what he had been working on.

ಬ

Inside the seemingly uninhabited house next to them, someone watched out a window, carefully examining her new neighbors.

" Who are they?" A young woman's voice came from behind her.

The woman looked at the young man who was sitting on the front step, packing his stitching into a bag. His whole body expressed his lack of enthusiasm for being there.

" They are a family who plans on fixing up the old place. Yet, I doubt that that young man is very happy to be here. "

There was a pause while both people observed the new neighbors. The younger voice spoke very timidly, " I like that one. He is lonely, so far away from friends."

" Careful, dear. You know how they will react."

There was another pause as they watched the Hendersons unpacking. " I still want to meet them."

ಬ

Several hours passed while the Hendersons worked heartily on their new home. The movers arrived about half an hour after the family found the place. Since then, there had been a deluge of boxes and furniture.

William could not keep from helping the movers, though they said they would rather do the work themselves. Marla started unpacking boxes, for there were a few things that they would need that night, such as dishes and towels. Joe stayed out of the way, sitting out on the wraparound porch. He had found an old handmade bench that was still capable of supporting him while he brooded and stitched.

Joe was cross stitching, or what is normally called counted cross stitch. This is a basic style that is done by simply using a needle and thread to make small x's on fabric according to a pattern. With different colors and hundreds of stitches, a piece comes together into a picture.

" Honey, you don't have to look so grim; it isn't the end of the world." Marla came out, wiping her hands from having washed some dishes for use that evening.

Joe continued stitching on the kimono of a geisha in the pattern. " I don't care; I don't like this place."

" You haven't even given it a chance." Marla scooted him over and sat down.

" What am I supposed to do, just fall in love with it over night? You uprooted me my sophomore year to move to Atlanta and it took me a while to get used to that place. Then we up and move here right after I graduate. It isn't fair." He sounded about ten years younger right then, and even he recognized it. "I'm sorry."

His mom smiled, " Joe, I know what your problem is. It's Jenna."

He frowned and worked out a slip knot that had formed on the back of the project.

"Who?" he said knowing the question was rather silly.

She laughed, "Honey, you can act like an idiot around your father all you want; he is not too bright when it comes to emotional matters. But you cannot do that around me. I know that you and Jenna had a pretty bad break-up and you blame the move for it."

He stopped stitching long enough to look at her directly, "You know, you may be right, but I don't want to talk about it right now."

"Fine, fine." she held up her hands in surrender; then she looked over his shoulder,

"What is that?"

He held his work out to her. It was a very intricate cross stitch project that would form a lovely Japanese Geisha with blooming Lotus flowers all around her. He had only begun, but the work was very impressive, even in its infancy. "Just something to keep my mind busy."

"It's nice. Perhaps it can remind you of the move, in a good way, that is." She tried to cheer him up.

William came up to the porch from the car with a large white bag in his hands.

"Hey, I got lunch."

Marla looked at her watch, "It's five."

"I got dinner. Whatever." He pulled out a wrapped sandwich and handed it to Joe, then he pulled out a whole apple and a small bag of potato chips. "There you go."

"What's this?" Joe smelled the sandwich; it smelled pretty good.

"That's from the little ice cream shop and deli, just around the corner from us. Might be a good place to go once in a while."

" Deli?" Joe opened up the sandwich to find homemade bread with freshly cut ham, fried and dressed with cheddar, onions, tomato and lettuce.

Marla took a sandwich, " Yeah, you know, that place that cuts meat, makes sandwiches and soup, and is part of Americana."

Joe rolled his eyes, " Whatever."

A loud bang could be heard from inside the house. A mover called out for William, who promptly handed the bag to his wife and ran for the door.

Marla set the bag down for a moment, " Joe, you are going to have to lose this negative attitude; it isn't accomplishing anything."

" But…" before he could make another argument, he noticed something out of the corner of his eye.

Out of the trees slunk a strange looking dog. It was an abnormally large dog that seemed to be a wolf, but possibly mixed with some other canine species. Its body was bony thin and sickly looking. Its fur was long in some areas and short in others. Some places seemed bare, though very short fur was there to cover the skin. The longer hair was disgusting to look at, filthy and decayed. Its lips were pulled back slightly, revealing gray gums and blackened teeth. It slowly approached the porch where they were sitting.

Marla jumped up, " Oh, goodness, is she ugly." The immediate response tumbled out of her mouth.

The dog paused at the sudden movement and seemed to frown, though that was a little less obvious on a canine face. She looked right at Marla, then looked at Joseph.

Joe looked at the dog. He was less afraid of the beast. It walked right over to him, its eyes fixed on him with a strange deliberation. " I think it is lost; maybe it belongs to someone around here."

Marla was less convinced, " I don't think so. That looks like some kind of wolf. It could be dangerous."

Joe leaned over slightly, looking at the wolf through the bars along the banister around the porch. "Wild or not, she has very interesting eyes." he looked at the turquoise blue/green eyes, which were very endearing and not the least threatening. " She also looks hungry." he took up the gala apple from where he had set it down.

" Oh, don't feed that thing. It might be dangerous. "

Joseph could not help himself; he liked something about this dog. He held out the apple. The wolf slowly approached the porch and stuck its head between the wide set bars. With only her teeth, she gently took the apple from him. She stopped for a moment and looked at him as though she was thanking him, then slunk away into the trees.

" Joe, what did I tell you?!" Marla let out an annoyed huff.

Joe looked up at his mother, " Don't worry. At least for a moment I wasn't complaining."

Marla held in her exasperation. " Well, if that thing comes back around, don't encourage it by feeding it again. I am going to see if your father still has his rifle." She promptly went inside.

Joe looked toward the trees. Part of him wanted that wolf to come back out, though he wasn't sure why. Another part of him was sure that his mother wouldn't use the rifle on the dog. She couldn't even aim a rubber band and she knew it.

☙

Later, after William finished setting up the beds, Joseph made his way up the stairs to the second floor. The house was two stories with the kitchen, living room, office, and other smaller rooms downstairs. Upstairs were all the bedrooms. There was a master bedroom and four smaller rooms with one restroom down the lone hallway. William planned on turning the three extra rooms upstairs and the two extra rooms downstairs into guest rooms for the paying visitors that would come to the B&B.

Joe noticed the wooden floor was sagging in a lot of places and creaking loudly with each step. He wondered if he were to get up at night, would he accidentally put his foot through to the floor below?

" Hey, dad, do you really expect us to sleep here tonight? This place is in terrible shape." Joe wiped his finger across the wall and gathered enough dust to mistake the lump for a mouse.

William came up the stairs with another box in his arms. " The city assured me that this place was safe for us to stay in. Don't worry. I have some contractors coming in tomorrow morning to check into replacing all the flooring."

" That is, if we survive the night," Joe muttered.

Marla came up after her husband, carrying only the night bag she brought with her toiletries. " Don't worry, honey; think of it as an adventure."

Joe rolled his eyes, which he had been doing all too much recently. " If you wake up and there is a giant hole in my room, check the basement, I might have fallen through."

" Ha. Ha." Marla sarcastically responded. " Just get some sleep. We have a lot of work to do tomorrow. Good night." She patted his face and then proceeded to the master bedroom.

Joe let out a huff and flicked the dust off of his hand and went into his room. To his surprise, the room had possibilities, though it could use a good thorough cleaning. "This old place was built well", he thought to himself. The room was basically a spacious box with a nice window that opened outward over the overhanging roof of the wraparound porch below. His father had graciously brought up all his boxes and set them at the foot of the bed. Marla had found sheets, a blanket, and a pillow and laid them neatly on his dresser for him to use before he went to sleep.

Joe walked over to the bed and tossed his stitching bag on it, then stepped up to the window. Though he might never admit it to his parents, he found the view spectacular. For the last few years his view had been nothing but houses near his home. Now he was looking out over the forest that graced the rolling hills behind their home. At this moment it was dark with clouds gently hanging about the sky. He looked at the roof just below his window; it was flat and wide enough for him possibly to go out and sit.

He returned to looking around his musty room. It was practically empty, save the mounds of dust and some leaves that got in God only knows how. Fortunately there didn't seem to be any spiders or rodents.

Just then a cloud moved outside, allowing in a shaft of moonlight across the floor. It seemed to glint off something buried by decades of dirt. Joe was curious and went over to where the wall met the floor and brushed away some of the dust. There was a picture on the floor that had fallen some time ago and broken against the wood floor. Inside was a deteriorated piece of needlework. Joe recognized the style; it was a blackwork butterfly with hardanger around the outside. He picked it up slowly, but found that the work was stable in his hands, not as disintegrated as he imagined it would be after all these years.

" This is incredible," he commented to himself; this kind of work was beyond what he knew how to do. Most people wouldn't even know what this was nowadays. Whoever lived here before was a great stitcher.

He brushed off the remaining dust and carefully set the piece on top of the dresser. He would study this and even find a way to re-frame it so that it could be saved from any more deterioration. Then he made up his bed and lay down for the first night in his new home.

ଚ

Chapter 2: Meeting the Neighbor

A few days had passed and the family was hard at work revamping the place for commercial use. William was joyously in over his head- so much home improvement and it was all his. Joseph was glad that his father loved to work on these projects. Without them, or any football on television, his father would be like a toddler without toys. Marla had gone into the surrounding areas to check out antique shops. She wanted to furnish the home with period pieces to give the place an historic feeling.

Today, a group of specialized painters were reworking all the walls on the second floor. The bed rooms were emptied of furniture and had mats spread around so that the new hardwood floors weren't spattered with the special colored paint. Another team of insulators were coming soon to check on the walls and attic, to make sure that the place would be warm in winter, and that what was there wouldn't catch fire.

William installed new wiring around the kitchen for modern appliances. The old wiring was dangerous. It hadn't been updated since it was installed in the early nineteen twenties.

Joe sat in the living room with a small towel tied over the lower half of his face, guarded from the smells emanating from all corners of the house. His room was being repainted as well. So he spent his time much like any other day, stitching and being patient.

A light tapping could be heard on the front door. William looked around from the door to the kitchen. " That can't be guests, the place hasn't even had its first advertisement."

Joe rolled his eyes, " Dad, there might be others who wish to greet their new neighbors," he got up and set his stitching aside.

Opening the ancient front door, he found a very kindly looking old woman with a tray of cookies in her hand. He greeted her with a muffled "hello" as he pulled down the towel tied to his face.

She smiled at him, " Oh, hello there. I'm Elsabethe, your next door neighbor. I heard all the commotion and was surprised to see the old place had sold."

" Elsabethe, I thought you might be a fable." William came out of the kitchen.

Joseph's eyes were on the cookies, which were thick and covered in shards of chocolate. " Yeah, we heard that you owned this place some time ago and then sold it to the city."

She held out the plate to William, who immediately took a cookie. Looking around, she smiled with amused astonishment. "Oh, yes. This belonged to my sister for a good number of years. But, when she moved on, I took ownership of it. But that's another story. I heard you plan on opening this place as a bed and breakfast. How nice."

William, talking through a mouthful of cookie, said, " Oh, yeah. The place is just perfect for a business."

" That is wonderful. This old place needs the company of guests. It has sat alone far too long." The charming sweetness of this woman was present with every word. "Oh, I see that someone here is a stitcher." She came in and walked right over to the couch where Joe had been working.

Joseph nodded, "Oh, that's me."

" Did your mother teach you?" Elsabethe looked over the partially finished piece.

William guffawed. "Marla, no. She never did anything like that in her life."

Joe frowned at his dad, " No, I learned on my own. I have ADD and needed something to keep my hands busy while I was in school, so a friend suggested this. I loved it from the start, though I'm not all that great at it."

Elsabethe smiled, " Oh, my dear boy, it doesn't matter how good the finished product is; it is what you learn in the process of completing it that counts."

Joe was charmed; he could not help but grin. " Well, yes, I guess you're right. I only wish I knew how to do work like this." He pulled out the piece he found in his room from his bag.

Elsabethe looked at it with awe, " Where did you find this?"

" In my room." He smiled at her. " If this place belonged to your sister, she must've done this."

Elsabethe nodded, " Oh, yes, my sister and I have been stitchers since we were young."

Joe held out the piece. "Would you like this back then?"

" Yes, please. " She took it from him carefully. " I am afraid my dear sister didn't do much stitching during the last few years of her life here. I don't have much of her work left. Thank you. Now how can I help you?"

Joe smiled back at her. " Do you happen to know of any good stitching shops in town? I just ran out of a color I need and my last good needle broke this morning."

She started back toward the door, " Yes, there are a couple of decent shops in town. But, if you need anything, come over. I have quite the stash and I do enjoy good company while I stitch."

" That is a nice offer, but I would hate to intrude, especially since we've only just met." Joe was being as polite as any Southerner.

She continued toward the door, " Oh, honey, I always enjoy company, and a stitcher is never a stranger to another stitcher. "

" Thanks. If you don't mind, I would love to come over and see if you have any of the color I need." He held up a sky blue thread that was only about five inches long, and the last of that particular skein.

Just then, Marla came in the front door, almost out of breath. " Oh, Joseph, I need help. I got an old Victrola and a set of Victorian dining chairs and....hello?"

Elsabethe smiled, "Hello. Well, I must be going back to my place. It seems that you need to help your mother. But do come over anytime you like. Maybe we can have tea and stitch together. It was a pleasure meeting you." She quietly slipped away.

" Who was that?" Marla asked, a little befuddled.

༄

Elsabethe entered her home in a decidedly gleeful mood. She enjoyed the company of stitchers and knew that this young man would be a nice person to have around. Besides, she had an ulterior motive and needed to encourage him to come over often.

She stopped and looked at the piece in her hands. Elsabethe had not gone back into that house for decades. She knew that some of her sister's things were still in there, but she thought she had found all of the stitching. " Oh, my dear sister, why couldn't you have just focused on this and not become so greedy?" With that, she put the piece away into a drawer full of finished works.

"I am going to need supplies." she thought as she walked through the old home, which was filled end to end with furniture, mostly antiques. The walls were adorned with the finest stitching one could hope to create.

She entered a side room that contained a very old foot-pedaled sewing machine with antiquated cloth scattered about. Archaic wooden boxes were piled here and there, each designed to hold dozens of skeins of thread for all sorts of purposes. Opening one, Elsabethe found many empty holes with small squares of wood that would hold a wrapped up length of thread for storage.

"Oh dear, I must mend this situation." Carefully she pulled out a special needle that had been safely placed in the collar of her blouse. The needle was clear, as though it were made of glass. When the light shone through it, it had a very faint blue tone. She pointed the needle at the boxes of empty spools. " Now, you know what to do. Many colors and make them bright." The needle left her hand under its own power and shot straight for the spools. One square holder lifted from the box and the needle circled it quickly. From the eye of the needle came a thread of sky blue. Almost as a spider spinning its web, the needle spun a fantastic thread of the most elegant Egyptian cotton. Around and around it went until the spool was filled to the brim. The new thread placed itself in the box and another spool joined the needle, which began to wrap this one in another shade of blue. One after another, the spools were filled. Soon enough a collection of colors, that would make a rainbow envious, was perfectly sorted into the boxes.

"Fine. Now for you." Elsabethe picked up an old dusty piece of unused fabric. It was dingy brown; at least what color could be seen under the decades of dust was brown. "Can't have this mess on the floor." While she whipped the fabric in the air, the dust scattered and the fabric sparkled with magic, turning a soft, eggshell white color. With another whip of the cloth, it whirled around and became a perfectly wrapped bolt, finally resting against the wall.

"Next please." She picked up another parcel of fabric and proceeded to alter it for use.

Soon, the old room was alive with fabrics, threads, and other sundry items for the avid stitcher. It had been many years since Elsabethe had needed more tools; for she had mostly worked on a single project. But now she had a reason to want more and she was very pleased to accommodate.

ഌ

Deep in the old trees of the forest, piles of leaves littered the ground. The evening skies had given way to the night, and darkness was cut only by the occasional shaft of milky white moonlight, crisp and cool.

A soft breeze blew through the trees, giving off a spooky whisper. The breeze became a gust, then a gale. A mound of leaves lifted in the wind and whipped about each other in a bizarre fashion. The mass formed a body, with arms and a head. It flowed across the forest floor with a fluid motion. The leaves fell away as wax falling down from a candle. Soon the humanoid figure was a shadowy person in a long black cloak and a deep hood hiding its head.

Turning to look back toward the old houses it was startled by something. "So, my sister performs magic after all these decades. Surely she has a good reason." The voice was sultry, old and wicked, as smooth as the way she moved. "I wonder what that reason could be?"

Moving further through the forest, the strange figure stood over a sleeping wolf-like beast. Beside its head was the rotting core of an apple; though eaten days ago, it was something special to this creature. Two other wolves slept nearby, snoring and lying all over each other.

" My sister protects you as much as she can, but you are mine. Your punishment will be everlasting so long as I live." The wolf awoke and sat up with a jolt, immediately transforming into a young lady in a shabby white dress, glaring at the figure over her. With that, the shadowy figure burst into thousands of leaves and blew away in the wind. A distant cackle echoed through the trees, horrible and depraved.

☯

Joseph stood at the window of his room, still wrinkling his nose at the scent of fresh paint. He opened the old glass outward to let out some of the smell. Pausing there he looked into the trees behind the house for something, though he was not exactly sure what. The cool wind of late New England spring blew in and on it a faded laugh that sent chills down his spine.

" Creepy." He shuddered and went back to bed.

☯

The next day, William pounded a sign into the ground announcing the coming of their new bed and breakfast. Marla worked with an electrician who was fixing what William had tried to install in the kitchen, which meant that once again, the family would be ordering in food.

Joseph came in after a long morning of posting flyers around town about their new business. Coming back home he found his father still struggling with the old stove while his mother waited on the phone with the license bureau.

Marla looked up with the phone still attached to her ear. She was on hold, which could mean awhile with this type of office. "You're done already?"

"I got as many up as I could manage. Some places didn't want to allow us to use their walls or windows without paying. I did get some up on the public boards and around the town hall. I still think that we will get more attention from the online advertising." Joe plopped a folder of the leftover flyers onto the table.

William grunted while he pulled out a rusted old rack from inside the oven. He sat down and looked at it with a touch of annoyance in his eyes. Then he looked at his son. " I think it will be great to have some online advertising. We just need to find someone to set it up for us."

Marla nodded. " Yeah. That's the next phone call I have to make, if I ever get through to these bureaucrats." She tapped her finger on the counter in irritation.

Joe shrugged, "I think I will go over to our neighbor and stitch for a while."

" Oh, well, dinner will be whenever we decide to order it. Keep your phone with you; we might need you." Marla listened closer to see if they were picking up on the other end, but the same round of canned music started again.

Joe picked up his bag, which he had prepared before he left that morning. " Sure."

༄

Joe stepped up to the door in front of Elsabethe's home. He could not help but notice that it was identical to the door to his home. It was very clear that both houses were constructed at the exact same time, by the exact same designer. It was charming in a way. He reached up and knocked on the hardwood door.

Elsabethe opened the door, a smile brightly covering her face. "Good afternoon! Joseph is it?"

He nodded. "Yes. I would like to take you up on the offer to stitch."

"Oh, please come in then. I always have room for stitchers. Would you like to see my supply room? I am sure you are eager to find what you need to continue your project." She led him into her home.

Joe followed happily. "Of course." He paused a moment while walking in. "Wow, this place is just like ours, only like looking at it through a mirror."

Elsabethe smiled. "Yes, it was created at the same time with the same thought. Now, come with me."

Joe walked with her through the living room, which was filled with antique furniture and many handstitched pieces adorning the walls. They walked down the little hall that would lead to the stairs for the second floor. The first room past the entrance to the hall was the stitching supply room and that is where Joe went next.

Elsabethe went right in, but Joe stopped at the door. This room was overwhelming. Supplies of every kind for the needle crafter covered the entire room with colors of thread he had never seen before and miles of fabric that appeared brand new. This was a very beautiful sight to the eyes of any stitcher.

" This is amazing. Do you run a stitching store?" Joe stepped in like he was walking into a museum.

Elsabethe chortled at him, "Oh, honey, I have stitched for decades. After so long, one tends to accumulate quite a stash. Take what you need; I will be happy to see it being used and not wasting away in here."

Joe was a child let loose in a candy store, "If you insist."

" Would you like some tea and cookies?" she asked while he plowed through the mountain of fresh supplies.

He smiled. " Homemade?"

"Of course." She laughed.

"Sounds perfect. I have eaten fast food for days." He picked up a box of thread and was amazed at the selection of colors.

"I will be back. And take what you want, I don't use it fast enough." she left him to his Shangri-La of stitching supplies.

After gathering a collection of stuff, Joe looked around the room's walls. Every space was filled with completed works that were positively amazing. There was Hardanger, black-work, cross stitching with intricate bead work, even some styles that he had never seen before. This woman was either the most amazing stitcher he had ever met, or she collected the works of other amazing stitchers.

" Tea time," she called to him from the living room.

He left, with a feeling of being a very small fish in an ocean of stitching. To his delight, he found a fresh pot of tea with warm cookies ready for him. Though he had not smelled cookies being made when he came in, he didn't argue.

" I must say, Elsabethe, that supply room of yours could outfit an entire stitching store. I have never seen so many colors of threads, and that silk thread is luxurious." Joseph sipped some tea while he began to pull out his project.

" Oh, an old woman always keeps a few bobbins of thread around so she'll be ready for whatever pops into her mind. " Elsabethe poured some tea for herself.

The Crystal Needle

He took up the bobbin of blue thread he had just acquired and cut a length of it.

" Those pieces on the walls are amazing. Do you collect them?"

"Collect? No, create. They are some of my favorite samplers." She didn't show pride often, but when it came to her stitching, she allowed herself a small amount.

His eyes widened. " They are something from a master craftsman. Are you a teacher?"

" Why, yes, I have taught this for many years. But those, they are just a long lifetime of work toiling over a needle. In time, you will have a collection yourself." She smiled at him like a grandmother.

He laughed, " Sure, in about a thousand years."

"You can get a lot done in a thousand years; I know I did." she grinned at him.

Joe laughed, not realizing the truth that was in that statement. " Well, I guess I just have to take it one stitch at a time.

Elsabethe started working on a sampler that was so long the top end was rolled up in a thick reel. "I see that your father was putting a sign in the yard this morning. Expect the house to be ready in under a month?"

" Yeah, they are working themselves to death getting that old place ready. Soon, we will have a constant flow of guests who will come for a visit with people they don't even know." his lack of enthusiasm was all over his face and in the tone of his words.

" Meeting new people can be a joy, especially those who are wishing to relax. I wouldn't worry too much. That old place needs the company." She cut one stitch and began another, always using a beautiful and unique needle.

Joseph looked at her work from across the room, "What's up with that needle? I have never seen a glass needle before. I would think that it would break easily."

"It isn't glass; it is crystal, and it has quite an interesting story behind it, if you have the time to listen." She seemed anxious to tell her story.

Joe smiled, "Perhaps a story would be nice."

She looked up at him with a startling smile, "Oh, it is quite the tale. At least, for those who are interested in listening."

" Go ahead."

" Once upon a time…oh that sounds silly. Well, perhaps it will work. Once upon a time, back before this country was a nation, many people came here from all over Europe to make a new life for themselves. Two of them were sisters, the stitching witches. Their work had been in teaching and carrying on the traditions of stitching all over the continent of Europe. But, as the people of Europe began to fear magic, the witches were no longer safe, so they left. One carried a needle made of pure obsidian, dark as night and shining with the glory of a star. It could craft objects and golems and cast very powerful spells. The other had a needle of diamond crystal. It could create thread, pierce any material, and it too could cast very powerful spells. Each needle could not harm the other. What one could weave, the other could undo. They were balanced and perfect. Both sisters came here and continued their work, teaching stitching and helping people where they could. Until…

Chapter 3: A History Lesson

The year is 1692; the place is old Salem, Massachusetts. Townspeople began to fear the worst of each other and this soon gave birth to mass hysteria. This was the height of the infamous witch trials, which convicted not a single, actual witch, despite the courts filling the jails and executing nineteen innocent people.

The village of Salem was not much more than simple log homes down dirt paths. At the center of town was a chapel which also doubled as the town meeting hall. The residents walked about without smiles and with a touch of panic in their eyes. All but one that is, for there was a kindly older woman among them, who never feared her neighbor was a witch. She was heading back to her home at this time carrying with her a basket filled with bags of freshly ground flower and cornmeal that she would use to make bread at home.

"Good morrow to thee, Elsabethe." A tall man tipped his hat to the woman.

"Good morrow to thee, constable." She bowed slightly to him.

"Would you care to sit in on the day's court hearings? I am sure that we shall have a judgment this day." Constable Richard Stoughton was a man who headed the teams which apprehended accused witches and brought them to court.

Elsabethe bowed again. " I would'st enjoy such an event, surely. But I must be going home and making bread for the week. My sister and I help the church supply bread for the needy."

He tipped his hat again, "Then good day to thee, Elsabethe." The constable made his way onward to the trials of this day.

Elsabethe retained her smile, but walked a little quicker to get home. She was not so sure that this invitation was merely for pleasure. This man had been keeping an eye on her and her sister for some time and that could spell problems for them.

Coming to a little log cabin that was slightly off the dirt road, set among the trees in the forest, Elsabethe quickly entered. Inside she found her sister standing at a window, peering out for any who would approach. Adel was tall, thin, and had a severe demeanor. Her hair was always up in a tight bun, and her dress was always dark and fitted to her thin figure. Yet, one could see that there was a kindness to her, at least there once was.

"You moved quickly. Were you followed by anyone?" Adel asked sharply.

Elsabethe set down her basket and untied a cape that she wore in the chilly wind. "I was not running from anyone, not this day. But I was stopped by the constable."

Adel's eyes widened. "What did he have to say?"

"Nothing serious. He simply invited me to sit in on one of their silly trials. I, of course, turned down the offer graciously. I only moved quicker after that due to a latent fear about the duties of that man. I am sure he wasn't concerned about us." She tried to ease her sisters concerns.

"Elsabethe, they will come for us, just as those Inquisition fools tried to come for us. We are no longer safe in this new world." The tall witch snarled slightly at the memory of those horrible Spaniards.

Her sister smiled, " My dear Adel, the humans will always fear what they do not understand. We must adapt and resist using magic outside these walls. Our goal is not to spread magic; it is to spread the art and knowledge of stitching."

Adel rolled her eyes, " You trust them and they would hang you with the very thread used in your needle crafts. Don't give them anything, especially your trust."

" No, I will not let go of my trust in humans. Besides, so far they haven't actually pointed to us; they have only pointed to each other." Elsabethe peeked out the window once again. "Besides, this will die down soon enough. Once they are done tormenting each other, they shall come to their senses."

Adel walked away, steaming at the thought of her sister being so blind. " That should be enough evidence for you. They kill their own over what we are. They will soon come for us; don't deny that you know this to be true."

Elsabethe frowned while she looked at her needle. "What would you have us do? Our magic is powerful and we will never fall into their traps, not while we control the needles."

Adel turned with a wicked smile, "That is precisely the answer. This new land is ours for the taking. We can use this magic to craft a nation of our own. No longer hide from the world, but be part of it. Sister, think of it! We could create a nation that follows the needles, that respects our magic."

Elsabethe looked out into the trees. She could see a deer walk by with her fawn cautiously trailing its mother. The late fall leaves were creating a beautiful blanket along the ground. "Love one another."

"What?"

Elsabethe looked at her taller sister, "Love one another, or have you forgotten one of the most important rules of life? How can you say such horrible things when those three simple words would defy you?"

Adel took a step closer to her sister. "What are you saying?"

" I am saying that we will not use our magic in such a monstrous way. We have always been there to help others, not to control them. And,.....I will stop you if you try."

Adel was furious. Pursing her lips, she tried to control her anger. "How dare you! I am your sister and you would side with those that wish your death."

Elsabethe, always the more diplomatic of the pair, smiled warmly, "My sister, don't be angry with me. I am only saying what you know to be true. But I also understand your concerns. Perhaps it is time we move on."

"Move on? To where?"

Elsabethe thought for a moment, then answered. "Let us leave here and build a city of our own. Perhaps nearer the mountains. A place where those who are afraid of others may flee. Where those who have admitted to witchcraft may come and settle, for we know that they are no more in league with the devil than we are. What better way to earn trust than to show kindness and compassion?"

" A place to start again while keeping an eye on the others." Adel tapped her chin. "Sounds interesting. Perhaps you have a good idea."

Elsabethe picked up a large bag and opened it. She gathered special items from around the room. Stitching supplies and finished projects of importance to her went into the bag. The bag seemed to have no end to what it could contain. Adel went around the room disenchanting any spell that they had used. First she tapped her needle to a rock that was charmed to generate heat and cook food without the need of a dangerous fire, and then she poured out a pot of water that was used to keep an eye on the events in the courtroom.

Elsabethe pointed at a window and it opened on its own. "Come, we should be going soon. I must admit that I have begun to see the strange looks and fearful eyes of some townsfolk. I wager that we might be questioned soon enough"

Adel took up her broom and mounted it properly as a lady. "I believe you are right. Into the evening with us."

Both took flight out of the window and into the forest around their log home. The kind old witch was correct. Not too long after their departure, the town constable and head of the witch hunting squad was at their door to question them, which would have inevitably led to prosecution. Fortunately for the sisters, their magic would shroud them during this time so that they could not be traced.

༄

"Little did I know that my sister maintained her devious plans and would carry them out without my knowledge." Elsabethe finished.

"Your sister?" Joe slowly worked in the last end of a thread before starting another.

"Of course, I am Elsabethe." she smiled at him.

"I see." He smiled back, believing this to be just another story. "You know, this is better than television."

Elsabethe stopped working on her sampler, "If you look hard enough, you can find a lot that is better than wasting away in front of a glowing box."

"Alright. What happened next?" He continued stitching, though his ears were open to the story, which he believed to be nothing more than a fable.

"Next, my dear, is dinner. Didn't you say you had to leave by five? It is already half past five now." She pointed to an old cuckoo clock on the wall.

Joseph scrambled to gather up his project. "Oh, I didn't realize it had gotten so late."

"Don't worry, if your mother was going to be angry, I am sure we would have heard something; she is only next door." Elsabethe put her work away in a nice, hand-stitched bag.

Joe got up and went straight for the door. "Thanks. May I come back tomorrow, if you don't mind."

"Oh, that would be fine. I spend my days stitching and company is always nice. Besides, I am sure you want to know what happened to the sisters."

"Yes, of course. Thanks." He left with a courteous bow.

ಌ

Joseph walked between the houses slowly, not caring if he was late for dinner. His mind was lost in thought about the story he had just listened to. He was also thinking about this place. He hadn't had a fellow stitcher who lived nearby for many years. It would be nice to come over and stitch with someone who obviously loved the art as much as he did. He only wished that there was also a nice girl about his age who would come over as well and keep them company. His girlfriends, Jenna in particular, never had any interest in stitching.

Just then the crackling sounds of footsteps against leaves caught his ears. Someone was in the trees. " Hello?" he turned around slowly. No one came out of the trees, just more sounds of something walking over the leaves. Leaning to the right, he could see a tail protruding from beside a tree. "Hello? Come on out." he knelt down toward the ground, as anyone might do for a dog.

The wolf he had encountered before looked out from around the tree. She moved out extremely slowly. Each step came after a moment of thought, though her eyes never left him.

"It's okay, I won't harm you." he held out a hand, showing his palm to display a non-aggressive stance.

With the slow movement he could see the wolf better this time. She was very unsightly; ugly was the kindest word to use. But something about her timid nature and endearing eyes offset her ugliness. She obviously had been hurt before, for her fear of humans was evident, at least this is what Joe thought.

She finally reached him and stopped where the very tip of her nose could touch his fingers, which she sniffed for a moment. After he passed that test, she sat down and looked up at him with a non-threatening face.

'"There, you see that I am not going to hurt you." He cautiously put his hand on her head and rubbed the wiry, hard hair.

"Boy, I don't know what you are, but you have been put through a lot." He felt the different types of hair on her, which were all harsh to the touch.

She seemed to smile at him; her tail even wagged.

" STOP PETTING THAT THING, IT MIGHT GIVE YOU FLEAS!" Marla hollered out from the porch of his home.

The wolf jumped back, looking at Marla with pure fear in her eyes.

Joseph stood up. "Mom, she was relaxed. You're scaring her."

Marla waved her hand, "Shoo, go away."

The wolf looked back at Joe then toward the trees, breaking into a run and quickly vanishing into the forest.

"Was that entirely necessary?" Joe made his way up to the porch.

Marla frowned at him, "I called the city about the wolf, but those idiots said that these woods don't have wolves. Next time, I will come out with the rifle. Maybe a body will give them enough proof to do something."

Joe rolled his eyes, " No, you won't. You're more scared of a gun than of that dog."

" Get inside, I told you five...." Marla marched her son back inside as if he were ten, not nineteen.

Chapter 4: Getting to Know Joseph

The next day, Elsabethe insisted on bringing Joseph into town and showing him around. He was still gloomy about being here and she wanted to help alleviate his unhappiness.

The main street, which was most of the town, was filled with the normal daily activities of people coming and going. Elsabethe showed him to the main stitching shop on the street, introducing him to the nice couple who had owned and operated that shop for many years.

Elsabethe stopped at a place simply titled Featherville Baked goods. "This is one of the finest bakeries in New England. The original owner opened it nearly three hundred years ago. He was one of the first residents."

Joseph stopped and smelled the air. "Wow, that is wonderful."

She smiled at him. "Have you never smelled yeast proofing?"

Joe shrugged. "Not that I can recall."

"Come in, let's get some good muffins to have with tea." She walked him inside, a small bell jingling when the door opened.

The owner immediately smiled at her. "Elsabethe, wonderful to see you."

"Luis, it is always a pleasure. What kind of muffins do you have ready today?" She walked into a store front that was nothing more than a counter with breads lining shelves behind an archaic register. The whole place was built from wood with signs displayed for each kind of specialty bread you could buy.

Luis Hane, a balding middle-aged man in horn rimmed glasses, smiled at her. "I got some fresh strawberries from outside of town yesterday, and made a wonderful cornbread-strawberry muffin."

"Sounds wonderful! Pack me up a bag." Elsabethe waited at the counter while the man went into the back to get the muffins from the cooling rack.

Joseph looked at the unwrapped, unsliced breads behind the counter. "I have never seen a place like this. Every bread store I have been in has been modern. This is something out of a fairy tale."

Elsabethe laughed. "Oh, you are just too modern. This is what a bread store used to be. Luis's ancestor who opened this place was a great bread maker."

Joseph sniffed the air again. "I simply love that smell." He kept inhaling the gorgeous scent while looking at the wall of bread. "Either he does a lot of business around here, or he throws away a lot of bread."

Elsabethe shook her head. "Oh, Luis does plenty of business. People love freshly baked bread and reasonable prices. But it is true that not all of his bread is sold. However, Luis continues a family tradition started centuries ago by his ancestor who opened this place. Any leftover bread is taken to a local church that uses it to feed the needy."

"That is very noble." Joe was genuinely amazed.

"Thank you." Luis had returned with a bag filled with five of the cornbread strawberry muffins.

Elsabethe took them and nodded. "Thank you, Luis, please put them on my monthly bill."

"As you wish." Luis didn't do anything, for he never charged Elsabethe for her little purchases, only for the big orders. He didn't tell her, for he knew she would argue.

Elsabethe and Joseph left, heading back out into town. She walked down the street to a sidewalk café with a hanging sign that simply read, 'The Brew Review.'

Elsabethe sat down, as did Joseph. She set out her muffins on the plates that were already on the table. Joseph looked at her with a curious expression. "You bring your own food to a restaurant?"

She laughed. "They don't mind. Besides, this place makes its money in its teas and coffee."

Joe picked up the small menu card and looked it over. "Ooh, they have gourmet coffee. I have missed some good coffee since I left Atlanta."

Elsabethe nearly snarled. "Never been a big fan of coffee. I would rather have tea any time."

"You don't like coffee? Have you tried different blends? My father wasn't partial to coffee, until he tried some more exotic blends." Joe was again amazed.

Elsabethe shook her head. "The last time I drank coffee was when they decided to tax tea to death and we couldn't get any good tea around here. I tried to get used to coffee, but I just couldn't. Fortunately for me, this place can get in some of the English blends that I like so much."

Joe was puzzled as he tried to think of when the last time there was a hike of taxes over tea. But his thoughts were interrupted by the waitress coming by to take his order. She was twenty two, blonde and cute, which he noticed immediately.

" Can I help you?" she asked with a smile.

He grinned at her. " I think you already have."

She blushed and Elsabethe rolled her eyes. The older lady ordered first. "Peggy, bring me some Earl Grey."

"Sure, Elsabethe." She jotted that down, then turned back to Joe, who was still grinning at her. "And for you?"

He handed her the menu, "One cup of your mocha latte."

"Be right out." She was off, still blushing at his flirting.

Joe watched her leave, then noticed some other twenty something girls 'observing' him. He was beginning to like it better here. He smiled at them and even let off a wink. One rolled her eyes, though she retained a smile; the other blushed and looked away.

Elsabethe cleared her throat. "You are quite the flirt."

He shrugged. "I can't help it if they notice me."

"I bet you can't." She sliced one yellow muffin in half with a butter knife. "So, tell me a little about yourself."

He leaned back and stretched his arms out some. "Oh, nothing much to tell. I was born in the Midwest, lived there for a while, then father moved us to Atlanta. Stayed there long enough to graduate from high school and then we came up here."

"Oh, I know your life hasn't been all that dull. Haven't you ever had adventure? Perhaps even love?" Elsabethe was prodding him into spilling more details.

The waitress came back with their orders and set them on the table. She gave Joe another glance and then returned to the kitchen. He enjoyed watching her walk back to the kitchen, then continued talking about himself. "Adventure? I guess, if you consider running for your life from tornadoes every spring. Other than that, my family is rather dull. Mother went to collage while I was in school, so I had a split experience, spending as much time with kids my own age as I spent with collage age people. About love…" he looked up, thinking about that. " I thought I was in love once, with a girl named Jenna."

" You thought? What happened? If you don't mind my asking."

The slight smile on his face faded, " She was my girlfriend throughout high school. Mother promised me that if I really wanted to stay there and go to college and marry Jenna, I could. But, when I even suggested it to Jen, she suddenly told me that she didn't like me like that. It didn't take me long to realize that she was really not in love with me and that I wasn't really in love with her. So, in a way, I guess I am happy that she reacted the way she did. "

' 'Don't be silly. A broken heart is a broken heart. But, it is true that perhaps you two would not have been a proper match. " Elsabethe picked up her tea and added some sugar.

" I guess. I want to get married someday. I just want to find the right girl." He drank some of his latte.

Elsabethe gently stirred the sugar into her tea. "What kind of girl do you think you will be interested in settling down with? If you don't mind my asking."

Joe looked at the cute girls at the other table, then back to Elsabethe. "You know, I don't have any idea. Somehow I think when I meet her, I will figure it out."

Elsabethe smiled knowingly. " I am sure you will figure it out, someday."

Joe shrugged. "Yeah, I guess."

They lingered a while longer over their drinks talking about Featherville. After the café Elsabethe showed him around a few more places and then took him back home. Even though he missed the thrills of the big city, it was kind of nice being in a place where you could walk from one end of town to the other in an afternoon and still have the evening to stitch.

After they returned home, Elsabethe gave Joe the rest of the muffins for breakfast and then retired to her place for the evening. Marla, after trying one of the muffins, immediately decided to have that bakery on speed-dial. She was so happy that Joe had found the perfect place to supply the breads for the guests. He didn't say it, but he had warmed up to this place a little more.

ಐ

Chapter 5 The Continuing Adventure

The next afternoon Joseph and Elsabethe were in her living room, working diligently on their projects.

" Would you like some more tea?" Elsabethe came into the room with another tray of cookies and tea, made from the tea she bought yesterday at The Brew Review.

Joe was always pleased to have some of her fresh cookies and tea. "Of course."

She set the tray down. " If you prefer, I can have coffee on hand since you like it so much, though I doubt I can make a Macho Latte."

He laughed, "It's mocha latte. You don't have to worry about having coffee around for me. I can save that for trips to that nice place. I enjoy tea as well."

"Good." She sat down and picked up the end of her massive project.

He set his project to the side to pick up his tea cup. With a direct stare he stated. "Alright, you have had enough time to think about the story. What happened to the sisters?"

Elsabethe paused for a moment to consider. "Well, I told you that they left Salem and wished to settle down where others might come and get away from the hysteria of the witch hunts. So, Elsabethe and her sister Adel both arrived in this area and found a perfect clearing in the trees for a pair of homes. Each stitched a house on beautiful fabric and buried it in the ground. In one night, two houses grew up from the ground, creating the cottages of the stitching witch sisters. There they founded Featherville. In due time refugees of the witch hunts came flooding into town. Each person was hoping to find a place where they might find peace.

The Crystal Needle

☙

Elsabethe and Adel walked down the streets of the newly forming community. Given the number of people rejected from the strict puritan communities, the town grew quickly. Most didn't ask too many questions, for they were more pleased to have a place to be than worried about who was helping them.

One day man came walking through the streets carrying a bundle in his arms. He had panic on his face and the bundle was wailing loudly.

Adel stopped him. " Mister Pestridge, what is the matter with thee?"

He looked at the tall sister. " My baby is ill. She will not stop crying."

Elsabethe smiled and held out her arms. " Please, may I see her?"

Edward Pestridge handed over his child, in hopes that this old woman could help. Elsabethe accepted the bundle with a smile. She looked at the red-faced infant. " Oh, my dear, what troubles you?" The baby continued to cry; she then reached out and grabbed at Elsabethes chest. The old witch smiled at her father. " My dear man, this child is not ill. She just needs to be fed."

Adel sternly asked. " Where is the baby's mother?"

Edward looked down. " Constance was accused of witchcraft and was hanged. They would have taken my child and killed me too had I not fled and found this place."

Adel let out a loud sigh, controlling her anger at this injustice. Elsabethe could sense her sister's rage and was happy that she kept it from spilling out. The witch with the baby walked over to a work table where a man had placed a wooden cup. The man, who was carving the cups, smiled at the kind woman. Elsabethe asked, " May I have this cup. It shall be returned tomorrow."

"Of course." This man, like many others here, owed these women a lot and was glad to help.

She took up the cup and without anyone's knowledge she cast a simple spell that filled the cup with milk that was especially good for the baby. She brought it over to Edward. "Here, take this and feed your baby."

The man took his child, then the cup. He was overjoyed, but stayed calm for his child's sake. " Thank you, many times." He bowed to her with his head and then left for the home where he was staying with others who had recently arrived.

Adel frowned while she watched him leave. "What are we to do? This cannot continue. "

Elsabethe nodded. " I agree. I suspect we will need to find a way to bring some livestock here. Milk, butters, cheeses, and even meat will be needed for a growing community."

Her sister let out a huff. "That is not what I refer to. These witch trials are going to leave orphans for no good reason. That child should not be without a mother. "

A man walked by with an armload of kindling for fires. He stopped and smiled at the two ladies and then went on his way. Elsabethe then answered. " I am sure that this hysteria will die down. The fervor is already slowing. I have heard rumors that some of the preachers and law men have begun to declare the trials foolish. I don't think that we will have to worry much."

Adel did not agree, and it could be seen in her sour expression. "If it isn't witchcraft, it's adultery or money or speaking against the church. These people ban their friends from society for the most foolish of reasons. With all the ridiculous ways they push people away, our little Featherville will become a city greater than that of Paris or London."

Elsabethe simply smiled. "Then we will welcome them in with open arms."

Adel rolled her eyes, "I don't think you understand. We must educate them, force them to understand what they do is wrong."

Elsabethe let out a sigh this time. "Sister, the only education we should concern ourselves with is that of embroidery. Helping these people live is a wonderful thing to do, but that is all. Their societies will grow and learn on their own, without our help. In time, they will see the foolishness of their ways and will be the wiser for it."

Adel shook her head. "Your compassion blinds you sometimes."

"Why don't you think about what you really want to do, and I will go and see how the work is coming on the chapel." Elsabethe walked onward to the newest building in town.

Adel walked along and watched the others construct homes. She also could see the work on the limited fields around their houses to grow food. She did have compassion for these people, each story of injustice making her angrier at those causing the injustice. These humans did not know how to manage themselves. In three thousand years they had hardly made progress, at least in her eyes. They needed leadership that is above them, wiser than them.

Just then a pair of women came up to the tall stitching witch. One held a piglet in her arms, the other was seething with anger.

"Lady Adel, would you help settle a dispute?" The one with the piglet asked.

Adel had been asked this before and was happy to provide some wisdom. "Yes, child. What seems to be the issue?"

"This piglet was born on my property and I wish to raise it for meat." The girl stated plainly.

The other protested. "The sow was mine that gave birth. I brought it all the way from Plymouth. She simply wondered onto her property and then gave birth."

The other girl then responded. "But that hog ate all the squash from my vine before giving birth, so I am owed this meat."

Now the other girl was about to give another counter argument, but Adel held up her hand. " Both of you raise this hog and when it is time to butcher, share the meat between you. Perhaps you will learn to be friends before that and not resent one another for what you have to do."

The two girls glared at each other, but each nodded. "Yes, Ma'am." They bowed to her and then returned from where they came.

Adel got a thrill out of telling people what to do. She knew that she knew better what should be done, and people seemed to respect her authority. So, she walked onward toward her home while considering what could be done to put herself into a position of power and bring these people to order.

☙

After inspecting the work done on the church, Elsabethe walked to the edge of their town. She was interested in the farms that had started out here. Some of the newest people were farmers who were eager to begin work on growing staple crops, such as grains. She was pleased to find that a small farmhouse had been built and a man was walking behind a new plow that he had crafted from wood. It was a crude method of tilling the soil, but it worked and that was all that was important. Behind the tall working man was a little boy who spread seeds into the furrows freshly cut into the soil.

The man stopped working and wiped his brow. Then he smiled to Elsabethe and walked over to her. " Good morrow to thee, Elsabethe."

"Good morrow to thee, Markus Hane. I see that you were able to get the plow finished in time for planting." She smiled at the little boy who waved at her, then continued planting.

Markus nodded. "It is not what I am used to, but it will do this season. When winter comes, I shall see to constructing a much more suitable plow for this field."

Elsabethe nodded. "I will see what help I can elicit from the community. The people around here will be pleased to have fresh grain for their tables. Oats?"

"And corn. I found a bag of fresh corn seed near my home. I am unsure who lost it, but it is a blessing, be sure of that." He took out a rag from his pocket and wiped his face again, the sweat dripping into his eyes.

Elsabethe smiled at him. "I spoke with your son last eve, when he came into town. He said that you were not a farmer in Jamestown. He spoke of your bakery that was doing fine business."

Markus nodded and smiled at his little boy. "He speaks the truth. My father was a baker, and so I followed the trade when I came of age. If I hadn't spoken against the church, I might've been training my son there in the bakery as well. But I was a fool and…"

Elsabethe shook her head. " You are never a fool to speak your mind. The greatest men of our world spoke their minds with honesty. I believe that even the Son of God was well known for speaking his mind without concern for common etiquette, when what he said needed to be said. I am sorry that those of Jamestown didn't listen and forced you to flee from a good life there. I can only hope that we will bring you some joy here."

Markus laughed. "You are a wise old woman, Elsabethe. Perhaps I shall open a bakery here when we are more settled and the farm is producing well."

" I am sure of it. Do not fret Master Hane. This land is fresh and ready for a good kind hand." She bowed her head to him and then walked back toward her home.

She didn't often interfere with the work of the farms the humans tended. But, she knew how desperately this community needed food, and so had she conjured a bag of corn seed and carefully left it for him to find. Sometimes a miracle can be worked through one person helping another, with the trick being to remember humility above all else in acts such as that.

☼

Joseph worked through his piece slowly, more interested in the story than quickly finishing his project. "So, how exactly did these people make it all the way out here? If they were all rejects from the colonies, then they wouldn't exactly have a lot with them to get here. In fact, I can't imagine many survived the untamed wilderness."

Elsabethe, cutting some fresh thread, nodded. "Featherville is a magic place, for it was founded by magic. The sisters knew that those seeking refuge would be lost. Anyone who was lost and needing a new place such as this was brought here by a spell."

"You mean that they were led here by some kind of magical GPS?" he laughed.

She rolled her eyes, "Not exactly. Let's just say that if people were seeking us, even if they didn't realize it, the distance from us to them was made shorter."

"Wouldn't they question something like that? I mean, these people weren't exactly all that accepting of magic." Joseph loosened his work and shifted it over on the holder.

She laughed. " Honey, when you are desperate for help, you don't ask a lot of questions. Besides, to those brought to us, the magic was seamless. One moment, you are walking into a great forest, another you are walking out of it into the edge of our town. They didn't know, or care, how they got here, just so long as there was a warm fire, fresh water, and good food."

"So, what happened? What does all this have to do with that needle?" He tightened the holder and started working again on his project.

Elsabethe smiled, for this was coming to one of the best parts. " As I said, this town blossomed overnight. Many people came here from all the settlements. Everyone seemed to have a similar tale, rejected from their community for one reason or another. But, others came, others that the sisters didn't expect."

꙰

Back in Featherville 1692:

Elsabethe held out her needle and pointed it at the ground near the front of her home. A rose bush broke through the soil and started climbing up the side of the house, creeping around the banister of the front porch. It stopped growing and hundreds of blossoms sprouted out and popped open with beautiful flowers.

Adel came out of her home, standing on the porch, " Lovely, dear sister, you always had an eye for color. Though, a thorny plant like that on the banister isn't wise."

Elsabethe turned to her sister with a warm smile, " Oh, but sister, this is a special thorn."

" You didn't...." Adel came down her porch and approached the rose vine slowly.

"You did. You found the spell for the needle bush." she carefully picked a thorn from the vine and held it in her palm. In moments, the thorn stretched out and became a perfect stitching needle; it even had an eye for thread.

Elsabethe nodded, " Of course, sister, if we are to continue our work, we must have the perfect supplies. Besides, the roses will add such a lovely scent on hot summer days."

Adel nodded and set the needle down on the banister. She pulled out her obsidian needle and pointed it at the ground. " I also have some ideas for flowers." With a wave of her hand, a line of tulips grew up out of the ground along one wall of Elsabethes home. Each tulip budded quickly and then opened up into a flower of brilliant color.

Elsabethe smiled, " Spool blossoms, I completely forgot about those." She picked a petal from one of the flowers and held it in her palm. The bright red flower petal quickly curled up into cylinder shape, the cylinder closed tightly, then transformed into a perfect spool of thread in the exact color of the petal. "It is wonderful. You also always have had a keen sense of color, sister."

Adel smiled " Yes. The yellow is my favorite. I have never found another yellow quite that color. It will be a pleasing sight to have as thread."

Elsabethe set the spool of newly created thread next to the new needle on the banister. Then she held up her needle for another spell. "Oh, and let us not forget the Thimble Blooms. They were one of my favorites back in Athens." Her needle started to cast a strange mist of purple magic in the air while she crafted the spell for this plant.

"It's magic. I told you it was magic." Someone spoke behind them on the path that led out to the road, startling both sisters.

Elsabethe quickly hid her hand behind her, the purple mist vanishing on the breeze. Adel held her needle down, though she was prepared to use it in self-defense. Both turned to face whoever was behind them.

To their surprise, they found a tall handsome man with three children. His hair was autumn red with frosted white tips. The children also had lovely red hair with white tips. All four wore odd robes like nothing the sisters had ever seen before. The boys looked to be around fifteen, perhaps a little younger. Their sister was obviously near twenty and very lovely.

"Can we help you?" Adel asked sternly.

The man bowed his head slightly to them, " My name is Tonbo Kitsune and these are my children, Yuki, Oki, and Yoshi. We are not human and we are lost."

Elsabethe came closer to him, " what are you?"

The man stepped back and knelt down to one knee. In a flash, he became a fox, a glorious beast with lovely fur. Sitting down, he looked up at them and spoke with the same voice he had while in human form. "We are fox people from Nippon. We mean you no harm. Can you help us?"

Adel smiled, "We offer you a home for now. We are stitching witches. Our magic is limited and we cannot send you home, but we can keep you safe from outsiders. Where is your wife?"

He became quiet and very sad. The children looked as if they were about to cry.

"My wife was discovered and shot by a hunter from the human kind. "

Hearing this Adel became angry and exclaimed, "Could you not fight back?"

" It is not our way to harm others. They took us by surprise and we fled in fear. My wife was injured, but still able to run. We tried to heal her, but she could not recover and died on the journey. Hunters followed us into the forests and we had to flee. All I seek now is a place where I know my children will be safe. We need no house, just the trees without hunters to find us."

Elsabethe was moved by their story, "Please, stay behind our homes in the thicket. Your safety will be guaranteed. I should like to prepare a warm supper for you if you wish."

The fox turned back into a man and bowed to her, "Yes, that would be nice, especially if you have any hot tea."

" Of course, do come inside." She led them into her home.

Adel smiled at the children while they passed by her. Something began to burn in her that had started so many years ago, quickly growing into a great blazing passion. Her sister sensed Adel's anger. She knew that something was wrong, but she chose to ignore it. She loved her sister as any sister should, and she did not wish to believe such evils could boil in the heart of her own kind. But she was wrong, deadly wrong.

ಐ

Elsabethe sat in her living room with the Kitsune children and their father. He sat on the chair offered by Elsabthe while the children insisted on sitting on the floor around him.

"Would you like some cookies? Dinner will be a moment while the stew finishes making itself." she held out a silver tray with maple cookies from one of her own recipes.

Oki and Yoshi both looked at their father with wide eyes. He nodded to them slowly. Elsabethe handed the tray to Yuki, who kept her brothers from acting like fools around the sweets.

Elsabethe sat in her favorite chair. "Tell me, what a Kitsune is?"

Tonbo smiled, "We are magical fox creatures from Nippon. In the past, our land was only inhabited by magical beings and animals. But humans began to come over and settle, much like here. We have earned their respect and they have ours. Yet, it is usually a good thing to keep our two cultures separate, we do have honest contact with them, even some trade. There are those who consider us minor kami, or minor gods. But that is only because they do not understand magic."

"I see. What brought you over here?" Elsabethe was fascinated.

Tonbo answered, " Explorers from this side of the world came to our lands. We learned about their ways and their unique lifestyles and wanted to learn more. So, we assumed our human forms and agreed to go back with them to their lands, as guests. "

"Then, everything went wrong." Yuki added.

Tonbo nodded, "Yes. We forgot ourselves too often and used magic within sight of humans. They hunted us and called us witches. We had no idea what a witch was, but we were sure that it was not a good thing to be called by a human. We tried to find a way back to our homeland, but there was none without the possibility of being discovered by those hunters. We learned of the humans who were leaving their lands for this new world and decided that it was the safest way to get out of danger. But, when we came here..."

" The witch hunts." Elsabethe answered.

"Yes. Have they hunted you?" Oki asked.

Elsabethe looked at an old map of Europe, one she used for centuries while traveling over those lands. "Your story is very similar to ours. The humans over there hunted us. We were in danger of being discovered any day. So, we too fled here in hopes of being safer. Then, the humans over here became paranoid and started another hunt. That is why we founded Featherville, to get away from persecution."

Tonbo smiled again, "I am pleased that we have met. You and your sister will be good friends to have. We will do whatever we can to repay you."

"We will do whatever we can for you. You need not repay any of our kindness. I only wish that we could help you find a way home, but I am afraid…."

Tonbo held up a hand. "After seeing my wife killed, my only desire is for the safety of my children. If you can help me in that, that will be more than I hoped to find."

Elsabethe wiped away a tear. She was very sympathetic to their plight, especially with the loss of their mother. She smiled again, "Well, I do believe dinner is ready. Please come into the kitchen." she stood and held out a hand of invitation for them.

૯౧

Chapter 6: Revenge

Weeks passed and the new little town of Featherville garnered more and more residents, all fleeing from the insane hysteria of the witch hunts. Some were accused witches, others were falsely accused adulterers or criminals. The strict ways of the puritan life made getting into trouble easier than staying out of it. So, out of compassion for others, the sisters accepted people into the town and helped incorporate them.

All the while, the Kitsune family was carefully protected as promised. The children, especially the two boys, would often go into the town to meet the people and learn about the world. Tonbo was more cautious than his children and he didn't venture out much, only allowing his children to go into town if one of the sisters was with them.

One such afternoon Elsabethe was going into town to meet at the church and teach a class in stitching to the young girls who would use this skill to craft lovely table cloths and other items. The three Kitsune children were ordered by their father to go and learn stitching from the kind old witch.

Adel didn't often teach stitching as she had for centuries in the other parts of the world. She was more of a leader; listening to the townspeople's issues and helping them solve problems. She took a strong interest in hearing the stories of why the people came to Featherville.

This particular afternoon she sat on her front porch and waited. None of the towns people were coming by today, so she took this time to meet with a special individual.

Tonbo, as a fox, walked between the houses. He seemed to pace around today, but this was not unusual.

"What bothers you this day, Tonbo Kitsune?" Adel stood at the edge of her porch.

Tonbo looked up to her and then became a man. To him it was inconsiderate to be in his fox form while speaking with non-fox people. He bowed his head to her "Lady Adel."

Adel, who didn't mind the title he often called her by, smiled, " Master Tonbo. You seem anxious all too often."

Tonbo gave off a little smile. "I am always anxious when my children are away from me."

"Your lovely children are with my sister. What danger could they be in?" Adel was curious, and she also had an ulterior motive for seeing him today.

"I am sure that your sister can keep a good eye on them. But during our time among the humans in the western lands, it was my sons who gave us away. They are young and sometimes forget themselves around those who are unaware of our nature." He let out a sigh. "I love them greatly, but sometimes their foolishness is more than I can handle."

Adel nodded. "It is hard to be magical in a world that fears it. I sympathize with anyone who has magical abilities, but is confined from using them. It would be a better world if the humans respected magic for what it is."

Tonbo was curious about this. " What is it?"

She just about answered him with what was truly in her heart, but simply said. " It is what it is, magic. A musician makes music, a painter paints, a magic user creates magic. Yet only one of those is feared for what nature provided."

"That is true. I just wish they were here with me, so that I could be sure of what they were doing." He looked back toward the road with the impatient eyes of a father.

Adel sat down in a chair on the porch. "I am glad you are here. I was going to send for you."

He looked over toward her. "What can I do for you?"

Adel smiled at him. "I have a special mission for you."

He frowned, "Mission? What kind of mission?"

With a thin hand she pulled a small envelope from under a book on the table beside her chair. "This is a message I need delivered promptly. I have seen what kind of magic you have and know that you can travel over the land very quickly."

He nodded, "Yes. I can make it to Salem and back before the sun sets."

"Good. Please, if you would, deliver this to Captain Stoughton in Salem." She held out the envelope to him.

Tonbo took it slowly and looked it over, "May I ask what is inside? A peace offering?"

She smiled a terrible smile. "In a way. I mean to voice my opinion on the current situation among the settlements. I feel that a wise voice must be heard or this anarchy will continue until Featherville is the only suitable place left to live."

"And you believe he will listen to your words?" Tonbo was not convinced.

Adel continued to smile, "My good man, I have a way with words, especially to these foolish humans. Let him read it, but do not linger. I would not wish your poor children to be deprived of another parent."

He took the letter and bowed to her. "I would be honored to grant your request. Your protection of my family has not faltered and I owe you more than this."

"That you do," she whispered faintly. "Now, please be on your way. I would like to have tea with you this evening."

Tonbo nodded and transformed into his fox form again. With the letter in his mouth, he disappeared into the forest slipping through the tress with unnatural speed.

Adel closed her eyes and thought of the delicious victory this was going to be here.

"And what have you done this afternoon?" Elsabethe came down the path with the three fox children behind her.

Adel looked to her sister. "I have simply made sure that all is well in the world for this day. Oh, and children, your father told me to tell you that he would be out for a bit, on an errand of which I know nothing. But he will be back by night fall."

Yuki, who was joyous over her own small stitched creation, looked up. "Father is out? How odd, he never leaves the thicket."

"I am sure he will be fine. Perhaps he is becoming more adventurous. Now, why don't you come in and have some maple candies I conjured up this morning."

The boys didn't need a second request to rush in for the candy. Yuki bowed her head,

"Thank you." she too went inside, but not quite as hurriedly as her siblings.

Elsabethe walked toward her own house, then stopped, "I sense a dark spell. Have you been conjuring?"

Adel cocked her head, " I am sure I don't know what you are speaking of."

Elsabethe was rattled at her sisters attitude, but once again she chose to ignore it.

"I am sure." she went inside, an uneasy feeling creeping in with her.

&

Late in the evening, in the middle of Salem, the good Captain Stoughton of the constabulary found an envelope addressed to him on his stoop. Taking it up, he walked inside to dinner with his wife and children.

The tall British gentleman entered the log house and took off his hat. He was greeted by a little girl in a blue dress, who hugged him furiously about the neck, and his wife, who was always happy to greet her spouse.

She kissed him and then asked sweetly. "How goes the day, Richard?"

"We had four trials this afternoon. Not one confession among the accused, but the truth will come. What is for dinner?" He put his daughter down, with the letter still in his hand.

" Stewed deer, the one you shot yesterday. But I am afraid it isn't quite ready." she walked toward the large cooking pot in the corner of the kitchen.

He unfastened his heavy coat. "That is fine."

"What is that in your hand? Another accusation?"

He looked at the letter. " I am not sure. It was on the door stoop upon my arrival home." He slowly opened up the wax seal on the surface. It was a seal he didn't recognize.

Inside was not a letter or any sort of parchment he knew of. It was a small piece of stitched fabric. The stitching was unusual at best, spelling out words in a tongue he had never seen and certainly could not read. When he took the fabric into his hands, it vaporized into the air and left an odd burning sensation on his palms.

"What is this? Witchcraft!?" he said with exasperation.

"What is...." Before his wife could ask him anything, she found that his face had become quite pale. Swaying slightly on his feet his arms fell to his sides. His eyes rolled back into his head and he collapsed onto the ground in a heap.

"FATHER!" the child screamed upon seeing her dad fall.

"RICHARD!?" His wife ran to his side and shook him, but it was too late. He was dead. The spell was completed.

☞

Weeks passed and more people were found dead after receiving mysterious letters of their own.

In the courtroom of Ipswich, a panel of the highest authority was gathered to see to the matters of this session. An old, gray-haired judge held out his hand for a man to hand him the papers for today.

"What do we have this day, your honor?" Constable Thaddeus Walcott stood in the middle of the floor, with many people around who waited to hear the first case.

The judge looked over the papers for his work today. " Nothing unusual....wait, what is this?" he found a strange letter, not anything like the others.

"What is that?" The constable looked at the letter, noticing that his name was written on it, but it was addressed for the court to read.

The judge examined the wax seal, "I do not recognize this mark. Perhaps we should read it first." He opened the seal and pulled out what was inside.

"What in heavens name is that?" Thaddeus stepped up, unsure if his eyes were tricking him or if he were looking at a piece of embroidery.

The Judge put on a pair of spectacles to examine the piece. It was a poem stitched inside a border. The border was made up of strange glyphs that no one recognized. He read aloud,

"'To Thaddeus Walcott, constable and persecutor. Lives destroyed though no crime committed, punishment to thee that is justly fitted.' I am sure I do not unders....WHAT IN HEAVEN'S NAME?!" The piece of embroidery vaporized in his hand.

At that very moment, Thaddeus started to shake and foam filled his mouth. He came down to his knees and gagged slightly, finally falling face forward onto the ground. No one would come to his side; they were so afraid of what had just happened. Thaddeus Walcott was dead. The spell on him completed.

༄

Far off in Charlestown, in the county of Middlesex, a toddler girl played in a patch of wildflowers. Her mother was speaking with a friend about trading some bread for a cut of the pig that they had just butchered.

The child was having a fun time looking over the wildflowers growing at the side of the road. She picked one and plucked all the petals off of it, then scattered them about. Looking down for another flower, she found a letter lying on the ground. She could not read, so she did not know that it was addressed to her. Being a small child she didn't question the circumstances, and ripped the letter open to pull out what was inside.

After having finished their discussion about the trade, Martha Sewall continued gossiping with her neighbor. " I cannot say how she bewitched me, but I was sure that she was in league with the others."

"Were you not bewitched before? Is this the second witch to try and harm you?"

"Yes. The last witch fled with her family into the trees. The constables could not find her but surely she found the devil and returned to him. Fortunately, we are going to be able to bring justice to this witch. "

The other woman gasped, "How awful for you. I pray that you are well and that the witch didn't do you any harm during her trial?"

"Oh, no, I am free of her. She was made to confess and will be punished accordingly. I am sure that I am safe now." Martha nodded.

Sarah shook her head. "It is no wonder that she would be found to be in league with the devil. Only last year she spread that rumor about you and William Cornish, I believed not a word of it, of course. But she was so insistent on besmirching your name."

Martha nodded. "Yes. She tried to harm me with her words and then she bewitched me. Now she will pay for....what is it Abigail?" the little girl was pulling on her mother's dress.

Abigail held up the piece of stitching she found inside the envelope. But her mother hardly looked at it.

"Abigail, that is a nice quilt square." Martha looked back to the woman she was gossiping with.

Abigail looked at the piece, which she only now turned over to the front. The piece seemed to shimmer and then vaporize in her hands. This made the little child cry.

"I was so worried….what is it, Abi…." Martha coughed and seemed to choke on the air. She grasped her throat and the stumbled backward, falling onto the ground while still struggling to breath.

"MARTHA!" Sarah opened the small door in her fence to help her friend.

Martha writhed about on the ground, trying to take in air. Then she became still, no longer struggling. Sarah screamed and ran to find help. But it was too late; Martha Sewall was dead. The spell on her was completed.

ಬಿ

No evidence of the letters origins could be found and nothing made sense. Not even those who spent time accusing their friends and neighbors were able to point a finger at anyone. Those in power chose to keep this as secretive as possible, for the outcries and hysteria could easily have turned into uncontrollable anarchy.

Tonbo, in payment for the witches' protection, had unwittingly delivered these messages of death. His first and only concern was for the safety and well-being of his children. Due to his devotion, Adel knew how useful a tool he could be and would be sure to use him for even more goals.

Chapter 7: A Broken Family

Early one seventeenth century morning, Elsabethe walked outside of her home. She had with her a large roll of something held within a long cloth bag. The bag itself was special, a material that could not be harmed by the elements. Whatever was inside was highly important.

The morning was fresh and sweet with the sunlight just beginning to warm everything. A fine mist hovered above the ground and clung to the leaves and blades of grass. The dew gave away everywhere that a spider had spun itself a web. Though the creature desired not to be noticed, the delicate process of water droplets gathering upon the finely spun threads displayed the amazing work a tiny weaver can accomplish.

But none of the wonders of the natural world seemed to catch Elsabethe's eye this morning. Her focus was direct and her concern was obvious. She found her way to the edge of a small valley formed by a river deep at its base. The fog above the river filled this valley, making it appear that a cloud had slept there the night before.

The old witch pulled out her crystal needle and pointed it at an eagle flying over her head. The majestic bird swooped down and landed on the ground before her. She knelt down and held out her package. "Take this far away to someone trustworthy; do not return it until it is safe."

The white headed raptor seemed to understand her, for it picked up the bundle in its beak and then took to the skies. It flew fast and high, going out of sight quickly. The old witch seemed to relax slightly as the bird left her view.

" What are you doing out here this morning, Elsabethe?" a friendly voice startled the old woman.

Elsabethe turned to find a beautiful fox standing behind her. It was Yuki in her creature form. "Yuki dear, you startled me."

"I apologize." The girl stood up, transforming into her human form.

"That is quite alright, my dear. I was lost in thought. It is such a lovely morning I had to come out and enjoy it. What are you doing up so early?" Elsabethe strolled along as though she had been simply walking all this time.

Yuki smelled the fresh, moist air and then replied, "When I was younger, my mother and I would come out early and watch the sunrise. I come out early each morning, so that I can remember the best times with my mother."

Elsabethe stopped walking. "I am truly sorry for your loss. I only wish that I had been there to help. Somehow, I feel that I am not always where I am needed most. My sister and I started this place to be free from persecution, but it didn't stop the persecution from harming others."

Yuki smiled, "No, you could not have changed what happened. You may feel that you fled, but you have created a haven for those who would have died otherwise. If we had not had this place to come to, those hunters might have killed father too, or my brothers, or even me. I am thankful every day that I still have my father, though I will mourn my mother's loss all my days."

Elsabethe turned to see the sun's rays shine over a hill and fill the area with warmth. It was an explosion of light and life, though no sound came from it. "It is a beautiful sight. I have been in many places in my life, and the sunrise never changes. No matter what comes in this world, what strife we must endure, there are some things that never change."

Yuki nodded, her eyes closed while she absorbed the warmth. "Yes. From my homeland to here, that warmth has not deviated."

Elsabethe was about to say something, but she noticed that Yuki's eyes were quivering under her lids and a bit of a tear was filling each. "Yuki, dear, what is the matter?"

Yuki opened her eyes and wiped them quickly with the back of her hand. "Nothing."

"What brings tears to your eyes, or need I ask?" Elsabethe took Yuki's hand.

Yuki sniffed hard and then attempted to force a smile. " I cannot allow myself to dwell in sadness. My father and brothers need me to be strong."

Elsabethe looked her right in the eyes. "Strength can be a cover for reality. Have you wept tears for your mother yet? "

Yuki shook her head, still trying to hold back. "No. I shouldn't."

"Oh, my dear child. You must. Don't let sorrow eat at you. Please, come here." She pulled the girl to her and put Yuki's head on her shoulder. "Remember your mother."

Yuki, who had not freely shed one tear yet, sobbed. She had wanted to cry for weeks, but she could see the same pain in her father's face and knew how it would hurt him to see her weep. Then, with the tears flooding, the memories of her mother's smile, words, and life came all over her. She wept for the woman who loved her as much as her father loved her. She wept for the grandfather back home who would never see his child again.

"Elsabethe, Yuki, what is the matter?" Another fox approached, this time speaking with a deep male voice.

Elsabethe smiled at him, with the girl still held against her. "Father Tonbo, please come here."

Tonbo, who had just arrived from another mission for Adel, stood up into his human form. "Yuki, what is the matter?"

Elsabethe gently moved Yuki off of her and looked into her red eyes. "Please, hold your father, he needs you too at this moment."

Tonbo put his arms around Yuki, who had not turned to him yet, "Yuki-chan. What is the matter?"

Yuki turned to him, but looking at his face only made her cry again. She put her head against him. "Oh father, I miss mother so."

He held her and put his head on top of hers. "I do too, my child, I do too."

Elsabethe took out a handkerchief from her pocket and wiped her own tears now. She then quietly excused herself and left them in their memories and the mists of the morning dew.

That afternoon Yuki worked with her brothers in Elsabethe's living room. The witch was teaching them more extensive lessons in stitching. Yuki had a talent for this kind of work and enjoyed it more and more. Her brothers were forced to continue so that they might garner some patience, or at least that is what their father hoped.

"I heard that that boy from town was asking about you. I think he wants to court you." Yoshi spoke to his sister.

Yuki frowned, "Are you speaking of William Young?"

"I heard he said you had the prettiest eyes." Oki said this in the mocking tone of a little brother.

Yuki rolled her beautiful eyes, " Humans. He is nothing but a tail chaser."

"He has seen your tail?" Yoshi asked sarcastically.

She pointed a needle at the twins, " No, and he never will. I have to take care of father now that mother is gone. I don't have time for courting."

Elsabethe smiled, "Oh, my dear, you shouldn't give up on love. I know your father wants you to find a nice man. He has mentioned to me that he desires you to be happy and have children someday."

Yuki cut some fabric from her piece, "Why worry about having my own when I have these two to deal with?"

As if on cue, the twins started in on each other. "Hey, I wanted to use that." Yoshi grabbed a pair of scissors from his brother. Oki snatched them back, "I wasn't done." Yoshi punched him in the shoulder and took the scissors before Oki could make the simple snip he needed to cut the thread loose from his piece of work. So, in response, Oki pummeled his brother off of the sofa they were sitting on and both wrestled on the floor.

" Children, children. " Elsabethe attempted to intervene.

Yuki, who had seen her two brothers do this all too often, held out her hand. A blue flash of light fell over them and they were completely frozen. "Stop or I am telling father of your actions in someone else's home." She let them go from the field of magic.

Both brothers snarled at each other, "Yes, sister." They were obedient to a fault, at least when they knew that their father would not be happy with them.

Oki got back on the couch, grabbing the scissors again, "Where is father anyway? He has been gone a lot lately."

Elsabethe frowned, "I have noticed this too, but I am unsure of his ventures."

"Oh, didn't you know? He is running errands for your sister." Yoshi sat next to his brother and snatched the scissors again.

Yuki looked to her brother, " Have you been spying again?"

"Of course. And what I have seen is very curious. Each day your scary sister gives him something and he runs off into the woods toward that awful settlement we ran from. "

Yuki set her stitching down, "I am sure father wouldn't be putting himself in harm's way. He wouldn't be that unwise." She was terrified and didn't hide it well.

Elsabethe came over and tried to comfort her with a cup of hot tea. " Oh, my dear, I am sure that master Tonbo is alright. He would never put himself in danger. Now, continue working, your cutwork is impressive."

Yuki snipped a few threads from the fabric and blushed, "Thank you, sensei."

"If you will excuse me, I must check on something." Elsabethe left the room, knowing that Yuki would keep an eye on her rowdy brothers.

She entered her stitching room and picked up a small piece of material with a beautiful blue bird stitched onto the surface. Holding the fabric in one hand, she waved her other hand over it. The bird came to life and rose up from the fabric, appearing exactly as if it had flown in through a window.

" Go, little one, and bring me news from the outside." The bird was given its command and followed through with precision, flying out the window and toward the other settlements nearby.

༂

That evening the children and their father were reunited and slept in the thicket in their fox forms. Adel sat on her front porch and held her obsidian needle in her fingers, looking at the way the moon light shone through it. She had not stitched anything, other than her spells, for some time and she considered working on a project for the art of stitching.

"What brings you out this evening, Sister?" she asked without looking up.

Elsabethe was halfway between their houses and stopped when she realized her sister was aware of her approach. "Sister, what have you been up to these past few weeks? I have barely had time to see you and we haven't even shared a pot of tea."

" I have been….busy." Adel stuck the needle through the fabric of her sleeve, planting it for safe keeping.

Elsabethe smiled as sweetly as she could, "What have you and Tonbo been working on so diligently? Has the handsome fox garnered your interest?"

Adel stood up and came to the edge of the banister, looking out over the night sky that was encroaching upon them. " Oh, he is far too young for the likes of me. We have simply been…making contact with the outside world."

"I know." Elsabethe held up her arm and the bluebird she had conjured came from the top of her house. It was holding a letter in its beak, one that Adel had sent out. It dropped it into a waiting hand.

Adel became noticeably agitated, " Where did you get that?"

" I retrieved it from the stoop of the colony's governor this afternoon. What would you possibly want with contacting such a man? He doesn't even know of this town's existence, at least that is what I believe. What is inside, I wonder?" She let the bird go and opened up the envelope.

Adel stepped back, momentarily at a loss of what to do.

Elsabethe took out the stitched piece and knew exactly what was written on it in the ancient lettering. The stitching, as designed by the spell, vanished into her hand, but it didn't do anything to her or the man it was designed to kill. She knew full well that nothing crafted by the obsidian needle could hurt her, not in the mortal way that this was created for. "A death note. Forbidden magic. I never thought my dear sister would deal in such horrendous acts."

"Don't be a fool, Elsabethe. Those humans don't know the first thing about ruling this world. They have stumbled upon a continent that could be great. We both knew that when we came here. But, instead, they return to their foolish ways, hurting each other in pointless attempts to assert their puritan morals. I was simply taking care of the worst of them." Adel came to the edge of her porch and started down the steps.

Elsabethe didn't fear her sister and she stood her ground, "What next? Would you kill any that disagreed with our ways? Would you use your powers to create a new world here, one with you as the leader?"

Adel approached her sister slowly with a smile like a snake about to eat. "Oh, dear sister, you are too clever. Yes, I would rule this continent and more in due time. But you would not be left out. We would rule together."

"So, you rid them of their leadership and take over. It would not be so easy."

Adel looked up to the first stars of the night, "Oh, it would be easy, dear sister. With their leaders gone, those foolish humans would turn on each other. Anarchy would erupt and soon they would long for leadership, any kind of leadership. We would step in and take over. They would fall on their faces and no longer hate us."

Elsabethe was aghast, "They would fear us."

"They hunt us and our kind like animals. They kill their own in vain attempts at retribution for acts that were never committed. Have you not forgotten that those poor children you teach to stitch lost their mother because of these human bigots?" Adel turned on her sister, angrily stating her case with force.

Elsabethe shook her head, " Every time I look at Yuki I wonder if she looks like her mother. I see sadness in their eyes each time they see their father and she is not beside him. But this is not a reason to kill, not a reason to conquer. It should be a reason to rebuild, to focus on the future, and not dwell in the past. "

"Well, you can look at the future. I am living in the here and now. And it is time that we do more than stitch pretty flowers on fabric." Adel walked back toward her house.

Elsabethe stopped her, "Sister, I will not allow you to do this. I will fight you."

Adel stepped up to her porch again, "With what? We both know that you are not a fighter. Besides, the crystal needle cannot harm the obsidian needle."

"Oh, sister, think of what you are saying, what you are doing. This is not our way." Elsabethe pleaded her case to her sister one last time.

" It is my way. From now on, this is my life. Good bye, sister." Adel walked into her home, leaving her sister standing out in the cold night air.

ஐ

Chapter 8: A Fox in Wolves' Clothing

"What happened next, what happened next?" Joseph was annoyed that Elsabethe stopped telling the story right there.

She packed away her stitching and poked the needle through the collar of her blouse. "Next is time for you to go home. Your father asked me to send you home early so that you could be ready for tomorrow."

He frowned, "Oh, yeah, the grand opening. It is amazing that it was over a week ago that we had lunch at that coffee place."

"It is hard to believe that you have been coming over for a month. My story must intrigue you greatly." She was amused.

Joe nodded, "Yes, I always enjoyed a good fantasy. Besides, it adds a little mystique to this town."

"Oh, there is a lot of mystique here, I should know." She stood up and picked up the tray where she had made tea earlier.

Joe looked up at her, "Why have you put yourself as part of this story?"

"Is it that odd? Perhaps the story isn't a myth. Perhaps it is real and I am the Elsabethe of the stitching witches." She said this with a hint of playfulness in her voice.

He laughed, "Yeah, right. Maybe you should write this story down. It would be a fun legend to tell around here, especially around Halloween."

"Oh, stitching witches have nothing to do with Halloween. That is a foolish human celebration." she said this and her eyes bugged out, having caught herself in a moment of acting as who she really was. Fortunately, he laughed again, not believing her.

"Well, I will be back tomorrow. I have no interest in the open house mom and dad are holding. The place still stinks of paint. " He got up and was about to leave.

"Oh, if you could, I would like to make you dinner tomorrow. I am sure your mother is far too busy with her open house to worry about fixing any sort of supper for you."

Her request sounded urgent and Joe noticed. "Why?"

Elsabethe grinned slyly. "I have a friend coming over tomorrow evening. A young lady who won't be by until dark. And I would like you to meet her. "

"Elsabethe, are you trying to set me up?" he rolled his eyes.

"Oh, don't be silly. She is just another stitcher, like you, and I would like you two to meet. Besides, she has heard this story before and might know more of it that my old mind is forgetting."

Joe nodded, "Unless mom has something desperate she needs me for, I will tell her I am having dinner here. Would you like me to bring anything?"

"Just yourself. Now, get along, your father is probably waiting for your help." She prodded him on his way.

Joseph went for the front door of the house that felt more like home than the place he had been living in for the last month. He stopped and looked back to her, "Thanks."

"For what, honey?"

He smiled warmly, "For allowing me to come and showing me that I can enjoy this place. I no longer hate Featherville; I look forward to each day. I guess I just needed to find a close friend."

"Oh, a young man like yourself doesn't need a foolish old woman like me as a close friend. You need a nice young girl." She grinned like a grandmother.

"I see. I will be here tomorrow, though I am not sure when." He waved goodbye and left her to her plans. It was odd leaving while there still was daylight, but he had work to do today and he wanted to get it done. Little did he notice the wolf watching him walk to his home, but she watched him more often than she allowed anyone to know.

ಬ

Elsabethe carried a tray of tea cups and other dishes into her kitchen. She let the tray go in midair and it floated over to the sink, whereupon it proceeded to clean itself.

She was tired and ready for bed, especially with the full day she was planning for tomorrow.

"Elsabethe." A cautious voice came out of the darkness.

The old witch turned with a smile on her face, for she knew this voice quite well.

"Yuki, dear, come out and have something to drink."

The ugly, mangy wolf came out of the shadows and sat in the kitchen. " No, thank you. What did you ask me here for?"

Elsabethe cleared her throat, not sure how Yuki might respond to this. "Well, I asked the young man next door to come over and have dinner with us."

"Us?" the dog looked at the old witch with astonishment.

"Yes. He will be staying after dark, and you will be in your human form, and…"

"And I am not coming." Yuki turned to leave.

Elsabethe snapped her fingers and the door to the back porch locked. " Wait, please. I have spent time with him; he is a good listener and a great stitcher. He is also kind and loving. I can sense it, so can you. This is why you have an interest in him."

Yuki turned back around and sat with her eyes cast down to the floor. "Yes, I met him on the first day he was here. He was nice to me, like no one else has been when they first see me."

"I also saw you come out to see him the other evening." Elsabethe gave the dog a knowing smile.

Yuki looked away. "Alright, I was watching him and he caught me. I was interested in how he would act."

"And?" The old woman was pushing.

"Okay, he is nice, and cute, and charming. He needs a good girl, but that is not me." Her cute smile turned back into a frown.

"Please."

Yuki gave the old woman a confused look. "What is so important? Why now? "

Elsabethe took a deep breath. She knew that this wouldn't be a fun idea. " I have been telling him the story of how you and your family came to Featherville. I haven't gotten to the part where you and your brothers were cursed. I thought that you might help elaborate on it so that I get all the details right."

Yuki frowned, "You mean the night that father was killed."

"Yes. I know it is a painful memory but you must face it sooner or later."

The wolf let out a sigh, "To face the story and that boy at the same time. I just don't know."

"Oh, don't be so worried. Just sit and stitch with us. What could be wrong about that?"

The wolf looked up at Elsabethe. "Well, if he acts like everyone else does when they meet me, it won't be a new experience. Maybe you're right and he will be the one."

Elsabethe got a bowl out and filled it with the rest of the tea from the pot. She set it on the floor for the dog. "Just be yourself."

Yuki stepped over to the bowl of tea, lapped a few times, then sat down to look up to her oldest friend. "Your sister stirs in the forest."

"I know. It won't be long now." Elsabethe looked out her window to the woods behind her place.

Yuki let out a sigh, "I guess my time is almost up. One way or another, this may be my last chance."

The next day, William, Marla, and Joseph welcomed as many strangers as they could gather into their new bed and breakfast. People from town and tourists passing through stopped by to see the place and consider the vacation possibilities.

William walked around with a tray of goodies for people to munch on while they looked over the very professional brochure about the bed and breakfast accommodations.

Marla guided people throughout the house and explained all the historical nuances of the place, from the unique antiques to the history of the house and town.

Joseph stood by a wall, attempting to stay out of the way as much as possible. He looked over a piece of stitching he had done back in Atlanta. It was a Chinese peony with a small box of Chinese writing next to the flower. The style was a type of canvas work that used specialty threads and long stitches to give texture to the piece. His mother really liked the color and had it framed and hung in the room. Joe found it humorous to have an oriental looking piece framed in an antique frame and set in an early American decorated room.

"That is nice." A woman's voice surprised him.

Joe turned around. "Oh, thank you. If you are looking for the restrooms, they are down that hall." He had directed so many people today it came out without thinking.

She shook her head. "No, I am fine, but thank you. Do you sell any of these pictures? I would love to buy one."

Joe shook his head, though a beam of pride was bursting to get out at the thought of someone liking his work that much. "Oh, no. This is just a hobby of mine. Fortunately, it makes for free art for my parents."

"You do needle work." A rude boy laughed at Joe.

Joe turned to the young man he had not noticed before. "Excuse me." He became just as abrupt, having dealt with this type of attitude before.

The teenage boy sneered at him. "What?"

The woman who was admiring the work grabbed her son's ear. " Be nice. Come on, Max." She dragged him out none too gently.

Joe shrugged. He had come across some rude teenagers before and was used to this. A lot of testosterone-filled boys think they can mock a stitching guy. He simply brushed it off, hoping to never see that rude mug again.

"Son, could you go and get another box of doughnuts?" William ran by to greet another couple coming into the front door.

Joe walked into the kitchen, which was a nice quiet place from the crowds in the living room. On the counter were a dozen boxes of doughnuts that had been delivered earlier in the morning.

"This is going to be a mess." He commented to himself. Although he was warming up to the area, he still didn't like the idea of the bed and breakfast. Who would want to always have company? Your life would be nothing but keeping others happy. Fortunately, this was his parents' idea, not his. So, he would accept it for now and wait for the first good opportunity to leave.

Unsealing the package, he set out the overly sweet pastries onto an antique serving platter that his mother had found. While he was doing this, something caught his attention in the window. Right outside the kitchen was the edge of the little forest. Mostly green grasses, vines, and trees, it was a lovely thicket to have behind this old cottage. Yet, even during this midweek of June, a collection of colorful leaves were swirling around on the ground. It was odd that they had not been covered by the new growth during spring, and even odder that they would look so freshly fallen when Fall was months away.

"Whatever," he muttered and finished his work.

The leaves outside gathered into a single area and nearly blew away from the edge of the forest. But something caught them as a wall of light appeared at the tree line. For a fraction of a second the light shimmered and the leaves were pressed back into the forest. Joe looked up again, the leaves' activity having caught his attention. He could not explain it, but somehow those same leaves were blowing in the opposite direction than they had been moving only moments before.

"That's it; this place is just creepy." He took up the tray and rejoined his father in the living room.

☙

"I don't care. That was a long day. Although mom and dad did get a lot of reservations for the fall and winter months." Joe sat in Elsabethes' living room while she worked on a very fine smelling dinner in the kitchen.

She came into the room with a tray of tea and little butter cookies. "How nice. I expect that they are pleased that the business is launching so efficiently and the place has never looked so nice. I will have to come over and see what's been done on the inside."

"Oh, it is a nice place. Dad and mom worked hard to make it perfect. I just hope it all pays off. A nice opening weekend doesn't always mean a good run for a show." Joe took a cookie, relishing its warmth and fresh baked softness.

Elsabethe rustled around in a bag she had picked up that morning. From it she produced a nicely framed piece of stitching. " Here, I had this done today. It is a house warming gift for your place."

Joe took it and looked at the stitching of a lovely garden patch with the word Welcome stitched among the flowers. All the work was done on off white congress cloth and framed in a nice green stained wooden frame. "This is beautiful!" Joseph exclaimed admiringly. " It will be perfect in the living room. Thank you."

"Oh, think nothing of it. I stitched that years ago and I am very happy to have it to give to you today. After all my years in the needle arts, I have a stock room full of finished pieces that need to find good homes. " Elsabethe looked out a window, she seemed to be checking something.

Joe ate several cookies trying to quite his rumbling stomach. " When are we eating? It is getting awfully late and all I have had today are sweets and pastries."

She smiled, " Soon. I have a nice stew on the stove, with cornbread muffins coming out of the oven soon."

" That sounds good" Just then, the door chime rang.

Elsabethe nearly ran to the door. Joe wasn't sure if she was excited or worried. She opened the door and looked down first and then straight ahead. "Oh, good, you're here. Do come in." She stood aside to allow the newest guest to enter the room.

A strange figure came into the room. It was a small person, wearing a large black cape. A deep hood was settled over the head and face, blocking Joe from getting a good view.

He stood up, trying to be polite. "Hello."

A soft feminine voice came from under the hood. "Hello." She kept a little distance between herself and Joe. " What smells so good?" she asked Elsabethe directly.

" Dinner, which will be ready in a few moments. Make yourself comfortable. You should get to know Joseph, for he is a great stitcher." Elsabethe sort of pushed her in his direction.

" Oh, I'm not all that great." He smiled, hoping to get some kind of response from the girl under the cloak.

She simply moved over to the long couch and sat at one end. Under her coat was a cloth bag that she sat next to her. Inside were stitching supplies, something that Joseph could detect by the orts (bits of thread left over after stitching) hanging out from the top and the material neatly placed on a tube like holder.

He sat back down when Elsabethe left them alone. "May I ask your name? Or are you too shy to answer?"

She looked up. He could see a face, though it was heavily guarded by shadows. With a small voice she answered him. "Allison." Yuki had decided on different name, one that was more common today.

"Allison, that is a nice name. What are you working on? Has Elsabethe been teaching you?"

"Oh, she taught me a long time ago. I haven't decided on what to stitch next. I don't get much time to work with my needle." She hadn't moved her bag or its contents yet.

Joe smiled, " I would guess so. If you work this late, then you must not have a lot of time to do much stitching. But any stitching is enough to be worthwhile. I have too much time, I think that's my problem." He pulled out his project, "That is why I have so much of this done."

His work seemed to spark her interest. "Oh, she is lovely." The stitching was the Japanese lady that had taken him months to make any progress on. The woman and half of the scenery were done, but he still lacked a lot of the side details of the image.

Joe got up and walked over to the couch so that she could get a closer look. He wanted to give a humble impression, though he was darned proud of his work and enjoyed others admiration. " It is a geisha, from Japan. That's what the pattern is called anyways."

Allison took the piece from him. " Oh, no, this is a bride, or a courtier, not a Geisha." She pulled back her hood to get a better look at it.

It was then that Joseph saw what she'd been hiding. It was a shock at best. All over her body, at least the bare skin he could see, were gray spots covered with bristly, dusty gray hair. Some of the hair was long and spindly, while at the base of each patch was a mass of thicker, short hair that looked as thick as grass. There was a particularly large patch over half of her face engulfing part of an eye. The hair on her head was a lot like the longer, shaggy hair, thin and messy looking. Her fingernails were long, almost black, coming to points. They did not appear to be fake.

Allison looked up at him and saw the look of shock on his face. Something about his reaction startled her, though she had seen this look many times before. Plopping the needlework back into his lap, she stood up. With a quick motion, she flung the hood back over her head and readied to leave.

Elsabethe chose that moment to come back into the room, "Leaving so soon?"

"I see no reason to stay." Allison took up her bag and was about to leave.

"I wish you wouldn't leave." Joseph stood up now.

She turned around, honestly curious. "What? So that you can have something like this to stare at?"

He smiled, "Yes. Please, take off your hood."

Allison wasn't sure what he was up to. She had seen people who had thrown things at her and others who threatened to call the animal patrol. But she did as he asked and pulled down her hood.

Joe stepped closer and looked directly into her eyes. A gentle smile crossed his lips.

She frowned, "What?"

"You have the most beautiful eyes I have ever seen." He looked into her turquoise/green eyes. "They shine like crystals held in the sunlight."

Elsabethe let out a great sigh. Allison's frown melted slightly. She had been ready to insult him back, but she wasn't ready for a compliment. Looking into his eyes, which were looking kindly at hers, her frown turned into a shy smile followed by blushing. She cast her eyes down and said, "Thank you."

Elsabethe had never been happier than she was at that moment. " Now, if you aren't leaving, I do have a nice supper waiting in the kitchen."

Allison set her bag back down and took off the cloak. She tossed it on the end of the couch and followed the others into the kitchen.

☙

Joseph took the large bowl of stew from Elsabethe and handed it over to Allison, who smiled again at his politeness. He then took a bowl for himself.

While Elsabethe went for a tray of cornbread muffins Allison leaned over and nearly put her face in the bowl of stew. She stopped herself when she realized what she was about to do. With some quick thinking she slowly lifted her head and smiled, " Oh, this smells divine."

Joe nodded, "Yes, this is very nice. Reminds me of some good southern cooking."

Elsabethe sat a bowl of hot cornbread muffins on the table. "Well, I thought that you might enjoy something from home. Besides, it is a wonderfully easy dish to make."

Allison took a cornbread muffin from the bowl and looked at it like it was an alien object. Joe smiled, "Haven't you ever seen a cornbread muffin?"

She began to peel away some of the paper cup, " I can't say that I have. At least not like this. But it does look nice."

"Well, then you're in for a treat. Cornbread muffins and stew are one of my favorite dinners. " He took up a muffin and proceeded to take off the wrapper. He couldn't understand why, but this girl reminded him of that wolf he met when he first arrived a month ago. It could be the scraggily fur, or lovely eyes, or even the way she was vigorously eating the muffin. Joe would never say anything to this effect, but it was on his mind.

Allison stopped with her face nearly buried in the muffin that was cradled between her two hands. She glanced over and said with a mouthful of food. "What?"

He laughed softly, "Well, I do like muffins, but I don't think I ever ate one with such gusto. I prefer to crumble half of it up in the stew, adds a little body." He cut the muffin in half and took only half of it in his hand. He mashed it up and then sprinkled it into the stew. The other half would be for buttering and eating.

She smiled, feeling a little odd about all of this, and did as he was doing. Both took up spoons and tried the thick brew. Allison's eyes lit up with her first bite. "Oh, this is wonderful!" she started to shovel in the concoction with speed and abandon.

Joseph laughed, "Slow down! You're going to make yourself sick."

Elsabethe added with a more serious tone. "Yes. Please, remember some manners dear."

Allison stopped and looked up at Elsabethe. It dawned on her how she was acting, and she swallowed the last mass of stew she had forced into her face. With a cloth napkin, she cleaned herself and looked over to Joe. "Sorry. In my family, you have to be quick. I have a pair of twin brothers who are wolves when it comes to eating."

Elsabethe cleared her throat, loudly, and set aside the bowl of stew in front of her. "Would you like to hear more of the story?"

Joe nodded while he started to eat. Allison looked to her old friend with less enthusiasm, for she knew the end of this story all too well.

"As I said, Adel was focused and her anger was becoming hatred. She wanted to control those who would harm our kind, at any cost. But she was fully aware that her magic could be perfectly countered by the magic of the crystal needle. So, she reached out to her new friends and sought the magic of another."

Chapter 9: Betrayal

1692

Adel strolled into the trees behind her house. She walked down a hill and over a little creek that ran through the small valley. The fall leaves were gathering around the base of the trees becoming lovely blankets of nature's creation, rustling and billowing about when the chilly breeze flowed through. She held a thick cape around her shoulders to guard off the cold, yet it didn't seem that any cold could match that which was in her eyes and in her heart.

Finding her way to the place where the Kitsune family stayed would take time on foot. She could fly on her broom much faster, but believed a gentle approach would seem less threatening.

৪০

Yuki crouched in the midst of the trees. With an explosion of motion, she leapt forward and started striking at a smaller tree with precisely placed fists. Then, with a twist of her body, she spun with her leg sweeping the air behind her.

"Good, good dear, you are quick. Now, I want you to close your eyes and find your way to the top of that tree." Tonbo was reading while teaching his daughter the basic fighting techniques of the Kitsune back in Nippon.

Yuki took a slow breath and closed her eyes. She waited a moment, listening to the breezes around the trees. Suddenly she dashed for a tree beside the one he was talking about. With a kick off from the trunk, she bounced back and forth between three separate trunks, each leap taking her higher and higher into the branches. When she got to the very top, she stopped on the highest branch that would support her weight. Pausing briefly, she stiffened her body and held her arms out perfectly level to her shoulders. Slowly she fell backwards and began to descend straight down. Coming in contact with another tree's branch, she caught it and spun over and over, then let go to catch another. Again and again, she did this until she was back down on the forest floor with a precisely placed landing. All the while, her eyes were closed and she was blind to her surroundings.

Yuki opened her eyes and smiled. She was happy to have learned so much from her father. He did not praise her, but she never expected him to, for it was not their way. Humility is a teacher like no other, one that can lead to wisdom. She simply sat down at the base of the tree she had just descended. Next to her was her stitching, which she proceeded to work on now that her daily practice was finished.

"I see that you are continuing your education in the literature of England, Master Tonbo." Adel stopped beside the tree he was sitting against.

The elder fox looked away from his book, his usual serene demeanor gone. Looking up at her, his appearance became fierce. "Yuki, take your brothers and go visit Elsabethe."

Yuki gathered up her stitching and stood. With a courteous bow, she answered.

"Yes, father." With that she and the twins were gone.

Adel smiled. Though she had no romantic designs on this man, she found him very pleasing to look at, even with an angry expression. He closed his book and stood up, fairly towering over her. "What do you want?"

Adel walked around the tree, looking at his handsome figure from all angles. "I suspect that my dear sister has told you about my work."

"Yes, she told me that you surreptitiously had me deliver spells that took the lives of humans in the surrounding villages." The harshness in his voice matched the fierceness in his eyes.

"Oh? You sound as though you were not pleased to deal with the murderous humans. Should they not pay a price for wrongly killing?" She twisted words well.

Tonbo walked away from her, not wishing to look at her. " Go away, leave this forest and my family alone. I will no longer be a device for your horrible plans."

"Have you no honor?" Adel knew this would garner a response.

He turned and marched back over to her. "How dare you! I will never have my honor questioned, especially by the likes of you!"

"How then can you let the people who killed your dear wife, and mother of your children, not pay for their crimes? Your wife didn't do anything to them. Yet they, no doubt, would parade her pelt before each other as a victorious trophy. How can you stand the thought? The honor in you must be screaming for vengeance." Adel looked right at him with no fear in her eyes.

Tonbo looked away. What she said, what she illustrated, made his heart ache. For a moment, and only a moment, he felt the rage of retribution in him. But, casting his eyes past the old witch, he looked into the scattering leaves of fall. In his mind he could see a beautiful woman standing there, with raven black hair and a smile that could melt the heart of any man. She had brilliant turquoise eyes and incredible skin. He whispered in the breeze, "Keiko," as a single tear ran down his face.

A hand reached up to brush the tear away, a thin, cold, sharp hand. Adel looked up into his wounded eyes. "What is it?"

He looked down at her, "What would you have me do?"

A wicked grin spread across her face, "I have great plans for this land. I would destroy what little they have and rebuild with my own vision. I will not do this alone. I can sense you have great power, and I need a king at my side. We will be married and I will set forth a new leadership that will shape the destiny of this entire world. But all this cannot be done while my dear sister remains, for her magic is equal to mine. Deprive her of her crystal needle and bring it to me. With the crystal needle and the obsidian needle together, I will become more powerful than ever. Elsabethe will be lost and we will rule this world."

Tonbo was silent. He looked into the trees, where he had envisioned his wife only moments before. "I will do it. I will retrieve the needle tonight while Elsabethe is entertaining my children." He bowed to her.

Adel smiled. Her face revealed that she didn't entirely trust him yet, but she was pleased that he was still listening to her. "Fine. Bring it to the woods and bring your children as well, for they should be witness to the new revolution of mankind."

Tonbo bowed again, "As you wish." He turned and walked toward the edge of the forest. He could move faster as a fox, but he wanted time to think.

"One more thing." Adel took out her dark needle. Tonbo turned around. She whipped the needle in the air with the movements of a conductor and a black thread flowed off the end heading straight for him. Before he could respond, he felt a horrible sensation on his left forearm. It was as though she were piercing the flesh with her needle and running the thread under his skin. When it was done, he looked down to find a strange piece of stitching embedded into his arm.

He held his arm in agony while it seemed to continue to burn. "What is this dark magic?!" he demanded.

She smiled still pointing her needle at him. "That, my dear man, is a pact spell. Promise me you will do what I ask."

Tonbo glared at her. "Will you leave my children unharmed?"

Adel smiled at him. "Of course. If you complete the deal, you and your children will be safe from harm. This I promise. But, if you break this pact, you will suffer the consequences."

He bowed to her one last time. "I understand."

She lifted her hand with the needle and the pain in his arm was gone, though the stitching was still embedded. Adel slowly planted the needle back in her collar. "Fine, then we have a deal."

Without another word, Tonbo left her in the forest.

☙

Elsabethe worked hard in her kitchen making some sweets, with a little help from magic of course. She had left the living room with the children who had come over that afternoon. The twins were at each end of the couch, with their arms folded and surly expressions on their faces. One had a black eye; the other was sporting a little blood from his nose. Each was trapped in a transparent magical field that their sister had created.

"He started it." Yoshi muttered.

"Oh yeah, you were the one who said that I couldn't catch you." Oki muttered back.

Yoshi looked across the room at a glass figurine of a dancing lady. It flew at Oki and shattered against the force field surrounding him. Oki jumped in surprise. "Ha" Yoshi shot at his brother.

Oki pointed his finger at a picture on the wall and prepared to levitate it at his brother, but something stopped it from leaving the wall.

Yuki, who was sitting in a chair across from them working on her gloves, looked up at the picture. She was more powerful than both of them individually and with only a glance she could stop their spells. Together, they were stronger than her, but they hardly ever worked together that well, which was good news for an older sister who was in charge of keeping them from killing each other daily. "Stop this, or I will turn each of you into a nezumi."

"HE STARTED IT!" Both cried while pointing at the other.

She let out an annoyed sigh and snapped her fingers. The glass figurine which was scattered all over the floor came back together and replaced itself on the shelf. "Fine, I will let father deal with you."

Immediately their demeanors changed.

"Don't tell father." Both pleaded.

She picked up her stitching and continued, ignoring their desperate pleas.

"What is all the commotion in here?" Elsabethe came in with a tray of cookies and hot tea.

"Cookies." Both boys announced in hungry excitement. Yoshi hit his head on the force field, Oki hit his hand. They said 'Ow' in unison.

"I see we are being punished." Elsabethe chuckled. " Sister, could you please let them have some tea and cookies? These will only be warm for a while."

Yuki looked at her brothers. "Alright. Now promise that you won't attack each other again, or break anything in here."

"We promise." They had an annoying habit of talking at the same time.

She waved her hand and the force fields broke. Both boys instantly went after the food, careful not to hurt each other, for now.

"Honey, I have something for you. It is a dress that you will look lovely in for the event in town. I am sure it will be absolutely gorgeous with those gloves." Elsabethe handed the tray over to the boys.

"What event?" Yuki set aside her gloves.

Elsabethe smiled. " There will be social this Saturday in town. I organized it to help all the new people get acquainted. I do believe that there is a young man in town that would appreciate being introduced to you."

Yuki blushed. "Oh, Elsabethe. I am not sure if I am ready for that."

"Oh, pish tosh. Now, would you like to see the dress? I would be honored if you would at least try it on."

Yuki smiled and nodded, "I would be honored to wear something crafted by a master."

"Honey, I am not a master, just a simple stitching witch. But I would like to see if it fits or needs any adjustments." Elsabethe went to her stitching room, to collect the dress she had crafted with the crystal needle.

Yuki felt rather embarrassed. No one had ever made her a dress like this. She had had others make her kimonos before, but that was expected. A lovely dress was something special, especially on this side of the world.

༄

Tonbo walked up to the house. He knew his children were inside, he could hear the twins. Elsabethe was so kind and accepting of them that she allowed them to enter at their will. He pushed aside the door and looked into the living room. Both boys were on the couch, fighting over the last few cookies. Elsabethe was standing with her back to him, working on something. He could not see Yuki, but he knew that she was in the room, he could feel her.

"Father!" The boys stopped fighting long enough to bow to their father when he entered the room.

"Oh, master Tonbo. I was not expecting you." Elsabethe turned and bowed to him as she had learned from Yuki.

Tonbo returned the bow, but he was very silent. Something was weighing upon him. Anyone could see it in his eyes.

"Father. I am glad you have come. What do you think of this lovely dress?" Yuki spoke from behind Elsabethe, who stepped aside so Tonbo could see her.

Yuki was standing on a short pedestal so that she could be pinned and checked. She was wearing a dress made of the finest crafted material that the magical world could create. It was a simple dress, one that accentuated her figure, but covered her from neck to floor and down to the wrists. There was a wide ribbon tied around the waist with a beautiful bow in the back. The whole dress was blue with a hint of mint green. The colors made her brilliant red hair all the more beautiful against her perfect complexion.

He stepped over to her, the sadness in his eyes all the more present. He took her hand and held it in his strong palm for a moment. " I never realized how much you look like your mother."

Yuki blushed and grinned. Her mother was considered one of the most beautiful women in all of Nippon, especially by the man who called her his wife. "Thank you, father."

"I think I can have this done in time. If you please." Elsabethe took up her crystal needle and waved it in the air. The dress transferred to the dress form in the stitching room. Yuki was again in her simple, conservative attire. She stepped down and sat back where she had been stitching.

Tonbo paid close attention when Elsabethe used her needle for magic. He looked around the room at his children while they looked back in confusion.

Elsabethe stepped up to him. "Master Tonbo, what is wrong?" She could sense her sister's magic on him and it was a powerful spell.

He closed his eyes and thought hard about the spell he would cast. Holding up his arm, he opened his hand. There in the palm appeared a scroll, rolled up and tied closed.

"Your sister desires the crystal needle to further her plans." He said this very plainly.

Elsabethe stepped back from him. She knew her sister was growing in greed for power, but she never expected this. Holding up the needle, she prepared to defend herself, but she didn't know what the children would do. In her mind she quickly envisioned what could happen next. Would she be forced to fight him and his children? She had come to care deeply for these people and the idea of hurting them was almost too much. But she knew what must happen, regardless of her feelings. "Master Tonbo, I will not harm you, but I will never allow my sister to take this needle."

He looked at her, his face stone cold. Something in him was unsettled. "Children, leave the room. But do not leave the house."

Being very obedient to their father, the three got up and bowed out. He looked down to the frightened witch. " I will do everything in my power to see to the safety of my children. " This statement came out as his own justification for what he was going to do next.

Elsabethe remained in her defensive posture, "What does my sister ask?"

"Only for your needle and I have no choice." He held up his arm to show her the spell stitched into his flesh.

Elsabethe didn't know the details of the spell, but she knew it to be of extremely dark magic which would inevitably take a person's life. "Oh, dear Tonbo, I am so sorry. Here let me try to undo that." She pointed her needle at his arm, but the magic only caused him to flinch in pain. "What is this? What did she do to you?"

Tonbo held his arm where it hurt. "It is a pact spell, one that I agreed to so that my children would be saved from her."

Elsabethe closed her eyes, anguish written all over her features. "Oh, I am so sorry. A pact spell cannot be undone. Once you agreed, you sealed it from being countered." Then she opened her eyes, speaking with great sorrow for what she had to say. "I cannot let you take this needle to her. For the sake of all people I cannot allow this to happen."

"I have absolutely no intention of taking the needle from you. A world with her in power is a world that will not be safe for my children, or anyone else." His expression was deadly serious.

" I am sure I do not understand. What do you want then?" Elsabethe didn't put her needle away just yet, still unsure of the situation.

Tonbo untied the scroll and opened it to be certain that it was the spell he had in mind. With a grim smile, he looked back to her, " I understand that you can no more harm your sister than she can harm you. This is why she recruited me for this mission."

The old witch nodded, "That is correct."

"There is an ancient style of magic from my homeland, binding magic. This spell, with myself and even help from my children, will bind her powers and stop her from being able to harm anyone ever again." He handed her the scroll, not sure if she could even read the ancient kanji. " It is not that complicated, but it does require more than one person to cast."

She looked at the ancient scroll, blind to the words on it for it was a tongue that very few on this side of the globe had ever seen. However, she was aware of binding magic. She had learned about it from a sage witch four or five hundred years ago. " Binding magic, that is extreme." It hurt her deeply to consider doing this to her sister.

Tonbo stepped closer to her, nearly covering her in his shadow. "That woman is a threat and I will stop her. I can do this without you, but I am sure that it will be more successful with your help. And I know that you have insight into her way of thinking."

Elsabethe nodded slowly, something sticking in her throat. Perhaps it was her heart at the thought of what she was considering. She had to do this and she knew it even more than Tonbo, though she didn't have the conviction of a dedicated father. "I will help. You are quite right, that woman is no longer my sister, she is a monster who must be stopped."

Tonbo went right into tactical mode, " Fine. Oki and Yoshi can help you learn the spell. They are good with reading and translating kanji into your tongue. Yuki will come with me and help me get Adel's attention. We have until sundown."

Elsabethe nodded slowly turning to go and get the children. Stopping, she looked back at him. "That spell on your arm, I am sure you know what that is?"

Tonbo stopped her. "I understand what my fate will be. I only ask that you look after my children when I am gone. They will need guidance in your world." His passionate determination was wavering at the idea that this would be his last day with his children.

Elsabethe nodded once again, "I promise to keep them under my protection as long as they are with me. And……I am sorry for what my sister has done to you and your family. It is not our way, at least it used to not be." Her heart was breaking, for she knew that his life was spent and it was Adel's hand that had cost him his future with his family.

"Thank you." he bowed to her. She returned the bow and then left to gather the children so that they might be informed of what was to happen that evening.

Chapter 10: A Fathers Love

Elsabethe, Tonbo and the children all spoke of a plan that involved a unique coordination of magical talents. Yoshi and Oki stayed with Elsabethe in her home, helping her learn the spell. Yuki and Tonbo left to begin what had to be done.

Tonbo, knowing that Adel would come for him soon, walked with his daughter toward the center of the forest.

He looked to his little girl more than once. Usually he was a very stoic man, one who was hard to read when others looked upon him. His strength was a virtue that protected him and his family. But, at this moment, that firm attitude was broken and so was his heart.

" Father, what is wrong?" Yuki stopped walking, wishing to force her father to say something to her.

Tonbo stopped a few steps ahead of her. He paused and took a deep breath. "My little child, I am going to miss you." He whispered, so low in fact that Yuki didn't hear him.

"What, father?" she came around to him, only to find something she had not seen but once on the face of her father, tears in his eyes. Only when their precious mother died had he shed tears.

He looked at her, anguish written all over him. "I love you and your brothers dearly, I pray you understand this."

"Yes, of coursen father." she was a little frightened by the way he was talking, for she was unaware of the spell Adel had cast on him.

Tonbo took her in his big, strong arms and held her tightly. "I wanted to be sure that you knew this above all. My love for you transcends any magic."

Yuki closed her eyes and pressed her head into his chest as she did when she was very young, when they would lie together as foxes in the den. "I know, father, and I love you too."

He cried, while running his hand down her soft red hair. "Be a good girl, be a happy girl. Find a mate and have children to love."

At that moment Yuki began to understand. Somehow she came to the realization that this was the last time they would embrace this way. Yuki also knew that what was to happen was irreversible, and she had to accept this.

"I love you, father, I always will." she looked up into his eyes with a smile.

He returned her smile, setting his resolve to make sure that smile was not taken away by anyone.

At that moment, as if called by their embrace, the winds became cold and a darkness fell over the forest. Both Kitsune knew that the obsidian witch had arrived.

"It is time to finish this." Yuki announced.

Tonbo nodded, "Whatever happens, do not let harm come to yourself or your brothers."

Yuki bowed her head, " I promise. "

"How touching." Adel stepped out from behind a tree, which seemed impossible for the width of the tree was only half her size. "Such a beautiful sight, the love between a father and a child."

Tonbo stepped in front of Yuki. "I do not have the needle."

Adel smiled, she was holding her needle up, playing with it between her fingers.

"I was under the impression you were a loving father and husband. But, I didn't know you were this foolish, exacerbating my anger by coming here to taunt me."

"I am not here to taunt you. I am here to ask that you relinquish your powers and stand accountable for the lives you have already taken. If you do this, I promise that you will not be harmed."

Adel smiled wickedly. "Oh, you impudent dog. I have no intention of relinquishing anything and nothing you do will convince me otherwise."

"I thought not. YUKI!" Tonbo stepped aside.

Yuki held out her hands and a wave of white energy shot out at the witch, hitting her in the chest and taking hold on her. A stream of this brilliant energy connected the two, with Yuki in control. Adel was taken by surprise. She really didn't expect Tonbo to use his children like this.

"I WILL NOT BE TAKEN SO EASILY!" Adel swung her needle in the air, about to cast a counter spell.

But, at that moment, another white beam of energy hit her right hand, grasping it in mid-motion. Oki Kitsune hovered through the trees, holding his hands out with the magic light connecting him to her. Another beam came from the other direction, pulling her left arm up and lifting her off the ground, holding her against her will. Yoshi was holding her in place, opposite his brother.

Adel was motionless, but with a smile on her face. "My dear foxes, if you are going to stop a stitching witch, be sure to deprive her of her needle first." The hand with the needle thrust upward breaking their hold on that arm. With one singular motion, she swiped her hand through the other two beams, cutting herself free.

Landing on the ground, she dodged a pair of air blasts from the boys. Jutting both hands out in their directions, she caused the earth to shoot rocks at them. One dodged the blow, while the other was hit right in the center of his chest throwing him against a tree. Landing hard on the ground, he passed out.

"LEAVE MY CHILDREN ALONE!" Tonbo yelled while he furiously hurled lightning bolts at Adel.

She pointed her needle at the incoming attack. When the energy came in contact with her hand, she threw it aside, burning holes in the ground. " Oh, I thought that you Kitsune never harmed anyone?" Her voice was filled with taunting.

Yuki held up both of her hands, "We never kill, unlike you. But we are capable of so much more." All the leaves on the forest floor came together and trapped the witch in a thick ball of foliage. Then, the ball slammed against the ground, with the intention of knocking the witch senseless.

Tonbo ran over to Oki, who was still knocked out on the ground. "Oki…Oki." he held the boy for a moment.

Oki opened his eyes, "Did we get her?" he asked with a smile on his face.

Yuki stood up, not sure that her attack was good enough to stop such a witch, yet there was no motion in the pile of leaves. "I am unsure brother." she walked over to the mound and prepared to cast an entrapment spell.

Suddenly, a hand shot out of the leaves and grasped the young lady's throat. Adel rose out of the leaves, lifting Yuki with her as she ascended into the middle of the trees. Yuki struggled, but could do nothing in this position. Leaves, twigs, and other natural debris began to flow around the old witch. A storm was forming born of pure rage.

"FOOLS!" Adel's voice boomed over the entire forest. "I have been practicing magic since the days of the first Pharaohs. You never stood a chance. Now, watch as your betrayal is met with its punishment." She looked at the horizon and saw that the sun was just about to set.

Just then, a silver needle flew through the air. Behind it was a thread that was being produced by its eye. The small object spun around and around Adels wrist, then stuck into a nearby tree, pulling her hand down with it. The motion caused the old witch to loosen her grasp on Yuki's throat.

"What is this?" Adel looked at the tethering thread.

More needles flew through the air. Hundreds came, each creating their own thread, and each spinning around Adel to fasten her down. One by one, the needles would tie her up, and then pin themselves into a tree trunk or into the ground. In due time, an amazing array of threads bound the dark witch like a spider pinning its victim.

The Crystal Needle

Elsabethe stepped out from behind a tree, her crystal needle shining with the magic she had just cast. With a smile, she answered her sister. "You are not the only one who has been in this business for centuries."

"You!? You would betray me like this?" Adel furiously struggled against the ensnaring threads.

Elsabethe came to where her sister had been pinned between all the trees. "I have no intention of allowing you to harm anyone else. Our magic was never meant for the dastardly deeds that you create. It is time that I took a stand for the humans and for this lovely family."

Adel was so enraged she could only sputter as she struggled. She writhed around, breaking loose one of the threads. Her needle glowed as she began to break free of each of the spells cast on each of the attacking needles.

Elsabethe stepped back, "She will be free momentarily. We must bind her now."

Tonbo, Yuki, Oki and Yoshi stepped up, each taking a position around the witch in the four cardinal directions. They started to chant in unison a spell in the ancient tongue of Nippon. Elsabethe waited. She had learned the words, but she didn't need to cast the spell while four were there to do so now. The color of the skin on Adel's left arm was draining as her magic was being taken from her.

"NO, I WILL NOT ALLOW THIS!" Adel struggled harder, cutting more of the threads.

Elsabethe stepped up to her sister, but spoke to the others. "Keep chanting; I will make sure she doesn't harm you."

Adel stopped for a moment. Something other than the spell caught her attention. She looked at the sunset. "No, I think that I have won."

Tonbo's arm jolted and he looked at it. He suddenly realized that the spell was taking effect. He waited a moment, but nothing happened to him. Then, as if ice had just filled his bones, he heard all three of his children screaming. A black smoke was rising from their flesh and they were all being taken by the death spell.

"NO!!" Tonbo screamed, raging towards Adel.

"I warned you there would be payment for betrayal. Watch, fool, as your precious children all die before your eyes." Adel cackled wickedly at the sight of what was happening.

Tonbo had little time to think. He held his hands out and started casting a spell of his own creation. This was a magic that needed no words, no training, just enormous love. The black smoke on his children blew away, and he began to burn with the same darkness. The three children were still in pain, but they were no longer dying. He fell to his knees and cried out in agony, the pain of this spell was tremendous, but he knew he had to endure until it was finished or it could possibly still take one of the children along with him. So, he fought with strength that he hadn't realized was in him.

Adel broke through the last of the threads, heading straight for her sister. "I will not lose this day!"

Elsabethe wanted to help Tonbo, but she had to stop Adel too. So, she made her decision. Holding up her needle, she started chanting the spell the boys had translated for her. Adel stumbled as more of her magic began draining from her.

"I WON'T BE STOPPED!" She held up her needle to respond to the attack and watched as it exploded into a black mist, having all of its power bound by the spell.

"You can't stop me!" Adel gasped struggling even harder to reach her sister.

Then another voice joined Elsabethe's. Yuki was chanting and holding out her hand to Adel. The boys were both unconscious, having nearly died.

Elsabethe continued chanting with tears running down her face. Tears of sadness for the children, tears of pain for Tonbo, and tears for what she was being forced to do to her own sister.

Adel was nearly upon her sister, her arms ready to tear Elsabethe apart. But when the very tip of Elsabethe's needle touched the enemy, Adel burst into thousands of leaves, scattering in the wind.

It was over. Adel was bound by the spell. All that remained was a cloud of leaves flooding into the forest.

Two wolves lay on the forest floor, almost dead. Elsabethe closed her eyes and gathered herself as best as she could.

"Yuki?" she looked around for the one who had helped her complete the spell.

She found the poor girl kneeling down and crying over the body of a fox. Tonbo was dead, his life spent as the payment to keep his children alive. The act was more than heroic, but that did not make it any less painful to those who loved him.

Elsabethe walked over to Yuki and knelt down, putting a hand on her shoulder.

She wanted to tell her how very sorry she was for her sister's actions, but the words weren't enough. A silence fell over the forest with only the weeping of a daughter to be heard on the gentle autumn winds.

༄

Chapter 11: So much more left

"What happened to the children? You said that the spell was redirected by their father, so why are the brothers passed out?" asked Joseph, who was now stitching with Elsabethe and Allison in the living room.

Allison responded, "The spell was a clever, evil concoction of magic. Even without it causing what it was designed for, it still left lasting effects. The children were cursed, transformed from beautiful foxes into horrible wolves."

"But the sister was not a wolf?" Joe cocked his head thinking.

Elsabethe nodded, "Yes and no. The boys were permanently transformed into wolves, but the sister was only partially cursed. She could remain a human in the night, but when the sun came out, she would become a wolf."

"Could they not use magic to undo this?" Joe sipped his tea, not seeing Allison's watering eyes.

Allison answered, rather harshly, "No, they could not! The damned curse locked their abilities and distorted them into ugly beasts even while in human form."

Joe looked at her with surprise. "It is only a story."

Elsabethe rolled her eyes. She had thought that he would be a little wiser than this, especially after seeing the girl. " Unfortunately, she is right. A spell like that would lock the abilities of the less mature magic user."

"I guess I understand. But couldn't the other witch undo it?"

Elsabethe held up her clear needle. "Yes, she could undo any normal spell. But, a pact spell is something special. It binds the caster and the recipient. Master Tonbo bound himself to the spell so that no one could undo it. When his children were attacked by the magic, they too fell under the conditions. Believe me, I wish it wasn't so."

Joe smiled. "Well, it is only a story."

Allison looked away, tears running down her face again. "I...I need to leave." she got up and ran out, leaving all her stitching behind.

"Is she okay?" Joe watched her leave.

Elsabethe, who had not realized how much this would hurt her, felt terrible. "I am sure she will be fine. Sometimes a story can bring back memories that one doesn't wish to remember."

Elsabethe and Joseph continued stitching. He passed the time by asking more questions about the story. Truthfully, he was waiting for Allison to come back in.

"So, what happened next?" Joe cut the thread on the last stitch of the kimono part of his pattern.

Elsabethe smiled, "Next? It isn't over yet."

"I don't understand? When does a story not have an end?" Joe remained oblivious.

"My dear boy, the spell that bound Adel has a limit. It will break in due time, and Adel will return. These trees will be dangerous when that day comes." Elsabethe put her work away in a cloth bag.

"What kind of danger? Will she come out of the woods and steal little children?" he was taking all this very lightly, for he did not realize how true it was.

Elsabethe shook her head slowly. "When the time comes, she will exact her revenge on those who bound her and on all humans she despises for actions toward witches."

Joe smirked. "Oh, I get it. One of those ghost stories to scare tourists with."

Elsabethe let out a sigh, " Adel is no ghost. But, you will have to discover that on your own."

Joe put his own work away. He wasn't sure what to make of her last statement. Surely she didn't believe in all of this? Yet it seemed so real when she told it. He set this aside in his mind and packed up his last threads of the day.

He stood up and stretched out his back from sitting and stitching all evening. Joe turned to Elsabethe and asked, "Does she mind this story?"

She looked up to him. "I don't see why not. Her role in it is very noble, though a little painful."

Joe was not sure how to take that. "I guess. I would imagine that she has been hurt too often and that kind of story might not be the best thing."

"You are concerned about her feelings?"

"Well, yes. I don't like to see anyone upset, especially a friend." Joe picked up his bags and prepared to leave.

Elsabethe grinned at him, "So, you consider her a friend, only having met her this one evening?"

Joe shrugged, "Perhaps. I always enjoy the company of a stitcher. "

Elsabethe turned out a light beside her chair, "Goodness, it's quite late." She noticed the time on the clock beside her chair. "I think it is time for bed. I hope you don't mind if I invite Allison to come back and stitch with us, though she won't be coming back until later in the evening."

Joe looked back to her, "I don't mind perhaps I will come a little later myself."

She smiled warmly, happy that he seemed genuinely sincere about this girl.

"Good night." Joe waved to her and walked out the front door.

༶

Walking between the houses, Joe stopped a moment to admire the velvety night sky. Though he missed his old town of Atlanta, he did enjoy the clarity of night that comes in a small town with no city lights to distort the stars. He even enjoyed the symphony of sounds created in the trees with no sirens, horns honking, or loud boom cars driving down the road.

In the distance, Joe could hear something completely out of the ordinary. It was a soft and deeply sad crying. He had a strong feeling he knew who it was bleeding those tears.

Walking around Elsabethe's home, he found the girl sitting on an over turned pail. She had her face in her hands and did her best to contain deep sobs.

"Allison?" He approached slowly.

She looked around cautiously, then nodded as if she didn't know her own name. "Joseph? What do you want?" She knew she was being rude, but couldn't help herself.

Joe stepped closer to her, "I would hope that all those tears aren't from something that I said. I never meant to hurt you."

She looked down, letting a tear run down her cheek, "No, it was nothing you said that brought this on me. I….I just can't talk about it."

Joe rifled through his bag and pulled out a handkerchief monogrammed on the corner with the logo from his family's new business. He stepped up to her and held it out. "I don't know what is so sad, but I hope this can help."

She slowly took it out of his hand. For a moment Allison looked at it with amazement. Then she dabbed at her face with the cloth.

Joseph smiled, "Well, goodnight." he turned to leave.

Allison blew her nose and then asked. "Why?"

He stopped and turned back around. "Why? Why what?"

"Why are you being so nice to me? You hardly know me." She sniffed hard.

Joseph set his bag down on a rather large stump that had been cleanly cut some years ago. "I can't stand to see a girl cry, especially one who has been unfairly hurt."

Allison smiled through her tears. "Thank you."

Joe smiled back and turned to leave. He took a few steps and stopped. "Uh….if you are heading home, I wouldn't mind walking you. It is awfully late."

She shook her head and gruffly stated, "Don't worry about me, I will be fine."

Joe gulped and then looked away. "I was just trying to be nice."

Allison closed her eyes. "I am sorry. I didn't mean to be rude. I really don't need to be walked home, I live very close by." She actually smiled at him. "But, thank you."

He looked down, feeling silly having just asked such a teenage question. "Well, I hope you will come back tomorrow. I like having the company to stitch with."

"I will, but I can't come until late." She wiped her face.

He laughed, "Have to wait for the sun to set, is that it?"

Her eyes widened and she looked around. Could he have made the connection?

"What do you mean?"

He realized he might have been terribly rude, "Oh, nothing, nothing, just a stupid joke. Sorry."

Allison smiled softly, "You're right. By the time I can come, the sun will have set."

Joe yawned and turned, "Well, good night." he left her to go to into his house, which was just a few feet away.

Allison watched him go inside. She could see the trail of lights as he moved from one room to another, finally settling on one room with the light staying on long enough to allow him to change and crawl into bed.

"I see that this young man has caught your attention." Elsabethe commented as she stepped out onto her back porch, not too far from the little wolf girl.

She looked away with a frown on her brow, "No, he is just another human."

"No, he isn't and you know this." Elsabethe wrapped herself in a thick robe and stepped out into the cool night air.

"He is a human, unless I have lost my senses for magical creatures." Allison was a little surprised.

Elsabethe shook her head. "True, he is a human. But he is so much more. Part of him is seeking a person like you, which is why he has acted the way he has. When was the last time a young man asked to walk you home?"

Allison stood up to walk into the trees, "I cannot remember the last time I even let a human man see me. They are all disgusted by my appearance." her tone became bitter quickly.

"He isn't."

Allison looked up to the stars, more tears welling up in her eyes, though it seemed that she had drained every last one already. " Just wait. He is just another human. If he were to see me in the light of day, as the dog that I am, he would throw things at me, call animal control, or even pull out a gun."

Elsabethe stepped closer, slightly annoyed. "Now you know that is not true. Hasn't he already proven that to you? You certainly didn't think that when you came over to him before, as a dog."

Allison held up the handkerchief, looking at it for a moment while she remembered an apple. "Perhaps."

"Why don't you give him a chance? I am not asking you to marry him tomorrow, only to stitch with him. Right now, both of you need a friend."

Allison looked back up to the room where he had gone to bed. "He may need a friend, but I cannot be anything to him like he needs. I am not the kind of girl a handsome man wants. He may be kind and nice, but he won't want me."

Elsabethe stepped off her back steps to the ground and walked over to her. "Please don't give up. Let him have a chance. If he has any sort of heart, he will learn you are a wonderful person." She heard a subtle scoffing sound from Allison. "Please, just come back, what harm could it do?"

"I...I will come back and stitch. We will see if he comes back as well."

Elsabethe stepped out further, the moon's milky white glow covering her face. "Why have you called yourself Allison? That is not your name."

"You have told him too much of the story. I don't want to confuse him. "Allison turned back around and looked at Elsabethe. "Please don't tell him any more about Adel, father, or any of this."

"But..." Elsabethe began to protest.

Allison shook her head, "I will admit that I sort of like him. And I don't want to scare him."

Elsabethe smiled knowingly at her friend, "Do not forget that you were interested in him first."

Allison looked down for a moment as she remembered the day that he and his family arrived. "I guess I was interested in him, but I have made mistakes before. Just remember what I said."

"I don't believe I fully understand. But I will oblige you as long as you come back and stitch with us." Elsabethe waited for the girl to agree.

"Yes, yes, I will. I need to go check on my brothers." Allison walked into the trees, heading for a well-worn path to a den that she had created centuries ago.

Elsabethe let out a long sigh. She knew what must happen for this to work out. But she wasn't sure that little Yuki was willing to believe it could be possible. She went back inside and stored the rest of the stew in a special bowl. With a minor spell, she sent the stew out to Allison's brothers, so that they would have a hot meal tonight.

※

Allison walked through the trees of the forest. The sky was partially blocked by the natural ceiling of leaves above her, which made for a dark night. Yet there was enough of the bright moonlight to let her see her path. She held the handkerchief in her hand while she walked, looking at it with a small smile on her face. She wouldn't entirely admit it to Elsabethe, but she thought that boy was awfully cute.

Stopping, she knelt down by the side of the pathway. Buried in the ground was a large, smooth stone. On its surface were hand carved-letters in ancient kanji. This was her father's resting place. She spent much time here, remembering the man she missed so often. Tonight was especially hard, for the story had been difficult to hear again. She thought she could handle it, but she really couldn't. A lump was forming in her throat at the memory of sitting over his body after he died to keep her alive. But what kind of life had she known since that horrible night? Three hundred years of simply waiting for the Obsidian needle to return with its caster at the ready to wreak her revenge.

She placed one hand on the grave marker, and cried. "Oh, father, I wish I were with you." With her other hand she wiped the tears from her eyes with the cloth. Slowly she moved her hand away from her face and looked at the cloth she was holding. It gave her pause to smell the scent of the boy who gave this to her. Why did this mean so much to her? Why did it mean so much to him to help her? Was he really this nice or was he just pitying her? She didn't know, but she wanted to find out.

"Sister?" A wolf walked up to her. His eyes were compassionately looking at her.

She smiled at him. "Hello, Oki. I was just thinking of father."

The wolf stood next to her. "I worried about you listening to that story again."

"Oh, my brother, we should never allow ourselves to forget what father did for us. Even if it brings tears to our eyes." She wiped her face again with the cloth.

"I know." Oki looked at the grave marker, a lump forming in his throat as well. He turned back to her. "Why don't we go back to the den. Elsabethe sent some nice smelling dinner."

She patted him on the head like anyone would their dog, which he didn't mind. "I have already eaten. Why don't you return and share with your brother, I want to stay out here a little longer."

"Are you sure?"

"Yes. Please don't worry about me. I will be fine. Now go, and don't fight with your brother." She waved at him to leave.

He smirked at her, or at least he formed a smirk on his canine face. "Sure, as long as he doesn't hog it all."

She laughed at him and watched him head back toward their long time home here in the woods. Allison would stay out here for the night, sitting beside her father's grave and pondering what might happen next. Never more in her life did she desire the sage wisdom of her father.

ஐ

Chapter 12: Just Friends

Evenings passed with Joseph enjoying stitching with Elsabethe and Allison. More than once he brought over some of his other works, showing off his talent. Elsabethe would roll her eyes at his display of ego, but Allison ate it up.

This evening, he sat in his new, usual place on the couch next to Allison with only their stitching supplies between them.

"You must like Japanese culture?" Allison looked at another piece of work he handed her. It was an ancient Japanese temple surrounded by mountains and trees, designed to look like an old Japanese silk screen painting.

Joe shrugged, "Yeah, it's neat. My hometown had a sister city in Japan, so I grew up with a lot of Japanese influence. Have you studied anything about Japan?"

Allison looked away before the blush to her cheeks could give away her thoughts. "A little." Elsabethe coughed a couple of times upon hearing that. Allison went on. "Did you bring anything else?"

"Yeah, this one was a special piece I did for my girlf...well ex-girlfriend." Joe pulled out another perfectly stitched oriental picture. It had a two tailed fox sitting near an old temple with cherry blossoms floating in the breeze.

Allison took it from him, her eyes sparkling at the sight. It looked just like a painting of her grandfather. "This is very nice. A fox, right?" she feigned ignorance of the subject matter.

Joseph really surprised her with his response. "No, that's a Kitsune. They are fox spirits, like the ones in Elsabethe's story. I think it has two tails because it's old, or something like that."

She casually corrected him. "No, they gain tails as they grow wiser. The tail splits, but usually it only happens with age, for that is how wisdom is gained." Suddenly she looked up with wide eyes, " Uh, at least that is what I have heard, before."

He was stunned, but happy. "Yeah, that was what one person told me at a Japanese Festival in Gwinnett."

"What is a Gwinnett? I thought you said you were from a place called Atlanta?" Allison handed him back the piece and picked up the project she had started when they first met.

Joe shrugged, "Gwinnett County has a nice convention center where they hold festivals and other events. It's near Atlanta." He casually changed the conversation over to her. "Where are you from?"

Elsabethe, who was quietly stitching in her seat across the room, looked up. She was not sure what Allison would say. Allison continued stitching not sure of what to say. "Uh, why?"

Joe laughed, "Nothing special, just curious. We have been stitching together for almost two weeks and I don't even know if you are native to the area. Your accent isn't really New England, though neither is Elsabethe's."

Allison smiled and created a misleading truth, "Well, my family has been here in Featherville for over three hundred years."

Joe looked up with surprise. "Oh, well, I guess I was wrong. You are quite the native!"

Elsabethe put away her work, "Young people, I believe it is time for bed. It is getting late."

Joseph hadn't noticed the clock all night. He was sure that his father would call him again, embarrassing him as usual. But it was already almost eleven in the evening so neither of his parents must be worried about him.

He packed up his current project and the extra finished pieces he had brought with him and said good night.

Allison packed up and put her stuff in a special place in Elsabethe's home, for it wasn't good to keep one's stitching on the dirty floor of the forest. She was quiet and had a slight smile on her face.

"I told you that he would come back." Elsabethe quietly commented.

Allison walked toward the door, putting a cape around her shoulders, but not putting up the hood. She stopped just before leaving. "Yes, he has surprised me."

"Good night, dear." Elsabethe watched the girl leave, hoping dearly that this was the beginning of something special for one who had endured a life of misery.

&

Joseph startled Allison who had stepped down from the front porch of the old house. "Hey."

She looked at him and actually grinned, "Oh, hello. Are you locked out again?"

He had been accidentally locked out a few nights ago, but this was not the case tonight. "Nope. I thought that we might talk, without needles and thread between us. Or, an old grandmother listening in."

At first she considered simply turning him down and going back to the forest, yet she wanted to stay. "Well, what do you want to talk about?"

"You." he walked right beside her, unashamed to be there.

Casting her eyes down, she slowly walked down the unpaved driveway of the two homes. Kicking a couple of the larger stones, she shyly asked. "Me? Why?"

Joseph looked up at the cloudy sky, only a few patches of stars could be seen. "All the time, we just stitch. I've shown off my collective work and talked endlessly about myself. But, you haven't said much about yourself. I want to know more about you."

Allison let out a sigh. He had hit upon the very subject she didn't want to talk about. Walking ahead of him, she sat on a large boulder that his father had put out as part of the yard décor. "Not much to say, really. I stitch and I live. What else do you want to know?"

He walked around the rock, kicking at dandelion fluff and watching it scatter on the breeze. "Do you have parents? Siblings? Where do you work all day? Of course, I am not prying and if you don't want to answer, I will understand."

She caught a fluff of the dandelion and looked at it, "I don't have any parents, they are gone."

He stopped, not realizing what he might have done to her. "Oh, I am sorry."

"It's okay. They have been gone for a long time. I still miss them, but I can accept it." She tried to sound less depressed. "I have two brothers, both a handful, but I love them. As for work, well, I am in charge of keeping an eye on the outskirts of Featherville."

"Like a forest ranger?" he asked very innocently.

"Yeah, I guess. It's a lot of work. Not much else to say."

"Alright. What about your future? My father has been bugging me about getting out and making something of myself. Of course, all he cares about is that I get in to a college that has a team that might make me want to go and sit through football games." He said this with a touch of humor, though it was truer than he wanted to believe.

"My future?" she looked at him with wide eyes. She hadn't given her future much thought, her curse keeping that sort of thinking at bay. "I don't know. I want to get out of Featherville."

"You and me both." he retorted.

She continued. " I have heard so many wonderful things about this country that I want to see it myself. The grand forests of the west, the desert, the plains, even the big cities."

Joe looked back at her in surprise. "You live in New England, and you want to go and see big cities?"

"Pretty much all I have seen is this place. It has been centuries since I even walked through a place like Paris or London." The words came out before she realized what she was saying.

He glazed over it like it was just a jest. "Yeah, well, as one who just spent four years in a place like Atlanta, I like big cities. This small town is quaint and all, but it lacks interesting stuff." He surprised her again and hopped up to the boulder right next to her. "Okay, what about other things?"

She looked at him with the same perplexed expression she gave him a few moments ago. "What?"

"You're worse than a politician who won't give answers. What do you like? What do you hate? Do you get into politics? Do you like football? I could write up a questionnaire, but it's more fun just talking." He leaned in with a cute smile, knowing perfectly well that he was flirting with her. But he often found that girls tended to respond to a handsome flirt.

She laughed. He was cute and the way he acted was so unlike anyone she had talked to in decades. "Music."

"Huh?"

"I like music. When I was younger my father brought me to a concert in London where a man played a violin, the 'Canon in D'. It was beautiful." she smiled remembering the event when she was introduced to Johann Pachelbel.

"Alright, that's a start. Classical music, it's nice." he looked up to the sky, which was slowly beginning to clear off.

"Baroque."

"Huh?"

"It was Baroque music. Classical is after Baroque." She grinned, and then began to laugh.

"Alright. So I stand corrected." He laughed too. It was possibly the first time he had heard her laugh like this. He liked hearing her laugh.

"Okay, so what do I hate? Lice, I hate lice." she said this without a second thought, even scratching at a patch of fur on her arm. Just the thought of those little bugs made her itch.

He continued to laugh, "Well, you and everyone else. A good shampoo should take care of them if there is a problem." he was prodding her with a joke.

"Sure, sounds easy enough." She understood he was joking, though little did he realize that she went through a drug-stores supply of lice shampoo once a year.

Joseph pointed toward the end of the driveway, "Hey, why don't we go to the little Ice Creamery; they stay open until midnight."

"Ice cream? I have always wanted to try ice cream." she smiled.

"Try? You haven't tried ice cream?" He was more than stunned.

She cleared her throat, "Well, no. It isn't something that I have had the chance to try."

"Great, then I would love to introduce you to something that I like. Come on." he was eager to take her there, as a friend, that is.

She grinned at the thought, but her happiness faded quickly, "No, I don't think so." The thought of going into a place with other people was too much.

"Don't worry, I can pay. Or if you think that's too macho, I will go Dutch." he was always persuasive with girls he was interested in.

Allison jumped down from the rock, "No, I don't think so. It is getting awfully late."

He came down beside her, "What's wrong?" he could easily sense that something was really bothering her about going and the last thing he wanted to do was hurt her.

She took a slow breath, then smiled to him. "Thank you. But I just can't. I really think we need to get to bed."

Joe wasn't sure about anything, but he knew when to back off. "Well, it's been nice. See you tomorrow evening."

"Yeah, sure."

Allison walked around the back of Elsabethe's home. She did this every evening that he was walking with her to give the appearance the she was not simply heading into the forest. This time, though, she walked into the forest after leaving his view and came to a tree that was large enough to hide her. She watched him from around the tree while he walked on home. He was smiling, actually smiling. Nothing about her disgusted him. She had never thought that could be possible. After he went inside and she heard the deep thunk of the lock latching, she turned and stood with her back against the trunk of the tree.

"No, I am not going to let this happen." She hit her head against the tree, then rubbed her head where she had just hurt herself. "That was stupid." She muttered to herself.

Then she turned back around and looked at the house, watching the window where the only light was on. It was his room. Suddenly she found herself wishing he would stand by the window so that she could see him once more. " What am I doing?" She backed away from the tree again, feeling silly. Then her wish came true and he was standing at the window preparing to open it. He stood there for a moment and looked up to the stars. He had removed his shirt and was unknowingly giving her quite the show. She leaned against the tree and sort of hugged the trunk. She wanted that trunk to be him, holding her. He was no longer standing at his window. In fact his light was off and he was most likely in bed now. But she remained, hugging a tree trunk.

"Yuki?"

"WHAT, WHO?!" She turned with a shot, startled by whoever was behind her.

Yoshi stood there, his face showing curiosity at what his sister was just doing. " Are you well?" he asked.

She cleared her throat and walked passed him. "Of course. Let's get back to the den." Without another word about the matter, she walked straight into the trees.

Yoshi stood there for a moment, and then he walked over to the tree and sniffed it. There was nothing on it, so he shrugged and headed in her direction.

ಐ

Chapter 13: Beneath the Surface

Joseph helped his father carry in several bags from the grocery store. They would spend the next hour making four large pots of chili for the few guests of their bed and breakfast. It would be a treat for these New Englanders to try Oklahoma chili, for that was where William learned to make this spicy beef concoction.

"So, you've been quiet today. Girl problems?" William spoke for the first time since they left the store.

"Huh?" Joseph looked up at his father while they walked into the house. "Oh, uh, what do you mean?"

They walked into the kitchen and set everything on the table. William began to empty the bags into the fridge, "I didn't want to say anything, but a couple of nights ago, I stepped out to get you to come home and I saw you sitting on a rock talking to a girl."

Joe looked around. He had been completely unaware that his father had seen him. It felt odd, in a way. "She is just a friend."

"A friend, I see." William had a 'pestering' attitude that showed up when it came to girls and Joseph.

Joe rolled his eyes. "Sure, she's a girl and we are friends. Nothing special."

"Do you want it to be?" William opened several packages of ground beef into a pair of large pots.

Joseph set out the spices while he thought. This was not the first time that the consideration of Allison being a possible girlfriend crossed his mind. But he really didn't have an answer. "I don't know. She is a unique person. I like her, but I don't want to make her uncomfortable."

William chopped up an onion to sauté in with the meat. "Uncomfortable? You're a handsome fellow, which, of course, you got from me, and I would think that any girl would leap at the prospect of dating you."

Joe let out an enormous sigh and nearly glared at his father. "There is a lot more to her than the flighty girls in high school. Just because I caught my fair share of attention doesn't mean that I can simply have any one I want."

"HA." William pointed a greasy wooden spoon at Joseph. " You said <u>want</u>, you do want to date her."

"What is this, an investigation?" Joseph picked up a bag of tea bags and hot chocolate packets and went over to the cabinet.

William stuck the spoon back into the pot with the cooking meat. " No, it's just a father who would like to see his son happy. You moped for weeks after Jenna dumped you, and you haven't even explored any since we moved. Now I find you with a girl, out in the romantic moonlight, and I was just hoping that it could be more. That's all."

Joseph crumpled up the now empty bag in his hands. "It…it isn't impossible. Allison isn't average and there is something about her that intrigues me. But that is all right now. Maybe I will get her to go out with me."

William smiled brightly while he opened some cans of tomato products. "Good. It would be especially nice to have grandchildren around."

"UUUGH! You're cracked. You know that? Simply cracked. I suggest that I might ask a girl out and you already have us married with children on the way. You're worse than mom." Joe opened the back door to toss the bags into the recycling bin.

"What's worse than me?" Marla came in at that moment.

William had to answer first, of course. "Joe, here, is thinking about asking a girl out."

"Oh, really. Well, that would be nice. Think about it, a New England wedding." She was acting foolish on purpose.

Joe sat at the kitchen table and put his face in his hands. " Now you know why I never brought the girls home that I dated. The first ten minutes with you would scare off anyone!"

Marla walked passed him while patting him on the head. "We wouldn't be parents if we didn't embarrass our son. Now, we are going to have a campfire this evening. Could you chop up some wood?"

"Fine, anything to get out of this loony kitchen." Joseph went out of the back door to go and get some wood out of the shed behind the house.

☙

The shed was near the woods and was nothing more than a place to keep wood dry. A nearby stump was used to split the wood so that it could be used for fires. From the many jagged edges in the stump, it had obviously been used for this task before. After piling up a good selection of logs, Joe took out a small axe and prepared a log. He paused and looked around. Soon enough a pair of cute twenty something girls would be jogging by. He had jogged along this road almost every day since his arrival and had passed these girls at this time of day before. He thought he might give them something to look at. So, he pulled off his shirt and stood so that he was in full view of the road.

Nearby, hiding behind one of the trees, was Allison. A wolf by day, she could not bring herself to come over to him right now. But she did come around the house every now and then to see what was going on. To her surprise, and delight, she found Joseph bare from the waist up. He wasn't a beefy man, but he was nice to look at. Years of dance and decent care of his body had given him a defined chest and strong arms. Of course right now, while he worked splitting wood, sweat was glistening off of him quite nicely. With her wolf's nose, she could smell him at a distance when the wind picked up. She would never admit it, but she liked the way he smelled, so masculine.

The back door opened and Marla came out. Allison had not realized that she had taken a few steps away from the tree, and she did not want to be seen, especially by his mother. So, she bolted before anyone saw her, or at least she thought no one had seen her.

Joseph was smiling at the road, waiting for the girls, splitting the wood slowly. Suddenly, just before he lifted the axe again, his shirt smacked him right in the face.

Marla, who had a pretty good throwing arm, was standing on the back steps with her hands on her hips. "You egomaniac, put your shirt on."

"Yes, mom." He stopped long enough to replace his shirt, having missed his opportunity to impress any jogging girls. He had however unknowingly impressed another girl.

&

Yuki, or Allison as she now called herself, lay on the forest floor in her cursed wolf form. While the sun shone overhead, she could not remove this form. Often she spent the days resting. Since her only time as a human was at night, she would spend that time awake. Most nights she continued her practice of combat training that her father had taught her. Night after night, she would perfect this, in the hopes that one day she could finally face Adel and be ready with every aspect of her being.

She had been a Kitsune fox for only nineteen years. For three hundred and seventeen years she had been this ragged wolf. The longing for her true form ached in her heart every day. One might think that it would wane over the centuries, but it hadn't. She also longed for her parents, even more than she desired to be a fox again. Now, though, a new thought would cross her mind. Something happy came along to fill in the gaps left by decades of sadness.

"Hey, sis." a young man's voice came from around one of the trees.

"Yoshi?" she sat up and looked around.

Two other wolves came to her, each trotting along with slight smiles on their snouts. "You going back again tonight?" one of the identical wolves asked.

She nodded. "Yes, I enjoy stitching with them."

"Going back to see that boy, aren't you?" The other wolf asked.

She glared at him, "Yes, what is wrong with that?"

"He is a child."

Allison smiled knowingly, " You know that we haven't aged since we were cursed. Which means he is about my age."

The wolf brothers sat side by side, always together.

Oki came back with, "Yeah, but growing older and experiencing three hundred years are vastly different things."

Allison let out a huff, "Alright, what is wrong? You two don't care about my age."

Oki looked back toward the cottages, "We went to see him."

"You didn't?" she asked, aghast at the thought.

Yoshi calmed her, "Don't worry, we only watched him from a distance. I doubt if he even noticed us."

"Well? What is the problem?" she could sense their discomfort.

Oki continued. "He is nice and all, but aren't you afraid that he will hurt you? He is a human after all, and they are superficial. One good look at you in strong light, and he will...hurt you." this was the voice of a deeply concerned brother.

She smiled, realizing they were honestly worried for her. "Don't worry. Elsabethe hasn't been turning off the lights when I go stitch with them. He has seen me in enough light to know what he is looking at."

Yoshi walked over to her, "Do you like him?"

Allison frowned, "He is a good friend."

"Annnnd?" Oki came over as well.

"And what? Do you want me to say that I am madly in love with him and want him to take me away from this forest. Then you will be in for a major let down. He is just a nice boy who seems like he can get past the way I look." She said this to convince them, but it didn't even convince herself.

"Oh, just a friend. One that you drool at when he is working without his clothing." Oki retorted with a smirk on his muzzle.

Allison would have blushed, if she were able to. "What,… uh,… you saw me?"

Yoshi nodded, "Yeah, we couldn't find you here and went looking. We saw you staring at him. We couldn't tell, was your tongue hanging out, or were you simply drooling?"

She growled at them, "I…I was….I was….just seeing what he was doing. He is just a friend, who happens to have a cute figure."

Oki rolled his eyes. "Girls."

Yoshi looked down, patting his tail against the ground. "Just promise me that you won't get too involved. That you will let him make the first move. I don't want you to set yourself up to be let down hard."

Allison smiled, "Don't worry. I do have three hundred years of experience to know how to handle a human boy."

"Good." Oki added.

All three rubbed their heads together affectionately. They were a family, strong and caring, regardless of the way they looked or what they had lost.

Not too far away from the three wolves, a shadowy figure crept around the trees, watching the whole scene.

"So, the little beast has found a love interest. What shall I make of this?" The old woman's voice was filled with calm hatred and pure evil.

With a gust of the midsummer's breeze, the figure burst into hundreds of dried leaves.

Allison shuddered, and looked around.
"What is it?" Yoshi asked.
She frowned, "A strange, cold breeze on the wind."

༄

Chapter 14: Lessons

Joe was at Elsabethe's again, just as he had been for many evenings already. This night, though, Allison offered to teach him a new technique. Of course this came with a little encouragement from Elsabethe.

Joe sat on the couch with a skein of yarn in his lap, the end in his hands. One hand held a crochet hook while the other was holding the thread. Next to him, sitting very close, was Allison looking over his shoulder.

"I have never been able to do crocheting. My grandmother tried to teach me and I just couldn't do it." Joe made loops and worked them together, creating a messy collection that was not exactly recognizable.

Allison reached over and held his hand, "Okay, first, you are holding this wrong. Here." She repositioned the hook in his hands. "Good, now, keep making that chain."

Joe worked and worked, but all he came up with was a mess that looked like a blind spider working against the wind. With a frustrated huff, he said, "I just can't get this."

Elsabethe, stitching in her little corner, spoke up. "For a boy who can do practically anything, you give up easily."

Joe held up his hands, covered in the yarn, "I think my hands are too big."

Allison leaned in even closer, taking his hands with hers. "Your hands aren't too big, you just need to learn use them correctly."

He grinned at her, "You might be the first girl who has said that to me."

Allison reached around and slapped him in the back of the head, " Focus." She retook his hand with the one she just struck him with. " If you put half of the energy you use to be cute into this, you would have finished a blanket."

He was stunned at first, but found himself with a smile on his face. "You know what is strange. I can tat, but I cannot crochet."

"Whats tat?" Allison kept her eyes on his hands, while she basically crocheted for him.

Joe watched her work with his hands. " Oh, it's another way of weaving thread with a shuttle. I will have to show you some time."

"Good. Now, look at this." She held up his hands, a perfectly even chain of crocheted yarn was between his fingers.

"Wow, I did that?" he joked.

She smiled at him, "Well, no, but you can. If I can use your hands to do this, then you certainly can. And, they aren't too big. Now you try." she sat back, letting go of his hands.

He slowly continued the chain, his new additions a little more sloppy than hers, but he was getting it. "Wow, this is amazing. I have tried to work with a hook like this for years and I haven't gotten this far before."

"Told you." Allison smugly retorted. "You know, you wanted to make a small washcloth, but with that length of a chain, you are heading for a blanket." she laughed while holding up the end of his long chain.

He looped again, "Well, maybe I will make a blanket."

Elsabethe chuckled. " Not with that. That yarn is old and won't be all that comfortable."

Joe stopped and tried starting on another row. "Maybe I will make it for that interesting wolf in the trees."

Both Elsabethe and Allison paused, looking at him. Allison asked. "What wolf?"

He looked up at Elsabethe. "There is a strange looking wolf in the trees out back. At least I think it is a wolf. She has come over to me a couple of times. I bet she gets cold in the winter." He noticed that they both seemed surprised. "What? You haven't seen it?"

Elsabethe looked at Allison, then back to him. "Oh, I think I know what you are talking about."

Allison seemed to move away from him slightly. She held her arm where the fur was showing, having forgotten to keep it covered. "Yeah, I've seen her."

Joe noticed the way that Allison was slinking away from him. "What is wrong? I need your help here." He held up the yarn, where he wanted to start connecting the rows.

She slowly moved her sleeves to cover her arms further, though the fur on the back of her hands could not be covered if she wanted to keep teaching him. " Well, first you don't make another row like that. Here, I will show you." she cautiously reached over his arms to take the yarn. For some reason she was more self-conscious now and he noticed.

"What is wrong? Are you okay?" He took her hand, holding it from moving away from him with his work.

She looked at her arm, then up at him. "It is just….I..." she cleared her throat. " I need that hand to show you how to add another row."

He let go of her hand. Something about her attitude intrigued him. He could not explain it to himself, but he really liked her. The way she showed strength and force, even slapping him when he was acting the fool, yet she was so insecure. He had seen other girls who were self-conscious about their appearance, but for some reason unlike with the other girls, he wanted to put his arms around her and make her feel better. Joe watched her work the thread, he even heard her words while she taught, but there was something else in him that was slowly changing from being 'just friends.'

ఐ

Joseph and Allison walked out of Elsabethe's home much as they had for so many nights now. He was looking at the small start on a crocheted blanket he had worked on. She was amused at his thrill over his work.

" I'm telling you, I have never been able to do this." He showed it to her again.

She laughed at him. " I know, you've already mentioned that. I guess I was able to keep your attention long enough to help you learn."

He slid the double crocheted chain down into his bag. By now, they were both at the steps that led up to his home; it wasn't exactly a long walk over here. Joe had a sneaky expression on his face, which Allison didn't notice.

" I guess I should be getting home." She bowed her head to him and turned to leave.

He didn't go up just yet, only setting his bag on the porch. " You know, I wish I had something I could teach you, after you were so kind as to teach me this."

Allison stopped and looked back, "What would you wish to teach me? Perhaps you could enlighten me to that tatting you talked about."

Joe laughed at that. "Me, teach you stitching, with the grand master of all things thread in the room."

"Huh?" she was not quite certain what that meant.

He walked out into the yard with her, "Elsabethe would be a much better teacher for you. I would feel like an idiot trying to teach you when she is probably miles above me in skill."

" She certainly didn't mind me teaching you crocheting, and I am well aware of her skill in that art." Allison was not sure where he was going with this.

Joe walked around her, all the while musing at the stars above. " Maybe. But I have never taught stitching before. I had something else in mind."

Allison's eyes bugged out. She was not sure what he was talking about. "What would you possibly wish to teach me?"

He smiled like a fool and looked at her with a hand held out to her. "Ball-room dancing."

" What?"

He waltzed over to her, literally, " Ball-room dancing. I have taught a lot of different dance styles, but my favorite is ball-room. "

She was charmed, though a touch scared. " How can we learn while there is no ball room, or even music?"

He took up her hand, " I can teach without music, so long as you can follow me."

Allison could not contain herself. She wanted to hold his hand and now was as good an opportunity as any. So she held out one hand to him. He surprised her by taking it and then pulling her to him so that he could put his other hand on her waist.

"Oh, this is close." She sort of leaned back from him.

He smiled at her. " That's okay. To dance as a couple you need to be close. " he positioned both of them just right. "Are you ready?"

She gulped, but still nodded " Yes, I think."

"Good. Now, this is a simple box step that is most common when dancing a waltz." He started moving with her around the yard, waltzing through the grasses under the stars. Each step he took he would have to guide her to follow just right. She caught on quickly, though she was terrified of stepping on his toes, or that he might step on hers.

Joe looked at her, staring down at his feet. She looked up at him with a smile. " I am getting it." The moon light glistened in her lovely eyes, enhancing her smile.

Joe stopped dancing and looked at her. "I like it when you smile."

She blushed and looked away. "Well, I have had little to smile about for so long. Thank you, Joseph."

He looked around, realizing that they had danced over toward Elsabethe's. So, he walked her back across the yard, her hand still in his. "It would be easier to learn if there was some music to dance to." Just then, the 'Blue Danube' started playing, seeming to come from above them. Joe looked around. " What the?"

Allison looked away and whispered. "Elsabethe."

" Huh?" Joe looked at her, not quite hearing that remark.

She shrugged. " Now you have music." She held up her hand that was still holding his.

He smiled, not questioning this, took her by the waist and started the steps of the most traditional waltz known today. Around the yard they danced, Allison following him pretty well, though she spent most of the time watching his feet while they danced. He didn't mind. He liked making her smile. He didn't know why, but that didn't really matter. With the last chords of the music, they stopped almost perfectly in the middle of the yard. Like the ham he was, Joe dropped to one knee and proceeded to kiss the back of her hand.

Just as he did this, the lights came on all over his house. At every window, except his, either guests or his mother and father stood. William had a boom box sitting on the window sill where he was. He also had a silly grin on his face. Everyone applauded, with a few whistling.

Joe took this in stride and turned to bow and accept the applause. Allison, on the other hand, was horrified. She looked at the people with wide eyes. Before Joe could say anything to her, such as the apology he wanted to say for his father's obvious attempt at embarrassing them, she let go of his hand and dashed for the woods. Joe frowned at his father, who gave him the 'what did I do' shrug. He then raced after her into the woods.

He caught up with her at the edge of the forest. "Allison!"

She stopped and turned to him, her face still red in panicked humiliation. "I'm sorry, I was just so…"

Joe came closer to her, "It's okay, my father simply loves embarrassing me. He thinks it is his holy duty as a father." He took her hand again, this time as a gesture of compassion for her feelings. "Are you alright?"

She smiled at him. "Yes, I'm okay. I was startled, that is all."

"You must've been, you were running in the wrong direction. Unless you live on the other side of these trees."

Allison looked around, pretending to only now realize where she was. "Oh, my. I guess I had better get back on track."

He pulled up her hand, not quite as gallantly this time, and kissed the back of it. "I hope you had fun. Maybe we can have a real date some time?"

She was now blushing at him kissing her furry hand. "I...I don't know. Maybe. Thanks, it was fun. Good night." She let go of his hand and walked out of the trees heading around Elsabethes home.

He turned and walked back home, this time actually making it inside. His mother and father were in the living room waiting for him.

Joe passed them with nothing more than a glare.

Marla stabbed her husband in the ribs with her elbow. William grunted and then proceeded to actually say, "Sorry, son, I didn't mean to scare her off."

Joe turned to them, "I am lucky that she is so forgiving. She doesn't blame me, so she will see me again, no thanks to you. Now, if you don't mind, try and curb this urge you have of embarrassing me and the girls I am with."

Marla leaned over to him and asked with a sly smile. "Are you really 'with' her yet, I mean is she your girlfriend?"

He rolled his eyes and shook his head. "I don't know. I was just teaching her something in return for her teaching me something. Now, if you don't mind, I am tired and want to go to bed." He walked away from them, purposely not giving them any more details.

From behind him he could hear his father ask his mother. "What do you suppose she taught him that would get him to dance with her?"

To which Marla replied, "Dunno, must've been good."

Joe rolled his eyes once again, while he marched upstairs to his room, all the way considering how he would repay his father for this.

ಬ

The next day, Joseph jogged down Needle Pointe road. He was wearing only a pair of skimpy jogging shorts, as he really enjoyed the way the girls blushed who jogged by him. At one end of the street, was a small park that sat next to Lake Eureka. Joe usually jogged down to the park and back. It was a three mile round trip and that was enough for each day, along with his other routines.

Today, though, he didn't see the blushing faces or even where he was going. His thoughts were on something else. He had not stopped thinking about Allison and the way she was last night. She was attractive in her own way. For years, he paid attention to how the girls looked that he was interested in, not in what they thought or how they acted. This accounted for the fools he got mixed up with all too often. Yet here he found a girl that he would probably not have even talked to before, and now he wanted to see her every day. Was this just a budding friendship? Was this more? He could not seem to come to any answer and that really bothered him.

"WATCH WHERE YOU'RE GOING!" A man yelled at Joe who had nearly jogged his way into the bicyclist coming from his way on the opposite side of the path.

"Sorry." Joe stopped and caught his breath.

Joseph had made it to the park. Concrete benches and tables had been placed about and were surrounded by trees and leaves. The lake was quiet today. Only a few motorboats could be heard in the distance. Joe walked over to a picnic table next to a well-used grill. He sat down with his back to the table so that he might look out over the placid waters of the lake.

"Why are you acting the fool?" he asked himself. He had never jogged across the road without realizing it. He also had never had a girl plague his mind like this. He looked at his hand, the feeling of her skin against his still fresh in his mind. Her hands were not smooth and elegant, but rough. Yet he wanted to feel them again.

At that moment, he heard a couple of giggles close by. The usual pair of girls jogged by, taking a good look at him while he sat nearly naked on a bench. They were lovely, well figured, and well endowed. He smiled back at them with the knee-jerk response from the flirt that he was. They passed by, never having stopped to ask his name or to say anything to him other than a coy giggle.

Joe looked up again at the empty path that wound around the exterior of the lake. He could see Allison walking down that path, at least in his imagination. For the first time he felt naked. He would have covered himself if she were there now. Why was this? He gave that thought a long moment. Then it fell on him like ice down his bare back. He respected her. Did he like her so much that he would want to show her respect and not just his body? Her comfort around him meant more than his showing off.

Real epiphanies happen rarely in one's life. They are a moment of clarity when the world seems to fall into place and the answer is so unmistakably screaming in your ears that you are unable to deny it. He had feelings for her. This was his epiphany. How much he liked her was still a question, but the truth was that he wanted to spend time with her in any way possible. Perhaps, in time, he would learn that he wanted her just as a friend. Or maybe, he would find he wanted more.

Standing up from the bench, he strolled back out to the jogging path which would eventually lead back to the road. Today he would not jog home. He was going to walk and think. He didn't have any more epiphanies, but he did come to a conclusion. He was going to get her to go out on a date with him. Joe knew that he wanted to see what kind of friendship was blossoming between them, and he wanted to find out without Elsabethe watching.

ಓ

Chapter 15: The Date

Several more weeks passed and the pattern continued. Each day, Joseph would come over and stitch for about half an hour before sunset. Right on time, Allison would be at the door just as the sun set below the horizon. Neither would completely admit it to the other, but they came to see each other more than to sit and stitch. This was obvious as the progress on their work was not what two people working each night for almost a month would have completed.

Allison was so eager to come that on more than one occasion she was at the door before sundown. Before Joe could see her in her canine form, she would run off and wait. Though she had yet to admit that she had a spark of feelings for this human, it was apparent to Elsabethe.

"What are you doing?" Allison leaned over to look at Joseph's work.

He was working diligently on a heavy thread with a shuttle, not a needle. He was weaving an intricate pattern like a detailed long, rectangular spider web. "It's called tatting. A friend of mine showed me this before I left Atlanta."

"So, that is tatting." Allison was very impressed.

Joe nodded, while still focusing on his work. "Yeah, this is what I told you about before. It used to be what they used for lace on hats and stuff."

Elsabethe smiled, "Oh, yes, tatting. I haven't seen that in quite some time. I taught sailors how to tat so that they could make nets to fish with."

Joseph continued to work. "Really? I would think that they would buy nets."

"Honey, this was before nets could be bought that would compare to a real handmade creation." Elsabethe didn't mind alluding to her age for she desired that Joseph would finally put the pieces of the puzzle together.

However, he was still as staggeringly oblivious as ever. "Well, I guess handmade is hard to compete with. I wish people would realize that nowadays."

Allison, who was still intrigued with his work, asked. "What are you tatting? Is it something you will attach to a sampler?"

"Wait a minute." Joe worked quickly to finish off the piece. He stopped the shuttle and tied off the end. Then, he attached a small tassel to the end of the rectangular web of threads. "It's a bookmark. That's all I learned how to tat, though I guess I could expand on it." He held it up to her.

Allison took it from him to examine. "Oh, this is nice. I would like to learn to tat like this."

Elsabethe, who was working on her long sampler, responded. "I am sure Joseph here would be pleased to teach you."

"Sure." Joe smiled to Allison.

Allison blushed. "Well, this is really nice. Perhaps you can learn to tat some table decorations for your parents' house." She held it out for him to take back.

Joe took it and pulled a book from his bag. It was a brand new book with a very shiny cover. He opened it and stuck the bookmark in the middle, then closed it. He held the book out to Allison. "Here, this is for you."

She didn't take it from him. "Me?"

Joe could see that she was stunned. So he showed her the cover, which read: Japanese Cultural Myths and Legends. "I thought you might like this. You seem interested in the Japanese stuff that I stitch."

Allison took it from him slowly. "I cannot accept this."

"Don't worry. It is just a gift between friends. Or, is that wrong?" He smiled at her, trying to make her smile back.

"I don't know what to say." she was embarrassed and captivated.

Elsabethe, who was enjoying their exchange, said, "Thank you would be appropriate."

"Yes, of course, thank you."

He pointed to the book. "Open it, right to where the bookmark is."

Allison had no idea what to expect but she went ahead and opened it. In the middle of the textbook sized book, she found a note that was hand written for her. All it read was, ' Please go to the Ice Creamery with me.' Her rosy cheeks turned red as she blushed furiously.

"Well?" he leaned over to her.

She slumped her shoulders. "I...I."

Elsabethe had had enough of this girl's resistance to Joseph's flirting. "Go ahead. Perhaps you will find that you will have fun."

"I...I." she looked at Joseph, who was still smiling and yet had a blush to his cheeks as well, demonstrating that he too was nervous about asking her out. She found this irresistible. " Alright, we can go."

"Great, let's go." he stood up and held out his hand to her.

"Now?" She looked at Elsabethe, hoping for some help.

"Go on." The old witch nodded.

Allison looked back at Joe. "Alright." she said hesitantly and held out her hand which he grabbed up immediately. Joseph pulled her out of the house so fast that he left behind all his tools and projects and even his cell phone.

"Have fun, you two." was all that Elsabethe could get out before they left.

☙

Joseph led Allison down the driveway until they were walking on Needle Pointe, the small road that eventually led to the main street of this cozy town. The ice cream shop was on the corner that joined main street.

Joe talked, as he covered his nervousness with a lot of verbiage, "After we first moved here, Dad went to this place and brought back lunch. I had never had a real deli lunch like that and decided to check the place out. I must've gone there a dozen times so far, but never this late. They make great sandwiches, and they have excellent apples. I don't know where they get them."

Allison smiled warmly, thinking of the apple he gave her on his first evening here. "Yes, I have heard they have good apples."

He laughed, "I may miss those great fresh Georgia peaches, but I do like the apples up here." He paused and looked over to her, noticing that she was not smiling any longer. "Allison? Is there something wrong?"

"I don't know about this." Allison was slowing down, closing herself up like a frightened clam.

Joseph, who was no longer pulling her by the hand, slowed down so that he could walk right beside her. "Oh, don't be so worried. I don't bite. In fact, I have been blamed for a lot of fun times." he gave her a childish grin.

She could not help but smile back at that face. "Is this place going to be busy?"

Joe shrugged, "I doubt it. Probably a few night travelers and maybe some other late dates. Why?"

Allison, who was becoming smaller and smaller as she walked, continuing to crumple up her body in resistance to the idea of others seeing her. Unfortunately she left her cloak back at the house. "You just don't get it, do you?"

"Huh?" he had a good feeling of what she was going to say.

"I'm....I'm not pretty." she said this slowly so that he understood her words.

Joe took her hand, "You are exactly who you are. That is all that matters to me. Is there any other reason that I should turn around and take you back?"

Though a dozen reasons came to her mind, they all ended with the same conclusion, and he had just shut that down. "No. Let's just have fun." For the first time she looked straight ahead.

Joe and Allison walked at a more normal pace again. Joe looked up. "It's clouding up, and the wind is cooling down. I'd say we are in for some rain tonight."

She smiled at him. "You seem to know your weather."

"Yeah, after living in Oklahoma for so long, you learn to recognize the habits of the weather. At least out here it is less likely to kill you. Though that wind is cooler than I am used to this time of year."

She nodded. "It's normal for around here, though it is a bit chilly."

He smiled at her and leaned in to her slightly. "You can have some of my warmth."

Allison rolled her eyes and joked with him, "Are you trying to get fresh with me?"

"Old habits are hard to break, although my offer is still there." He held out his arm to her. They both laughed at his antics.

Before they knew it, they were in front of the ice cream parlor. The place was an old diner from the late fifties that had been refurbished into this Ice Creamery and delicatessen.

"Look at this." Joe stopped just before opening the door. He was pointing to a little poster with details about an end of summer festival and carnival coming to town in a few weeks.

Allison stopped and read the sign, "What about it?"

"It's a thought." He opened the door for her, holding his hand out in a touch of over acting.

She didn't immediately run in. Stopping at the threshold of the door, she looked in to see how crowded it was. Fortunately, there was only a single truck driver at the far end of the long rows of booths, with his back turned to them. The only other souls in the place were a cashier and a man working in the kitchen. So she stepped in, her eyes still darting around fearfully.

Joseph came to her side and gently put his hands on her shoulders. In a whisper for only her ears, he said "Allison, don't worry, you are as beautiful as you feel." This was completely unusual and seemingly out of character for him. Yet it was profound.

She blushed and smiled. "Thanks."

He took her arm and walked her to the register. The man working there smiled, then flinched, staring directly at them, with his eyes scanning over the odd girl. For a moment, he could not tear his gaze away from gawking at the patch of fur on her face.

Joseph saw this and decided to do something. "Hey, I know that my shoes are sooo last season, but I wouldn't stare at you if you wore them." he joked, but with a slight edge to his voice to get the message across.

The man stopped staring, "Oh, uh, can I help you?"

Allison actually giggled at what Joseph had done for her.

Joe looked up to the menu, "Why don't we split a split? They have excellent banana splits here. I got one once and it was so big that I couldn't finish it on my own."

Allison, who had never tried ice cream before, nodded, " Sure."

Joseph ordered and then took his date to sit in a booth while the cook made their order. Soon enough, he brought out a bowl that could double as a fishing yawl with half a chocolate cake in the bottom. On top of that were four scoops of homemade vanilla ice cream, whipped cream, chocolate, caramel and butterscotch sauce on top. Four cherries, one for each scoop of ice cream, finished the dish. All of this was set between a banana that was split perfectly. Joe smiled eagerly at it, while Allison looked at it with a little fear.

" We eat this?" she asked.

He laughed, "Don't tell me you haven't seen a banana split before?"

"Not that I recall. Looks... interesting." she picked up the shovel they called a spoon. Then she had the next dilemma to deal with, where does one start on a behemoth like this? She poked the spoon into the scoop with caramel, but didn't take any. She then poked the chocolate covered scoop, this time taking up some. It was nothing more than what would fill half a teaspoon, but it was enough for her, for now. She cautiously put in her mouth and tasted it. "Oh, it's cold."

"Of course it is, that is where the ice part of ice cream comes from. Now, don't be shy, eat away." Joseph started at one end, while she started at the other.

Allison took up another spoonful, this time with cake, and a cherry. After eating it, she smiled elatedly. "Oh, this is wonderful. What is this called?" She was pointing at the red berry on top of the middle scoop.

Joe looked at what she was pointing at. "Oh, that is a maraschino cherry. It is very traditional on these dishes. Do you like it?"

She plucked another from the top of a mound of whipped cream and popped it into her mouth. "Yes, this is wonderfully sweet yet slightly tart."

After a while they had worked through a scoop of ice cream each, and were sitting back to talk while they nibbled. Joe got the cook to bring out a bowl of the cherries, which were dumped into the mess that was once the beautiful creation. Joe wasn't too keen on maraschino cherries, but she was enjoying them so much he didn't mind.

"So, if I can ask, why don't you have that fur removed?" he said this with as much couth as he could muster.

Allison stopped nibbling and touched a patch of the ugly fur that ran around her left arm. Her mood instantly shifted to gloomy.

Joe sensed this in her, "I didn't mean to…"

"It's alright, you are being sincere. I have tried everything but it grows too fast."

He thought about what she said, not sure what she had tried. But knowing that it could get difficult for her to talk about this, he stopped right there. What he didn't know was that when she turned into a wolf and then back into a human, the hair returned. She could spend five hours of her human time getting rid of it only to find it again the next sunset.

"So, I know you can dance, at least ballroom style. What other dance do you do? Elsabethe told me that you are quite skilled." Allison stopped looking at her arm and picked the spoon up again to find another cherry.

He frowned, "She hasn't seen me dance."

Allison looked at him with a knowing gaze, "I am sure you bragged about your skills to her at least once."

He laughed at her and took no offense at being called a braggart, for it was true. Then Joe sat back, feeling extremely full. "Tap, Jazz, Ballet, Irish jig, square, and line dancing. Mostly for stage."

"Wow, that's impressive. Have you done this professionally?" She fished out a cherry that was floating in the melted ice cream.

"Yes, but only for festivals and a few shows in small town productions. I was hoping to teach dancing and balance to people like football players and karate students. But they don't have much need for that in this small town."

Allison sat back also having eaten more than she expected. "You should go on stage. I hear that they have some good places to perform in New York."

He laughed heartily, " I don't think a small town dancer can make it so easily on Broadway. It takes years of professional training and a lot of talent. I don't think I have what it takes."

"You must have talent to have done so much already. Don't disregard yourself so quickly."

Joe grinned at her, "Now look who is talking about confidence."

She frowned, "But you don't have this kind of…… handicap."

"Handicap. No, you just have hair, so do I." He pulled down the collar of his shirt to show his furry chest. "It doesn't bar you from anything." This brought out a giggle from her.

"That is easy to say when you have such a nice body." The words came out before she could control them. Her wide eyes signaled that she realized what she had just said.

He grinned. "Oh, I have a nice body?" he teased.

"I…well…it is just…"

Joseph laughed lightly, "It's okay."

Allison was blushing and looking at him with a smile. "You do look good."

He shrugged, "I work out and spend time keeping this body in shape, maybe too much time. I spent high school with girls fawning over me, each wanting to date me, but they were flimsy flakes. I was no better. I fell into the trap of believing their words. I never gave the honest, smart, nice girls a chance. Girls like you. I was a perfect idiot. "

Allison was amazed at his honesty, "What changed?"

He let out a sigh, and tried to contain a burp, which was impossible. "When I was leaving town, I asked my girlfriend if she would consider coming up here and possibly think about marrying me. I thought she really loved me and would follow me. I even considered following her to wherever she went to school. But she told me that she would be happier if we split up and she would find a nice guy at whatever college she was going to. That was it. Like our relationship never happened. I was dumped for the prospect of finding another fool like me wherever she went. That made me think that perhaps I was just as shallow as she was."

"Didn't it hurt terribly?"

"Not really. What made me stand back and think was….I understood. We didn't have love, we had a standing date every Friday. We had each other to walk around with in the hallways. She never stitched with me or came to a dance recital. And I couldn't even tell you what her hobbies were, other than spending time at the spa and salon. She didn't care for me like that and the awful part was that I didn't see it until that moment. I made a lot of noise about not wanting to move up here, but I really didn't mind because I wanted time to rethink my life. An education is important, but without real love, what is the point?"

Allison smiled at him, "Joseph, you may have been a fool, but I don't think you were shallow. You learned from your mistakes. I doubt that girl has learned yet."

"Jenna? No, she is a born socialite. If the world wasn't revolving around ways to make her look better, she just moved on to where it would. Like an idiot, I was a tool in the game of *How to make Jenna look good.*"

She patted his hand, "Well, you can be sure that you are a better person today. I doubt that you would've even noticed me if I were around you during those days."

"You like being noticed?" He grinned foolishly again.

She rolled her eyes, "Okay so you have grown up a little, but that ego still needs work."

He couldn't resist teasing her, something he learned from his father. "Oh, you should come around during the day. I might take my shirt off and do a little work outside. Give you something to watch while you stitch, if you can tear yourself away from me long enough to poke a needle through the fabric." He was flexing up his chest while his hands were behind him so that he could pull his shirt to be tight over his muscles.

Allison rolled her eyes and looked away. "Boys." she retorted.

"What?" he acted like he didn't understand her attitude. But he got what he wanted. She was smiling and had not looked nervous for quite a while.

The happy moment was broken by the rambunctious sounds of a group coming in to the deli. Before Joe could even turn to see who had entered, the smell of cheap booze stung his nose and made him wrinkle his face.

Five teens came in, four boys and a girl. The boys were wearing high school team jerseys, though school had not been in session for well over two months. Two of the boys were obviously tipsy by the swaying of their bodies and the decibels with which they choose to speak. The others were laughing at the stupidity of their friends.

"Do you still have the key to your dad's liqu...liqu...booze cabinet?" One of the less tipsy boys asked the one leaning on a counter to stabilize himself.

His friend produced a key from the right pocket of his jeans that were so tight they seemed painted on. "Yup...hic....why?"

"I have some girls coming into town next week. We could show them a really good time." The crowd was completely comfortable speaking of illegal matters. Alcohol tends to soften the brain quickly as evidenced by this disgusting scene.

Joseph was about to suggest that he and Allison leave this place when one of the drunk kids nearly fell on him in the booth while he was dancing around the limited space of the restaurant.

Joe shoved him off, "Do you mind."

The boy staggered back up and leaned over the booth, "Hey guys, look, it's pretty boy from the South. His mommy and daddy run that old rat trap."

Immediately Joe realized he had seen this teen on the open house day. "If you don't mind, we are leaving." Joe tried to dislodge the boy's hands from the booth and table, that blocked him in.

The teen, under the spell of inebriation, was harder to move than Joe realized. He simply looked over to Allison and sneered. "Boy, for such a pretty boy, you have one UGLY date."

"That's enough, Max!" The girl exclaimed to the boy near Joe, embarrassed by all of this.

Joseph went for his cell phone to call the police, immediately remembering that he had left it behind. He looked over to Allison, "Do you have a phone?"

She shook her head quickly and nervously. Max the drunk leaned in to Joe, "Hey, who ya gonna call? Your mommy?" he snickered at his own pathetic joke.

Joe kept his cool, though his anger was boiling right to his eyes. He put his face right in the boy's face and said, "Move."

This was enough to scare the kid, as any bully is a coward at heart. Max stood up, with his hands out, "It's cool, it's cool."

Joe scooted out of the booth. "I will be right back." He looked to Allison, who was appalled at the scene. He was going to deal with this appropriately, by calling the authorities and having these miscreants hauled off.

Allison was as small as she could get, crouched down with her head low. She had never been more self-conscious. To her dismay, the drunken kid came around the back of the booth and hung over her shoulder, breathing down her neck with his toxic breath. "What kennel did he pick you up from, Rover?"

"Be silent." She warned him.

In her mind, she started to remember every reason why she avoided society. The way the men would stare and laugh, or the women would sneer. The Victorian age or today, all she remembered from her few excursions were people like these. There were not many like Joseph who would be nice to her. The heinous laughter in her memories mixed with the drunken chortling around her.

"What? Gonna cry?" the drunkest, rudest boy asked in a demeaning tone.

"Max, stop, you're being an ass!" The girl with this crowd announced, though she didn't do anything to actually stop him.

"Shut up, Linda." the boy yelled at her, much louder than needed.

The cashier came around from the back and was going to put a stop to this disgusting scene. "Sir, you are going to have to leave."

"Look, another pretty boy." the drunk laughed at him.

Allison was sinking in closer to her seat, the memories of the verbal abuse by outsiders raging in her mind. The cashier attempted to pull the drunk away from hovering over her. But the boy reached out and sucker-punched him, hard enough to knock him senseless.

"Yeah, take that from the captain of the team." he laughed at the unfortunate employee. Max then turned back to Allison. "What, don't like my breath?" he leaned in closer to her.

She wanted to cry and to lash out but she kept her cool. "Leave now."

The boy took her arm. "Come on, let's see if she knows any tricks." he pulled her out of the booth, bringing her to her feet.

"Desist at once." she warned him a third time.

Max laughed, "Desssit, sis, what kind of word is that? Why don't you just bark, dog."

"Max, stop it or I will tell your father!" Linda yelled at him again.

"Shut up Linda. hic, or I'll tell your mommy that you hit the bourbon too." He took both of Allison's hands. "Come on, dance, dog."

"Let me go at once." her final warning.

He didn't listen and started to pull her around. "Don't need no music to dance with a dog." He was laughing and jolting her left and right. "Annnybuddy got a camera? I wanna put this on my blog."

༽

Outside, Joseph was eager to make his call and then get Allison out of there. The phone box was an archaic device that had been damaged beyond use long ago. He picked up the phone, hoping that it still worked to at least contact the authorities; these things don't even require money when contacting police. But when he picked it up, the cord fell free of the box as it had been severed some years ago.

So he walked around the building, ready to get Allison out of there, sure that she wanted to leave.

"Come on, Allison, let's just get out of....WHAT ARE YOU DOING!!" He was about to come to her rescue when she displayed her true talents.

Moving her hand so that she now had the Max's wrist, she twisted his arm and then planted her foot into his stomach and sent him flying across the way into the wall.

"Why, you little!" he stood back up to come at her, but was soon taken by this master martial artist. She slid to his side, putting her leg behind his, bending him at the knees. He was doing his dead level best to stay standing, but she used both of her thumbs to press him down by the shoulders. Touching the perfect place on each bone she controlled his entire body. Even from a distance, one could hear the bones making popping noises. They weren't broken, but he would feel this for days. As she stepped away from him, he fell to the ground, writhing in agony from what she had just done. There was more than anger in her action. Years of abuse spilled out and she could have easily taken his life. But her morality won and spared him a very painful death.

Joseph was dumbfounded. " Allison, are you alright?"

She nodded and then promptly left the establishment. Joe looked at the boys and then at the cook who had only just come from the back. He spoke to the bewildered cook. "Uh, you might call the police or something." The stunned worker nodded quickly. Then Joe followed Allison out the door.

"That was amazing. I didn't know......Allison?" He found her standing just outside of the steps to the old diner. She was shaking and looked very stiff. When he got closer he could hear her containing sobs, but not too well. "Allison, don't let them hurt you. They are stupid, mean bullies."

Allison looked back at him with a red face and tears running down her cheeks.

"I..." she could not finish, the words stuck in her throat. She shook her head and ran away from him, out into the middle of the parking lot.

"WAIT, PLEASE!" he ran after her, the first droplets of rain falling from the dark night sky.

For reasons that she didn't know were in her heart, she stopped. "What?" the word came out with a deep, harsh sob.

Joseph stood behind her. " I cannot stand to see a girl cry. You do not deserve to be alone with this kind of pain. Please, what can I do to help?"

In a motion that surprised both of them, she turned and came back over to him. Just like she did with her father, she put her face against his shoulder and cried. He felt for her more at this moment than he ever felt for another person. He put his arms around her and held her. As if the sky wept in sympathy, the rain began to fall, showering them in the middle of the night.

She called out in a muffled voice, "I'm so ugly. You shouldn't..."

"Allison, you are not ugly, you have the most beautiful soul that I have ever known. I can see that in the stitches of your work and in the way you look at the stars in the night sky. Never let a fool make you feel bad about yourself. They do not deserve that kind of power over you."

Allison cried harder. Her pain was deeper than this one night. Yet for the first time in three centuries, she let another person see this sort of passionate display of agony. "You deserve a better person."

Joe rubbed her back, "You may not believe it, but you are the better person. You are the best person that I have known in far too many years."

She cried hard, holding him and letting the rain pour over them. It had been a long time since she let this kind of pain out. In fact, the pain was so deep that even the memories of her mother and father were part of this agony, not just the sadness of her appearance. His hold on her made her more secure than she ever believed possible.

She pried herself away from him and looked up into his eyes. "Why are you so nice?"

Joe smiled at her, "It's easy to be nice to a nice person. Now, may I walk you home on this cold rainy night?"

Allison stepped back and sniffed hard. She took his hand. "You may walk me back to Elsabethe's home. I will be staying with her tonight."

"Fine, that's a start." He liked the feel of her hand in his, even with the fur on the back. He never knew this feeling before. When he held hands with Jenna, it was only at times when others were watching and she was showing off her prize pet. Now he knew why those in love hold hands and he really liked it.

It rained all the way home and it looked to be this wet all night and into the morning. But, neither cared much. Once soaked, there isn't much more that the rain can do.

Joe noticed that Allison was keeping her head low, though he doubted it was from the weather. He wanted to tell her that she should not be so sad, but he could not break through that barrier in one night. Something about her, the way she was strong at one moment and then weak the next, seemed to appeal to him. She was in need, and he wanted to fill that need. For the first time in his life, he felt something for someone that was more than physical attraction. It was so much deeper. Yet, he also knew that she was afraid. Not of him, but of the world, and he couldn't easily change that. So, he would let her deal with this in her own way. But he planned to always be there to give her support.

"Well, here we are." They were standing in the clearing between the houses. Joe, who was still holding her hand, let go.

She stepped away from him and felt the back of her hand. He had been slowly rubbing his thumb with the direction of the growing fur, and she liked it. "Good night." she said softly.

Joe smiled, " Night." and turned to go back into his home.

" Joe." she said almost too softly for him to hear, but he did.

" Yes?" he turned around again and watched her.

She had her back to him, " Can you do it again?"
"What?"

Allison turned around, with her eyes still low. "Hold me."

He smiled and opened up his arms, rain water flowing all over him. "Any time."

She came over to him and put her arms around him. Laying her head in his chest, she embraced him. "It has been so long since I have been held."

Joe put his arms around her. He wasn't sure what this meant, if they were a couple now or not. He didn't care. A deep part of him wanted her to be happy and if holding her brought that happiness to her, he would hold her as long as she wanted.

Allison didn't care what she was doing. At first, she was thinking of when her father held her like this whenever she was in pain. But, now she was thinking about this young man. She never wanted to let go of him.

༙

Deep in the woods, a dark figure walked only in the shadows of the trees. It stopped at the very extent of the tree line and stood in the place of the darkest shadows.

"What have we here?" the cold, cruel woman's voice whispered on the wind.

She could see the pair embracing under the falling rain at this midnight hour.

"So precious a moment. Oh how exquisite the pain will be."

༙

William stood on the porch, wearing only his pajama bottoms. He was holding up his hand to keep the rain out of his eyes. "Joe?" he could see the couple in the rain. "Get in here before you catch pneumonia."

Joe looked back, then down to the girl who was holding tight. "Uh, Allison. I think I need to get home."

She slowly released him from her grip. "Oh, sorry. I...I should be getting inside too."

He watched her walk around to the back of Elsabethe's house. He assumed that she would go in through the back door. When she was gone, he turned and sloshed his way up to his porch.

"Are you insane? Its midnight and its pouring." William wasn't exactly happy with his son. " What were you doing?"

Joe shrugged to his father, "I was doing exactly what I needed to do." With that cryptic response thoroughly confusing his father, Joseph walked into his house.

༄

Allison watched Joseph and William from around the corner of Elsabethe's house. She could see that William was quite handsome as well, though he had neglected his figure somewhat. She didn't care. Joe could be short, fat, and bald for all it mattered; she liked him. For the first time in centuries, she felt a new sensation in her heart, one that was wonderful and complete. Right now she didn't care about the way she looked, because he didn't care. It made her feel so good that she never wanted this feeling to end.

With the sensation of walking on a cloud, she strolled back into the trees. The rain soaked her path and the winds whipped up now and then. All she felt was the warmth of his body against hers.

She stopped at a tree and leaned against it. The water was still pouring over her, yet she didn't notice the first drop. She held her hand and felt the fur on the back. For the first time in three centuries she didn't hate that fur. He held her hand, fur and all, and was content to do so. Her thumb rubbed the hair like he did while she remembered the feeling of his strong hand wrapped around hers. What a sensation, what a joy. Can this be real? These were the thoughts running through her enchanted mind.

"Sister?" Oki came around a tree, his brother not too far behind him.

She sank to the ground, sitting in the wet leaves. " I think he likes me." She said in a whimsical, infatuated tone.

Yoshi came up to her. "But, sister, the weather?"

She smiled and rubbed his wet head, "Isn't it a wonderful night."

Oki frowned and looked at his brother, "Either she is drunk or sick. Either way this could mean trouble."

She sat forward and hugged Oki. "Oh, dear brother, I am not drunk or sick. I am happy. He has made me so happy."

Yoshi was stunned, as was his brother who was being hugged about the neck.

"Uh, sister, would you like to come back to the den?" Yoshi asked.

She stood up and began to stroll toward their home. "Why not?"

They walked along with her, both seriously worried about the way their sister was acting. It didn't take either of them long to realize what was wrong with her.

∞

Chapter 16: Facing the Truth

"I don't know about this." Yoshi said while he carefully walked along the back roof of the Henderson's bed and breakfast.

"What?" Oki asked from another level of the roof.

Yoshi stood at the edge of his part of the roof and looked up to his brother. "We really shouldn't be doing this. Elsabethe said it would be unwise to show humans that we can talk and all."

Oki looked down at him. "You saw how she was acting. I want to be sure that she will be safe with this...boy."

Yoshi rolled his eyes. "And maybe we are being overly protective of her."

"Shut up and get over here, we need to see him." Oki commanded his twin brother.

Unfortunately for them, Joseph's room was on the second floor and the only way to get to the window was to sit on the overhanging roof of the porch below, which wasn't exactly meant for wolves. The only good thing was that the rain was letting up and now was merely a misty sprinkle.

༄

Joseph had dried himself off and placed towels over his pillow, so that he might not soak it with his wet hair. While he slept, he had a goofy smile on his face, something that had been etched in from the glee he felt inside. Even in his dreams he was still reliving the moment when his arms were around Allison.

To his surprise, he awoke to the sound of something tapping repeatedly on his window. "Huh?" he looked around, his wet hair a mess from sleeping on it. For a moment, he thought that it must have been part of his dream that was making the sound. But the tapping came again, this time followed by voices.

"Hey, Joseph." someone called his name from outside of his window.

Cautiously, he picked up a glass sphere paper weight from his desk and went over to the window. "Who?...huh?" his eyes were blurry so he was sure he was not seeing what he thought he saw.

Upon closer inspection, he was sure that he was looking at two wolves sitting on the ledge just outside his window. Both were staring directly at him as if they were waiting on him. "What on earth?" he proclaimed and came closer to the window, not willing to open it just yet.

"Are you Joseph?" One wolf asked through the glass.

"YAHH!!" he stumbled backwards and nearly fell on his butt, only catching a chair before crashing down.

He could hear them talking, "Yeah, that has to be him. The father is taller and fatter."

Joseph calmly set the paper weight down and then went to open the window. By now he was fully aware that this HAD to be a dream, even though he had never experienced this before in any other dream.

With the window open, he leaned out and looked at the wolves. "Boy, this is some messed up dream. What are you supposed to be?"

The twins looked perplexedly at each other and then back to him. Yoshi spoke first. "We aren't a dream."

"Sure. Oh, you must be the wolves from Elsabethes story. Pretty good likeness, I guess." He still thought he was dreaming.

Oki frowned, " We don't have time for this. Sis will figure out we're gone soon and she won't be happy with us."

Yoshi nodded. "Yeah. Alright, Mister Joseph, what are your intentions toward our sister?"

Joseph looked around, "Sister? Is there another wolf on the house?"

Again they looked at each other, "No. We're talking about Yuki."

" Yuki?" he pondered that for a moment. " Oh, Yuki, from the story. Yeah, what about her?"

"What are your intentions?" Yoshi asked again.

Joe frowned. "I don't know a Yuki."

"Yeah, you stitch with her every day. You were hugging her." Yoshi replied.

Josephs cool demeanor faded. "Yuki….Allison. You mean that Allison is your sister?"

"Allison? No, Yuki is our sister." Oki responded.

Yoshi looked to his brother. "Are you sure we have the right house?"

They both looked back across from Joe's place to Elsabethe's to be sure that they were on the right house.

Joseph was feeling a little more confused and starting to believe this might be real. "What do you want?"

Yoshi turned back to Joe, "Our sister is a very important person to us. And we don't want her hurt, especially by some human. "

"Yeah, so, what do you want with her?" Oki finished with a bit of sharpness to his voice.

Joseph thought about Allison, "I am not sure what you are asking. But if you are talking about Allison, all I want is to make her happy. What do you think I want?"

Oki cocked his head and glared at Joe, one eye more intense than the other. "You wouldn't take advantage of her, or anything? She is naïve about men, especially hormonal human boys."

Yoshi's eyes widened and looked to his brother. "Oki, that was uncalled for."

Joseph laughed at himself for the way he was acting. This dream was so real. "Well, if you want to know the truth, I won't do anything like that until I am married. So, you can be assured that she is safe with me. Now, if you don't mind, I would like to wake up soon, mom is preparing pancakes for breakfast." He joked.

Yoshi stood up and looked very proud of himself. " Well, I will take your word, for now. But, be sure that I will not be so kind if you do try anything."

Oki stood up too and began walking away, "Yeah, we are a dangerous duo. We can....yaaAHHI II I!!!" Oki had walked right off the end of the roof, having not paid attention to where he was walking.

Joseph leaned out, unable to see down to where the wolf had fallen. Yoshi walked to the edge and looked down. A small, embarrassed voice called out, "I'm okay."

Yoshi shook his head, then looked back at Joe. "Well, 'bye." he walked to the edge nearest the house and jumped to another ledge and then headed down the way they came, only with a great deal more ease on the descent than the ascent.

Joe was befuddled and a little amused. He went back to bed and hoped to wake up soon. In reality, he actually fell back asleep.

※

Allison sat against a tree, stitching on the white gloves she had started before her father died. The sun was shining overhead and her two brothers, as red fox kitsune's, tumbled about wrestling each other.

"Ow, you bit my tail!" one yelled

The other promptly responded. "You bit mine first."

Then they continued their playful romping and biting.

Yuki laughed at her brothers; they were fun to watch. At least they had one another to bite and wrestle with as she certainly didn't want to take part in this kind of silliness. Besides, she was diligently working on the gloves she would wear later to that event in town.

The leaves behind her made crumpling sounds with the footsteps of a man approaching. He came around the trunk and stood next to her.

With the deep, soothing voice of Tonbo, he said. "Those gloves are lovely, my dear."

Allison looked up, at first seeing the man she missed every day. "Father," she exclaimed happily. But the sun was behind his head and the light shown into her eyes. Covering her eyes, she stood up so that she could look upon him without the glare. "Father, the sun is so bright. Father?" Now, Tonbo was not standing here. Joseph had taken his place. Somehow, it didn't bother her. She was in fact very pleased to be next to him.

He took her by the arm and held up her hand where the gloves were resting.

"Their beauty pales in comparison to your own."

She looked away with a blushing face and a hearty grin. "Oh, I am not that beautiful."

Joe put his hand to her chin and gently turned her face to look at him. "Oh, but you are. You are very beautiful."

As if a bitter breeze had run over her bones, she started to remember what she looked like. "No, I...I am ugly." As she held up her hand with the gloves, the gloves grew old and disintegrated in the chilling air and the patches of gnarled fur began to appear all over her arms.

"Allison, what is happening to you? What are you?" Joe proclaimed in disgust.

She looked away, "I am a horrible monster. But...but you don't care. I know you don't." she looked back, only to find that he was gone, her brothers were gone and the forest was now as gray and dim as the way she felt in her stomach. "Joseph!" she called out, but her voice faded amongst the trees.

Then a shaft of light filled the trees and a figure stood in the shadows. "FATHER!? JOSEPH!? I cannot see!" The silhouette was holding something up, a musket. He began walking as the hunters used to when they hunted down her mother. Prowling through the trees with the end of their weapon ready to strike down anything they wished to kill.

"Oh, no." she started to back away, prepared to run from this man. Her legs failed her and she fell to her knees. "ELSABETHE!" she cried, but no one answered.

"Allison." a sinister voice taunted her. It sounded like Joseph's, but much more evil than he had ever sounded.

To her dismay, the man came very close to her, pointing the musket right at her. The shaft of light continued to cast the shadows that blocked his face.

"I will be merciful and put you out of your misery, ugly wolf." he said this without any feeling toward her other than contempt.

Tears welled up in her eyes and she was trying her best to move. "Joseph! Help me!"

"Oh, but it is me you are afraid of." The light faded and the face of her attacker appeared. To her horror, it was Joseph.

She stopped struggling and looked at him with tears falling down from her face.

"Surely you do not despise me?"

"I will hunt you down and kill you as the wolf you are." He moved right to her, with the gun in her face.

She closed her eyes and lowered her head. "Then, take my life."

Joseph's whole body, gun and all, was whisked away into the winds. Allison couldn't stand; her legs were too weak. She looked around, the forest vanished, and she was alone in a void.

Another voice came over the air. "What is this?"

"Who is there?!" she called out.

ଓ

"Who is there?" Allison woke up lying on the ground where she had fallen asleep. The sun's first rays were breaking through the trees and the morning would soon be upon her.

The leaves around her gathered up and took the form of a cloaked figure with a deep hood over her head. She pulled back the hood and looked at the girl on the ground.

"Adel," Allison gasped.

The woman smiled, "So, I see that you have finally found a special man."

Allison stood up and took a threatening posture. "You leave Joseph alone."

Adel simply smiled, "I cannot allow you to find this happiness."

"You have no power. Be gone." Allison pointed away.

Adel smiled wickedly, "I may have little power over witches and ugly wolves such as yourself, but humans are easily dealt with."

"BE SILENT!" Allison was becoming furious.

Adel continued. "I will use him against you. I will return to this world with all my power and no one to stop me. Then, my dear, dear little child, I will kill this man who has stolen your heart."

"NO!" Allison leapt at Adel, ready to mutilate her. She fell through the mound of leaves.

Adel, unharmed by the attack, turned to the girl. "I will kill him." she continued to say.

At that moment, the twin wolves came from their little excursion and both jumped at Adel ready to take her down. They did just as their sister had and simply scattered a mound of leaves. The only remains were the sounds of an evil cackle on the wind.

Yoshi and Oki were on the ground viciously biting each other's back legs and tails, unaware that they had missed their target.

Allison looked back to the sun as it broke over the horizon. She transformed into a wolf and sat down on the ground. "Stop it, you two. She was not really here."

Oki and Yoshi both stopped, each with the other's back right leg in their mouth. They each simultaneously spit out the other's limb and started spitting at the ground in disgust.

"Eww, you taste like dirt."

"Well you're no better."

Allison didn't say anything. She simply walked over to a tree and sat at the base.

Yoshi looked up, "Sister? What is wrong? What did she say to you?"

Allison looked down, mourning the loss of a man who wasn't even dead yet. "I…I don't want to talk about it."

ಙ

Chapter 17: Two Broken Hearts

"OOOH nuthin could be finer than to be in Caroliner in the moooooororning!" Joseph sang while he set out the basket of muffins and got the coffee for the patrons.

"Nuthin could be sweeter than my sweety when I meet 'er in the mooooorrroroning!" It wasn't bad. In fact he was trained in singing, though it was disturbing some of the guests at the sight of this young man dancing around like a fool while he worked.

"Joe? What on earth are you doing?" Marla watched her son dance into the kitchen with an empty coffee carafe.

Joe went over to the industrial coffee maker and began to prepare another batch of the dark brew. "Oh, I just had a wonderful time last night."

William came in from the laundry room with a pile of dish towels in his hands.

"Yeah, he was out at midnight, standing in the rain, hugging all over this girl."

"Oh, so you had a date. How'd it go?" Marla was pleased for her son. She trusted him at midnight with a girl, for she knew that he knew what she would do to him if he did anything immoral.

"It was an interesting night. Allison is a wonderful girl, so unique. She is one of the strongest girls I have ever known, yet she is insecure about herself. Ahh, a complex woman for once, one that is a treat to be with." He was smiling like a fool in love.

"You sure have her figured out, and after only one date." Marla took another pan of muffins from the oven.

"I have hardly begun to figure her out. That's the beauty of the situation." He rinsed out the carafe.

"Huh? You are happy to be ignorant about her? You sound like you know her quite well after just one night." Marla was still confused.

Joe poured the decaf coffee into the carafe while he talked. "We have only been on one date, but we have been stitching together for well over two months now."

"I told you, Marla, she's that girl that Joe was sitting out with until all hours of the night. I'm surprised it took him this long to ask her out. Lord knows she wanted him to." William had a lot of faith in his son's ability to woo girls.

Joseph shook his head, "I asked her out practically within the first week I met her, She turned me down flat," he said with a big smile on his face.

"She turned you down? How is that possible?" Marla was mocking him. She was a little wiser about this than her husband.

Joseph shrugged. "Allison was afraid of going out. I guess she has had a lot of disappointment in her life. But I convinced her, with stitching no less, and it was a night that I will always remember."

"YOU DIDN'T!" Marla's faith in her son started to slide.

Joe frowned at her, "Oh mother, I am not THAT stupid. I am not going to take advantage of an insecure girl. Besides, I will save that for the honeymoon." His frown turned back into a smile.

Marla laughed at him, "Oh, now who is talking about marriage, and after only one date."

Joe rolled his eyes, "I meant I will wait until I marry, whoever she may be. You sound like those two wolves."

William took a pot of the coffee and poured himself a cup. "Wolves? What wolves?"

Joe set a few coffee cups on the tray with the carafe. "I had the strangest dream last night. I was in my room and a pair of wolves came to my window. They told me that they were Allison's brothers and that they were worried about my intentions for their sister."

Marla stuck one eyebrow up, "A pair of wolves?"

"Yeah, it sounds like something out of that story that Elsabethe told me. I guess my mind was really tired after being out so late."

Marla walked passed him to get another bowl for the muffins. "At least your thoughts are in the right place. I always taught you to treat girls with respect."

William laughed, "It's funny you mentioned wolves."

"Why?" Joe stopped just before he left with the coffee.

"Last night, when I came out to get you, I could swear that I smelled wet dog." William looked up to find his son glaring at him. "What? What did I say?"

"Nothing." Joe turned and left. He chose to not tell his parents about Allisons problems. He wanted them to think of her as he did, as just another wonderful girl. Besides, he didn't want anyone to get the impression that he was acting so nice to her just out of pity. He really did have feelings for her.

~

Elsabethe was impatient today. She was very excited to find out what happened last night. Both people left and never came back, which could be either a bad thing or a good thing.

"Saucer, cup, come on, I don't have all morning." Elsabethe sat at her kitchen table waiting.

A nice china cup and saucer came out of the cabinet and sat on the table right in front of her. She pulled out the crystal needle from her blouse and tapped the edge of the cup. It instantly filled with hot tea, seemingly filling from beneath.

"Now, let's see...newspaper." she held out her free hand, and a rolled up paper appeared in it, the local gazette. She looked at it closely, "This is last week's paper, this week, please." she waited and the paper changed its words. The cover became a simple story about the workings of the upcoming end of summer festival. This year's was particularly important, since it would be the eightieth annual festival.

She had her tea cup up to her mouth when she heard something at the back door, at least she thought she did. It was awfully faint. "Hello?"

"Elsabethe." Yuki's small voice came from the other side of the door.

She got up and opened the door to find the wolf sitting on the back step with her head low. The old witch smiled and stood aside, "Come in, please, I am eager to hear about your adventure last night."

"I...I don't want to talk about it." Allison didn't enter just yet.

Elsabethe had a sinking feeling. "Oh, what happened?' then her tone changed to deep concern. "He didn't? Did he...."

"No, he was wonderful, a perfect gentleman." Allison was still looking down.

"And this is why you don't want to talk about it? Come in, please." Elsabethe nearly pulled the wolf in.

The sad wolf slowly walked inside. She jumped up to a chair at the table and sat there with ease. "Your dear sister came to me last night, in my dreams." Allison said this, knowing that it would draw a strong reaction from Elsabethe.

The old witch was stunned for a moment, "Adel."

"Yes. She has seen Joe and me. She sought me out to hurt me."

Elsabethe was dumbfounded. "But she has no power."

"She is regaining strength faster than we predicted. I suspect that she will be able to leave the forest come fall, perhaps sooner."

"Oh, I see. I guess I have become so complacent that I didn't want to believe that it could be here, now. What did she say to you?" Elsabethe was more than worried.

Allison looked down with tears in her eyes. "She said that she would kill Joseph. That she would use him to garner her return and then take his life."

"Is that all?"

Allison sniffed hard, a tear running down her furry face. "Isn't that enough?"

"Don't worry, my dear, I will see to his protection." Elsabethe tried to comfort her.

"Can you be sure? Without any shred of doubt?"

Elsabethe was confused, "What?"

"You cannot protect him all the time. I know that you are a powerful witch, but even you have limitations on what you can promise." Allison was trying her best not to cry.

Elsabethe frowned, "I am sure that I can protect him."

Allison looked away, "There is only one guarantee. I must never see him again. I must distance myself from him, so that he is no longer someone who Adel sees as a tool she can use." She could sense the protest in Elsabethe coming, "I would rather die than watch another one I care for die in my place."

"It doesn't have to be this way, Yuki. We can protect him."

"No. I will not risk his life."

Elsabethe calmly asked, "Do you love him?"

Allison paused for a moment, giving this thought. "I have never felt for a man as I do him. Last night, when it didn't matter to him, he offered his arms to me when I hurt. He gave me comfort. Then, after he walked me through the rain back here, he took me in his arms again, without hesitation, and held me for as long as I wanted. I do care for him."

The old witch looked a little closer at the wolf. "In his arms, in the rain. I think that there is more than just 'care' in you for him. Isn't there?"

Allison sniffed, trying to contain the weeping sure to come. "Perhaps. That moment in his arms took away all the pain. I never thought it could be that way. I never thought that any man's arms could feel as comforting as my fathers. My feet weren't touching the ground. I was floating on the moment of emotion. For a brief breath of time, we were together. It was wonderful, more so than I ever imagined possible."

Elsabethe actually smiled, "So, you would give up this for a fear that may or may not come true."

"No, that is precisely why I must give it up. The more I see him, listen to him, even touch him, the more I will fall for him. Each ounce of love I gain is an immeasurable amount of pain that Adel will weave, again. I don't deserve him, and he certainly doesn't deserve that horrible fate."

"My dear, please, don't do this," Elsabethe pleaded.

Allison got down from the chair, "I cannot watch another man I love die, especially one who knows nothing of what could happen. It is best that I distance myself from him, for his own sake." She left through the open door, heading back to the forest.

Elsabethe got back to her feet and followed, watching Allison leave the house, "My dear, do not do this. Without him, your spell cannot be broken."

Allison stopped halfway to the trees. "I understand the consequences."

"Do you? Are you willing to pine the rest of your days away for a man that you loved and obviously loves you? If Adel does not take your life, you will have innumerable years under this spell. That is a long time to reflect upon a mistake that was made willingly." She pleaded for the life of this wolf as much as this wolf was pleading for the life of the boy she loved.

Allison turned around, tears dripping from her face to the ground. "I must do what I feel is right." with that she ran into the trees, not wanting to hear any more arguments from the kind old witch.

Elsabethe closed her eyes and lowered her head as she whispered "Please, don't do this."

ଔ

"Strooolling with my girlie when the dew is pearly early in the mooorornning." Joseph nearly danced between the houses that afternoon. He could hardly wait to see Elsabethe and especially Allison today.

"Butterflies all flutter up and kiss each little butter cup at daaaaawaaning." he arrived at the front door and knocked.

Elsabethe, who had heard him all the way from his front porch, was ready at the door. She forced the most convincing smile that she could muster. "Oh, Joseph, you're a little early today."

Joe looked at his watch, "Well, this is still later than when I used to come, but I thought that maybe Allison might come early as well, and I wanted to be here."

Elsabethe continued to smile, though she felt terrible for him. "Come on in, your project is still where you left it. "

Joe stitched and talked all afternoon about what happened on the semi-date that he and Allison had been on, from the way Allison toppled those abusive punks to how they had hugged. He spoke of how wonderful it felt that Allison was smiling after the date. All the while Elsabethe tried to stitch, but barely achieved any work.

"Elsabethe, is there something wrong?" he noticed that her smile was fading and a sadness crept across her brow.

She cleared her throat and fixed her face, returning to a smile. "Nothing, just a touch tired. Would you care for some tea?"

"Sure. Allison should be here any moment. The sun is down and that usually means that she is coming." His eagerness only made her heart sink all the more.

"Joe...." She nearly told him the whole truth, just to make sure that he knew what was happening. She had been thinking about this all afternoon, how she would tell him and then he would run into the forest and tell Allison how much he loved her and didn't want to let her go away.

Joe smiled at her with a furrowed brow. "Elsabethe?"

She cleared her throat again. "Would you like honey for your tea?"

"No, just some lemon, thanks." He wasn't quite sure what that was all about, but he knew better than to pry.

When Elsabethe returned with a tray of hot tea and cookies, Joseph was glued to the front door with his eyes. "Honey, I am not sure if Allison will be here this evening."

He looked back to her, "What?"

Elsabethe tried to figure out how to say this. "You see, dear, she wasn't feeling well this morning. I doubt she will be up to coming this evening."

"Oh, that's right, she stayed here last night."

"She did? Oh, yes, of course, she did." Elsabethe was trying to keep up.

Joseph became instantly concerned. "Was she ill? Did the rain make her sick?"

"No, she just wasn't feeling herself. I am sure she will be feeling like coming soon enough. Now, why don't you have some tea and cookies." she sat the tray down on the coffee table between him and her.

Joseph poured himself a cup of tea. "I would like to help. If she isn't feeling well, I could bring her some soup. I make a smashing chicken soup."

Elsabethe sat down and looked at him for a moment. Again she considered telling him the truth, but that might not help, even if he believed her. Besides, it might worry him more which would do nothing to help anyone. "Joseph, dear, just be patient. Don't be too worried about her. She will be fine. Now, why don't you keep working on your project; you are so close to being done."

"Alright." He picked up the Japanese piece he had been working on all this time and began to stitch on the last segment of a little garden bridge in the background.

ಬ

Days passed and Joseph continued to come to Elsabethe's, hoping each day that Allison would come. The project she had been working on the last night he saw her was still on the couch, in the same place. He would sit right beside it, sort of saving a place for her. He didn't say it, but he missed her terribly and his attitude became more and more gloomy. Elsabethe felt for him, yet she could not tell him the truth.

" Elsabethe." Joseph said in a meek voice.

" Yes, dear?" He spoke so seldom that she was eager to converse with him. She hoped that even a few words might help his mood.

" Have you seen Allison at all recently? Is she still not feeling well?" He stitched slowly.

Elsabethe didn't like to lie, for it was not her way, but she wanted to make him feel better. "I... I don't believe she feels all too well, yet."

" I see. Well, if you see her, please tell her I am thinking about her." Joe began to pack up his work.

Elsabethe smiled, " I am sure she is thinking about you too. " she noticed him putting away his work into the usual bag. " Are you leaving so soon? The evening is young and we haven't even had tea yet."

He smiled at her, " I need to be getting up early tomorrow. Mom wants to make some apple butter to bring to the festival."

" The festival? Oh, the end of summer event the locals like to have."

" Yeah. Mom said that it would be good publicity for us to have a booth. We will sell some hometown favorites, apple butter, pickled squash, and chow chow, which all take a while to make." He quietly gathered the rest of his stuff and said his good evenings, then left, a little more morose than usual.

" I am sure that everyone around here will love what you make." Elsabethe felt terrible for him and Allison, both needing the other, but they were not together. The grandmotherly side of her wanted to do something to bring these young people together, but she knew that they had to decide when the time was right. Even magic had its limits. True love is well beyond magic. So, wishing things were different, the old witch simply continued stitching the enormously long sampler that she had been working on for over ninety years.

Joe came back in after having left only moments before. He was holding out a envelope.

" If you see her soon, please give her this."

Elsabethe smiled, and took the envelope. " I will."

He quietly left, without another word. Elsabethe knew that she had to see what was inside, for Allison's sake. She ran her crystal needle along the sealed edge of the envelope and it opened up without problem. Inside was a card. She pulled it out, immediately realizing it was a Get Well Soon card. Very simple and to the point, he had written a personal note inside, but she didn't read it. She had done too much in opening it. So, she sealed it back up and set it aside.

༂

Joseph walked back home, looking down at the ground. He stopped for a moment near the big rock that Allison had sat on the first night that they had really talked. He wanted to believe that she was ill, for he didn't want to believe that he had done something as offensive that she didn't want to be around him, for he really wanted to be around her.

First, he thought about what he might have done to upset her. Could it have been the hug? Was he too imposing? Could he have pushed too hard? No, she wanted to be hugged. She had even asked for him to hug her the second time. Could it have been the fact that those boys were harassing her and he didn't defend her? But he wasn't around to defend her. He would've if he hadn't been outside at the phone.

" What did I do wrong?" he said, then kicked the boulder with his foot. Immediately he hopped around holding his foot.

" Broke my big toe, that is what I did wrong," he retorted on his own actions.

Something in the trees stirred and caught his attention. There was a shadowy figure standing between the trees, human in shape and very menacing.

" Allison. Is that you?" he asked hopefully. He knew she had something to do with the forests around here.

The shadow seemed to fade and then all he saw was a bunch of leaves flying around in the wind, which wasn't blowing.

" This place is just creepy." he said again and hurriedly limped home.

☙

Chapter 18: Longing

The next morning, the bed and breakfast was active with the few guests that stayed for the week. Joseph and Marla worked heartily over a large pot of cooking apples. William worked outside of the house, chopping up more wood for another campfire evening under the stars.

Elsabethe stood outside the back of her home, barely out of sight of William. She was waiting on someone.

Soon enough a wolf slunk out of the woods. It was Allison. " Oki and Yoshi told me that you wished to see me?"

Elsabethe nodded. " Have you any information about my sister?"

" No, she has been very elusive of late. I haven't seen, heard, or felt her."

Elsabethe was very worried. " This can only mean that she is biding her time on something. I doubt that she is ignoring the world. "

Allison sat down and looked up to the old witch. " Your sister will return soon, and I will be ready for her. I won't allow her to harm anyone else, at least not while I live."

Elsabethe shook her head, " My dear, she may be too powerful to stalemate again."

" I do not intend to allow her to reside in this world. She is a danger and the longer we postpone her fate, the worse her anger and revenge will be." She looked away for a moment, for the next statement hurt to say, " I will kill her."

Elsabethe let out a sigh, " Your father would not be pleased to hear such a thing come out of his daughter's mouth."

Allison looked back to Elsabethe with a grim expression. " My father has been dead these past three hundred years and I will not step away from the woman who killed him. Be damned the traditions of my family, I will avenge his death and save any others from the same fate. This is my chosen destiny. I will make sure that Joseph is safe just as my father made sure that I was safe."

Just then, Joseph came out of his home and walked around the perimeter looking for his father. He called to him, his voice catching the ears of the two women.

Elsabethe looked down at Allison, who was looking across the way at Joe while he turned the corner and disappeared from view. " Should not your destiny be with him? He longs to see you again. "

" It is for him that I will fight your dear sister. I will fight for everyone that she might hurt to gain power." That statement came out stern and almost bitter, but the next words were softer and more from the heart, " What have you told him?"

" I have only told him that you have not felt well. That you are not yourself, which is the truth. You are not a killer and you are not afraid. You should come back. My sister's threats were meant to harm you and you are giving her that pleasure by denying what you have longed for all these years."

Allison looked back into the trees. " I cannot. He is too kind to be dragged into this."

Elsabethe held out the card that Joseph gave her. " He still thinks of you. He even gave this to me, in hopes that I might show it to you."

Something told Allison not to look at it, but she could not tear herself away. Elsabethe placed it on the ground and Allison looked into it. Inside was a simple get well soon message from the card company, but there was more written by the sender. ' I miss you, and hope that you are able to come back soon. Joe' Allison's lower lip quivered and she held her head low in shame for what she was doing. " Oh, Elsabethe, he misses me."

The old witch nodded, " Yes, he does. I have never seen a more love sick young man. He waits for you every night. I haven't the heart to tell him that you no longer wish to see him, and shred what little hope he has in love. "

" But, he....I....I just cannot watch another die." Allison was trying not to cry again.

Elsabethe repeated her promise. " I will do everything in my power to see to his safety. This I swear."

Allison took in a breath and looked away from the card. " I cannot drag him into our world. He does not deserve that. I must do what is right and stand vigilant in my duty. Adel must be dealt with when she returns."

Elsabethe shook her head, " I do not believe I shall ever understand your reasoning. But do not disregard him so quickly. Think about what you are doing. Think about what you might have if you give him a chance. As I said before, I will protect him with all my strength, if only to be sure that you and he are happy."

Allison stood and looked back to the old witch, "I must go, before he sees me like this. " She said nothing more, simply running into the forest, vanishing amongst the dense trees.

Elsabethe picked up the card from the ground. She looked at it, only now seeing what was written on the inside. " She is strong to keep herself together after reading such a thing from the man she loves. But she is also a fool. Damn you, Adel, you should never have allowed yourself to become such a weaver of misfortune for these poor children."

ଓ

Allison didn't exactly run back to her home in the forest. She made a detour to go to a tree that she had visited many times before. It had a nice thick trunk and could hide her from anyone's view while she watched them.

It would hurt terribly she knew, but she wanted to see him again. To her delight, Joseph stood near a pile of wood, talking with his father about personal issues.

Her thoughts trailed back to the day when he was showing off his body to the world. The way he looked with the sun on his bare skin was invigorating. Her tail even began to wag at her memory of the image.

Suddenly, she perked up her ears, because she heard her name being spoken.

" I don't get it, Dad, Allison can't be sick this long. Something is wrong and I don't know what to do about it.' 'Joe paced around while his father split another log.

William stood back up, setting the axe to the side. " Did you do anything or say anything that might've scared her off?"

Joe shrugged, " I don't know. Now I am beginning to question everything I did, or didn't do. "

" Women. They test everything that a man has. His good and bad virtues are displayed out there like a resume. One false move and they run like scared deer." Will pulled out a rag and wiped his brow.

Joe was a little surprised at the eloquence of his father. " I don't know. She seemed so happy, even after we hugged."

William laughed, " Hugged? You didn't kiss her. I kissed your mother on our very first date."

" ew."

" Hey, your mother was something else. Cute, smart, and sassy. She still is. She has the greatest legs a man could want. " William was smiling like a fool.

Joe repeated himself. " ew."

" Don't 'ew' me. You are just as sappy about this girl of yours." He picked up the axe and set up another log. " Okay, tell me about this 'hug'?" With a large grunt, he swung the axe and cleaved the log in two with one good shot.

Joe thought about it for a moment. " It was raining, she had just been bullied, and I walked her home. She asked me for a hug, and I hugged her. We hugged for a long time. She never moved until you came out. "

" Sounds innocent enough." William noted, and then set up another log.

Allison in the distance listened closely so that she could be absolutely sure what he said next. Joe kicked around a large chunk of wood that fell from one of the recently split logs. " I know. But, I am not sure anymore. Maybe she felt I was pushing too hard. Maybe she thought I wanted more. Maybe she thought that I would've done more had you not come out. I just don't know."

William split the next log and answered. " Stop coming to all sorts of wild conclusions Joe. Women are hard to figure out, especially when it comes to how they think."

Joe let out a large sigh. " I know. I just wish she would tell me something. Heck, I would be happy to just see her one more time."

They continued talking while a wolf sat behind a tree and listened. Her heart felt like ice in her chest. That moment of the embrace was something she would treasure for years. It was a beautiful moment, and now the man she cared for so much was feeling bad about the whole event. She wanted to jump out of the forest and tell him to not worry, that the hug was everything she had needed at that moment. But her common sense won over and she remained in the shadows of the old oak tree.

‽

Chapter 19: Revelation

Three weeks passed and Joseph continued to come to Elsabethe's each evening and stitch. His mood was more and more depressed with each passing day. Elsabethe wanted dearly to tell him what was really going on, but she respected Allison's wishes and she always kept her promises to a friend. So, Joseph was left to wonder what happened.

Joe thought hard about moving on, going out, and maybe dating someone else. But his heart would not allow him. He never knew this kind of affection before and he would not give up so easily. At least, not until there was no other option than to simply acknowledge the end of this relationship.

ಬ

Joseph walked down the mainstreet with his mother beside him. All the while he was unusually quiet. In his arms he carried a large hand woven wooden basket that Marla had bought for the bed and breakfast. Now, using him as her shopping cart, she was buying other items and piling them inside the basket.

" Thanks." Marla took a couple of large candles from a little old lady who operated a specialty candle shop. Without even asking, she held them out for Joseph to take and find a place to put them in his ever filling basket.

Without a word, he took the candles from her. She stopped walking for a moment and looked back at him. " Joe, is there something wrong?"

He shook his head. " No."

She cleared her throat, " Joe, don't do this. I know that look on your face and that attitude. Are you having girl problems again?"

Joe was about to reply with another 'no' when her words caught up with him. " Again? I haven't had problems like this ever."

Marla laughed, " Honey, every girl you broke up with left you gloomy and depressed. Yet, I don't think I have seen you under such a gray cloud for this long before."

" I don't want to talk about it." Joe moaned and then looked away.

Marla smiled at him. " Joey, don't be so worried. There are plenty of fish in the sea."

Joe frowned at her, " This one is different. "

" Huh?"

" She is special. I don't know why, or how, but she just is. Now, let's not talk about it." He started walking ahead toward the next shop they were going to visit.

Marla shrugged. " Teenagers." She then walked with him toward a little shop around the corner.

" Hello, Marla, what will it be today?" The local owner of a fresh fruit and vegetable shop greeted one of his best customers at the door.

Marla smiled, " Oh, I need about ten pounds of your best pears."

" Sure, have some great ones in today." George walked her inside where the walls were lined with produce from the local farms.

Marla picked up an apple and smelled it, " Oh, this one is sweet."

" What on earth are you making with ten pounds of pears?" George began to pile a cloth bag with fresh, light green pears.

"Pear butter. It is a variation of the apple butter I make and I thought that it would be nice to sell at the festival." She took one of the five pound bags from him and put it in the basket that was still in Joseph's arms.

Joe, grunting under the added weight, set the basket down on the counter.

"Mom, you could have warned me that was coming."

"Honey, couldn't you see it?"

"Not over all this other junk you've stashed in here." He rearranged the basket so that the produce didn't squash any of the other items.

Marla rolled her eyes and looked back to George. "Don't mind him. He is in a girl funk."

"Oh, Joe is having girl problems?" George smiled at the young man.

Joe let out an annoyed grunt. "Mom, don't talk about it, please."

"He is moping around about a girl…"

"MOM, please." Joe was getting angry at his mother.

George picked up a flyer from his counter. It was the little poster for the end of summer festival. "Why don't you invite a girl to this. The festival is a great place to get romantic. The Ferris wheel, fireworks, picnicking, even dancing. I am sure that you would have a lot of fun."

Joe took the flyer. He remembered seeing this very poster on the door of the ice creamery. A smile actually cracked on his lips. He began to think that perhaps he could charm another date out of Allison, even if it was through a mutual friend.

"Uncle, where do you want these?" A young man came out of the backroom with a pile of old photo binders in his arms.

" Samuel, be careful, those are old." George ran over to his teenage nephew and took half of the stack of binders before they all fell to the floor.

Joseph moved the basket down to the floor so that they could place the binders on the counter.

" What is all this? Going into the antiques business?" Marla fanned away some of the dust that arose from the old books.

George smiled, " I was cleaning out the basement of my late grandfathers house when I found all these pictures. They will make a perfect display for the festival this year."

" What kind of pictures?" Marla coughed from the cloud of dust.

George opened up a book. " This will be the 'End of Summer' festivals eightieth consecutive year. All the shops are putting together a display to recognize this. So, when I found pictures from the first ten years of the festival, I knew that I had a gold mine on my hands. This will be the hit of the show." He pointed to the first book.

The images were ancient compared to modern digital images. But they were very well made for the time. Some of the pictures were of the rides, attractions, and booths, but most were of the people at the first year's festival. Several pages were group photos of people in attendance, all waiting and smiling for their photo.

George was beaming in pride. " My great great grandfather was a photographer for the Featherville Gazette. These pictures were his shots of the festival. He only submitted a few to the paper, but he kept the others. Aren't we lucky."

Marla flipped over pages, " Oh, these are wonderful! I would love to have some for the bed and breakfast."

" We might find some that we can have copies made for you. I, of course, will keep all the originals." George started flipping through pages as well.

Joseph, who could care less, watched the pages flip by while he thought about how much he wanted to just leave. But then something caught his eye. " Wait." he stopped the old shop owner from flipping another page. " What is this?" he pointed to a picture.

George carefully pulled it out and read the back. His great great grandfather, being in the news business, kept good notes on the back. " Let's see, Crowd leaving last show August second 1929, eleven in the evening. Back when the festival started, the main attraction was a show where performers from all over the world would display music and skits. Vaudeville, I think they used to call it. This is long before large rides were the hot ticket."

Joseph carefully turned the image back over, examining it closely. " It cannot be."

" Joe, what's up?" Marla looked at the picture as well.

" I recognize them." he pointed to a pair of figures in the front row.

He could not believe his eyes. In the front row of the crowd, stopping to smile at the camera was a woman who bore a striking resemblance to Elsabethe. But that was not what really stunned him. Next to that woman was another girl, not wishing to look directly at the camera, with a dark patch on her face and patches on her bare arms. This girl looked exactly like Allison, down to where the furry patches were.

"Do you mind if I get a picture of this?" Joe pulled out his cell phone, which had a digital camera in it. " I won't use the flash, there is enough light in here."

George shrugged, " Sure." He set it out on the counter for Joe.

Joe positioned his cell phone camera well and got a really good photo of the old picture, then put the phone away.

" Hey, that looks like the woman who lives next door. Elizabeth, is it?" Marla asked.

Joe shook his head slowly, still fixed on the picture in front of him. " It's Elsabethe. And yes, this looks exactly like her."

" You've seen this picture before?" George asked Joe.

Joe shook his head. " No, I have never seen anything about the past festivals other than what they have shown in the commercials."

George looked at the picture closely, " I remember my grandfather talking about this one. It was the only picture that he showed me from this collection. I had no idea that he had all of these other ones."

Samuel came over and looked at the picture. "Yeah, that was the one that caused all the problems, at least that is what great granddad said."

Marla looked at it with a furrowed brow, " What is so controversial about this picture?"

George tucked it back into the sleeve in the page. " That girl." He pointed to Allison.

" Apparently people thought that the traveling circus sent her in to advertise for them during our town's festival. Grandpa wanted to publish this with the others, but the press was so angry with the circus that they didn't allow it."

Joe was astonished. " What happened?"

" The circus denied it and the girl was not seen again. I guess their little ploy backfired and they gave up. Don't know why they cared so much about a little town event. " George gathered up the books to take them to a safer location, considering their age. " Do you need anything else, Marla?"

She nodded and continued shopping while Joseph looked at the photo captured on his phone.

༰

That evening, Joseph came to Elsabethe's house again. He had not been in a few days and this time he was not carrying his stitching bag.

Elsabethe called out for him to come in. She no longer felt the need to answer the door for a friend such as him when he knocked.

" It is nice to see you. Are you well?" she asked with a smile.

Joseph was not able to smile. He opened his mouth to answer, but did not say anything. Walking over to the sofa, he sat down and looked at the picture on his phone.

" Joe, is everything all right? Where is your project?" Elsabethe was very concerned.

He looked at her, then back to his phone. "Elsabethe. Will you tell me the truth? "

" Of course dear, I would not lie to a friend or an enemy. Please, what is the matter?" her concern was quickly becoming a worry.

For a long moment he looked at her face and then looked down at the part of the picture he had focused the image on. He looked up again, feeling a little foolish with what he HAD to ask. " How old are you?"

Her eyes widened. She coughed and cleared her throat, then asked, " What was that, dear?"

" I would guess seventy five at the oldest, but something tells me that I would be wrong. How old are you?"

Elsabethe stood up, " How about some tea?"

Joseph stood up too, this time holding out his phone to show her the picture. She took the device from him and looked at it, the nice wide screen giving her a good view of what he saw. Anyone else might not understand the image, but she knew it quite well. Joe gave her a stern gaze, " You are not just a nice old lady. You are something completely different, aren't you?"

Elsabethe looked up, " Joe, I...I."

" Please, tell me." He wasn't sure he was ready to hear this, but he also needed to know.

Elsabethe looked at the picture for a long moment. Half a dozen lies came to her mind that might explain this away. But what is a true friendship if it is filled with lies? She knew that he would never trust anything but the truth, for he obviously suspected it. " Joseph, my dear child, I had hoped you would put these pieces together yourself. Now that you have some inclination, I guess you should be told the truth." Joe immediately became visibly nervous. Elsabethe nodded slowly, and answered with a soft voice. " Yes, I am Elsabethe, the stitching witch. Adel is my sister, and we have been in Featherville since it was founded in 1692."

Joseph sat down on the sofa, shaking and dazed. Now that he knew the truth, he wanted to deny what he had been thinking for the last few hours. "You....but... this cannot be true. That is fantasy, myth, nothing real."

" But it is. Watch." she took the crystal needle out of the fabric on the cloth beside the table and pointed it toward the kitchen. The needle seemed to flash at the tip.

A silver tray with a tea setting floated in from the kitchen, tea steaming up from the pot. It made its way between Joseph and her. She pointed to the floor and a small table appeared out of nowhere for the tray to set itself on. Then she waved her needle at the empty plate on the tray and a pile of the cookies he liked so much appeared out of nowhere. " I am afraid that the cookies never taste as good as home baked ones."

" YAHH!" Joseph nearly fell off the couch.

" Oh, please don't be afraid. I am a kind witch. I mean no harm to anyone. And I have never put a spell on you." This was a practiced speech, for she worried every day that someone would figure out her identity.

Joseph, who was still in a fog of disbelief, looked right at her. " Then, that story was real?"

" Yes. Adel really did try to control the world with magic. And, yes, she is still out there, but only a mere shadow of herself. Do not worry." Elsabethe was more concerned that he was going to fall over with a heart attack, given how pale he was becoming.

Joseph looked down to the picture. " Then, Allison….is Yuki."

" Yes. She was the cursed one, along with her two brothers. But, she too is not dangerous. She is…just another stitcher in this tapestry of life." Elsabethe was trying to make everything sound so plausible.

Joe stared off into shadows. " I…I…I don't know what to say."

Elsabethe put away her needle, " Honey, I am your friend, as I was yesterday and will be tomorrow. Allison is a person too. Though a wolf by day and a person by night, she is still a sweet girl." She noticed Joe was becoming short of breath. " Are you okay?"

Joe started to panic again while the reality was still settling in. " This changes my world. Everything I know is wrong. I just don't understand this."

Elsabethe put her hand on his arm. " If you would like, I am capable of erasing some of your memory, so long as you agree. You can be cleared of this and set so that you never met her, or me. But I am only capable of this if you agree to it; otherwise you will remember everything that has transpired."

Joe looked at her, trying to reclaim some composure. " You would take my memory away? Would I simply have amnesia of my time here in Featherville?"

Elsabethe let out a sigh, she never liked this option, especially for this young man. " Not exactly. I would set up your memory as though you only knew me as an old woman next door, and Allison would be a girl you met. But you would have to never see her or me again. The magic would fail the instant you saw either of us. Memory magic is tricky and difficult, but not impossible." She pulled out her needle again. " I am ready at any moment to…"

He held up a hand. " Tell me one thing."
" What is that?"
Joe looked right at her. " Does Allison love me?"
Elsabethe paused and asked, " What?"
" Does she care for me, as I care for her?"
Elsabethe nodded. " I am unsure if she can even admit it to herself, but she does. You have meant more to her than anyone else since her father died. "

Joe took a deep breath and let it out a little shaky, but he was gaining his confidence again. " Then I want to remember this. I think my feelings for her outweigh the shock of this."

She grinned at him, beaming in joy at his decision. " That is wonderful."

" 'Fantastic' is more the word, though I am still waiting to wake up from this dream." He sat back against the couch.

" Honey, it isn't a dream." She poured some tea, without magic, and held the cup out to him. " Why don't we have some tea and talk."

For a few hours, they spoke about magic and love. Elsabethe tried to answer every question clearly and concisely so that he felt more comfortable with a world he has only thought imaginary before today.

" So, you cannot see into the future? Crystal balls and psychics are all a bunch of frauds." He asked with the fascination of a child.

Elsabethe sipped her tea, " Magic users are just like humans when it comes to foresight. We can make logical assumptions from observations, but the future is unwritten. Of course, when one lives several thousand years, the outcome of a situation can be more obvious."

Joe set his tea cup down and looked at Elsabethe. " Can you tell me how I can win Allison back?"

Elsabethe let out a slow sigh, " No. I have tried to persuade her to rejoin you myself. She fears her connection to the magical world could do you harm. But she needs you."

" Me. Why?"

Elsabethe smiled warmly, " She needs love. Though I have cared for her and so have her two brothers, she needs a love that we cannot give her, but you can. The curse has left her very cautious about the outside world and you are the first to get past her looks. You are also the first one in many decades that has persuaded her to venture out into that world."

Looking again at the picture on his phone, Joseph began to realize how much he really cared for Allison. " Then, she really does care for me!" he stated quietly.

Elsabethe nodded, " It took her a lot of time to understand the emotions you elicited from her. But, yes, she does. The pain of her situation is so great that she does not wish to have you bear it as well."

Joe looked back up at her, " Tell me, can the curse be lifted? Can she be free of it?"

" Yes."

" How? " He asked.

Elsabethe closed her eyes and let out a sigh, "That, I cannot tell you. Breaking a binding spell is something that is secret and unique to each spell. If the way to break a spell is told, then it may never be broken. But I can tell you that it is a very easy cure, one that requires you."

" Me?"

She nodded. " Yes. You are capable of breaking the spell. But, you must figure that out for yourself. May I now ask, why you care about breaking this spell?"

Joe looked down at the timid girl in the picture. " It brings her pain and fear. I want her to feel joy without hesitation. I want her to feel as beautiful as I see her even now. "

Elsabethe was grinning ear to ear. " Oh, she is a lucky girl. If you were only a few thousand years older I might just date you myself."

Joe stood up, his knees nearly giving way beneath him. He wobbled for a moment and then started back toward the door. " I think I will go home and rest a bit. I still need to give this all a little more thought. It is a pretty big blow."

" Joseph, please don't worry. Yuki and I aren't all that different from you."

As he left, his mind raced with thoughts. How could it be real? Yet he had seen the evidence for himself. Could this be a dream? No, it was too real to be a dream. Or was it?

ಬ

Joe went into his home with his cell phone still showing the picture. His mind was racing as he thought about the story, Adel, Allison, the twins, Elsabethe, and just about everything else that only a few hours ago he though was just another story. What he considered a simple myth was turning into reality right before his eyes.

Marla, who was polishing some of the metal work around the room, held out a cloth. " Hey, Joe, why don't you give me a…" Joe passed her, his eyes still glued to the picture on his phone.

William who was coming down the stairs with his arms full of sheets and towels to wash, he passed Joe who was heading up the stairs. " Hey, Joe, can you get the laundry room door…Joe?" Joe was still oblivious to anyone else. William stopped and looked at his wife, " What's up with him?"

Marla shrugged, " I don't know. Something about that old picture has really caught his attention. He was like this all the way home today.

William continued toward the laundry room that was in the back of the kitchen. " Well, as long as he isn't still whimpering about that girl."

Marla stopped polishing and looked toward where Joe had just gone. She wasn't so sure that he wasn't still thinking about that girl. Somehow, she knew that his mind was still longing for her.

ः

Chapter 20: Acceptance

Joe sat outside his bedroom window. The overhang above the porch was flat and broad enough to support him. This was a good place to sit and think, for he could be by himself.

" YAH, HO-HA, TOUCHDOWN!" William Henderson danced around a pile of wood that he was splitting for future use. He often would split logs when he couldn't find anything else to do, especially when he wanted to listen to old football games.

Joseph laughed at his father acting like nobody was watching. William was so in love with football that he had the radio broadcasts of the good games, the ones where his team had fantastic wins, saved to an MP3 player. While he worked outside, or when he was bored, he would plug in the ear phones and listen. He must've hooted and hollered to the same touchdown fifty times by now. That was okay. At least he wasn't singing to his music. Nobody should have to hear a voice that is that off pitch.

While Joe was watching his father dance around, he noticed a tuft of short gray hairs sticking out on the edge of the roof. Pulling them out, he frowned at what looked like dog hairs. How did they get up here? Then he remembered those two wolves who visited him.

" But, that was a dream....oh, right, it wasn't. " He muttered to himself. It sort of made him feel more foolish that he had come face to face with the reality and still took all this time to realize it.

" Joe?" Marla startled him, nearly causing him to fall off the roof.

He looked back at her hanging half way out of his widow. " Mom, what are you doing?"

" Trying to find you. Is there something wrong?" She leaned further out of his window.

He tossed the dog hairs aside, not wanting to explain them right now. " Wrong? No, nothing is wrong with me. Why?"

She rolled her eyes at him, " Joe, you aren't that hard to read. One moment you are singing and dancing, the next you're sitting outside of your window, moping around. What's up?"

He sighed hard. " It's hard to explain."

" Girl trouble."

He frowned harder, " How'd you know?"

" Listen. I know more about life than you give me credit for. You don't let a lot of stuff get you upset, but girls have always been hard for you. Did she dump you? Did you say something stupid?" Marla was acting the mother.

Joe's frown faded and he let out a slow sigh, "No. I didn't say anything, and I don't think she has dumped me. She is going through something hard right now and she doesn't want to trouble me with her problems."

" Problems? What are they?"

Joe gave that some thought. He couldn't tell her the truth, but he hated lying to his parents. " Let's just say that they are pretty big."

Marla crawled out and sat next to him. " Maybe she could come and talk to me, I have been known to have my moments."

Joe shook his head, looking at the sun setting in the distance. " No. Her problems are special and I doubt she would even tell you what they are. "

" I see. Then you are in a pickle. Do you think that these problems will keep you apart from her?"

Joe looked up into the orange sunset against the high clouds. " I hope not."

Marla was silent for a moment, watching her own husband while he worked.

" How much do you like this girl?"

He looked at her, then back to the clouds. He had to think about that for a moment. How does one measure feelings? " I cannot say."

" Tell me something. Do you worry that she is feeling bad?"

" Yeah."

" Do you want to include her in as much of your life as you can?"

" Yeah."

" Good. Now, do you want to take her problems away and make her feel better, only because you are sad that she is sad?"

" Yeah."

Marla put her arm around his back. " Then, my son, you are in love. When anyone is in love, they worry that their problems and concerns will affect those they deeply care for. But, they sometimes forget that God has put the other person there for the comfort they need. Even when she says she doesn't want to see you because of her problems, she really does need you. And, with that bleeding, broken heart I see in your eyes, you need her comfort as well. Find her and tell her that you want to be part of her world, problems or not."

Joe laid his head on his mother's shoulder. "Where did you learn all of this?"

" I learned it the moment I vowed to stay with your father in sickness or health. Sickness sometimes is more than chicken soup. Many times it can be much deeper."

Joe cocked his head, " Why do you care? Whenever I had girl problems you guys always told me to simply move on and find another girl."

" No, that was your father's answer when you were dumped. He was right most of the time which is why I never got in the middle of your romances in high school. Joey, when I was younger I met a man who was odd, burly, loud, and cuddly. He seemed to have the emotional range of a football, but I knew he was more than that."

Joe stated, " You're talking about Dad."

" Yup. There were times that people told me that all he really cared about was football. But I knew that they were all wrong. I gave him a chance and we fell madly in love. He never wanted to show it, but he really liked me. He even gave up tickets to a championship game so that he could take me to Make-out Point."

" ew."

She laughed, " Yeah, that is kind of gross for you, but he was so sweet. If I hadn't stuck it out with him, you wouldn't be here and we wouldn't be the happy family we are." She looked down at the dancing fool, who was hopping around celebrating another touchdown that happened three years ago. " And I love that man. I don't want to know what life would've been without him. This girl just might not be the right girl for you, but it is far too early to give up hope. I want you to be happy in this world, just as happy as I have been, more if you can find it. "

Joe let out a sigh, " I think I have found that happiness."

Marla smiled and nodded. " Then, my son, don't give up. Find her, hold out your hand and tell her that no matter what her problem is, you are willing to give her strength. That is all you can do, and you will find that if she really loves you too, she will take your offer."

That answered all of his concerns. He would go to Allison and give this one last try. He would not give up until she told him that she really didn't love him. "Thanks mom." Joe smiled while looking at the rays of the setting sun in the sky above.

ೞ

Allison, as a wolf, walked into the deeper part of the cave-like den that she had been living in for centuries. She tapped a rock with her nose and it lit up under the spell that Elsabethe placed on it years ago. It gave warmth and light without a dangerous fire.

She laid down, placing the end of her muzzle on a small square of finely woven cloth. It was the monogrammed handkerchief that Joseph had given her the first night they officially met.

Yoshi walked up from a deeper part of the cave. He sat down and looked right at her.

" Yuki, I cannot stand to see you like this."

She glanced up. " Just leave me alone."

" You are wasting away in your heart sickness." He let out a sigh and closed his eyes. " You mustn't do this. Go, be with him."

She looked away, staring at part of the dirt wall. " You know why I can't."

" Yuki, a death of the heart is worse than a death of the soul. One lasts a moment, the other can last much longer. I will not permit you to die like this."

She retorted, " When did you become so eloquent?"

He smiled, " I am over three hundred years old."

She looked back to him, " Yoshi, I cannot bear the thought of him dying by spells of that old witch."

" I know. And I promise that both Oki and I will see to his protection. We will not allow her to harm him." he said this without fear.

Her sorrowful face turned serious. " You would obligate yourself to such a task? Why?"

He stood and walked away, returning moments later with a small, old book in his mouth. He dropped it in front of her. " Because father wanted you to be happy."

She looked at it for a moment, not believing what she was looking at. " Is this fathers journal?"

He nodded slowly, " Yes. I found it after father died. I never showed it to you because it is filled with his thoughts and feelings, and he often wrote about you and his desires for your future. I knew that it would bring heart ache every time you read it. But now I think that only he can advise you of the truth. Read it, the very last entry."

She had a lump in her chest at the idea of reading this, but she could not resist. Being extremely careful of the ancient binding, she opened the back cover to the last pages he wrote. The words were written in the archaic kanji of Nippon.

" I write this as possibly my last entry. I will defy Adel, as now I am aware of her actions and magical wrong doings. I will confront her and tell her that she will neither use me nor my family any longer. I will not be the tool of her death spells. Her anger and wrath is sure to be severe. I know that she is more powerful than I, for she is much older and more practiced in her magic. I pray that I may continue with my children, seeing them through the rest of my life, but I will also do anything to protect them.

My children have lost their mother and their home. I want nothing but their happiness in this world. My sons are fine men and I know that they will be strong. My daughter is a good leader and will make a fine wife someday. For all three, I wish them to know love as I have known it. If I am to perish, I will perish, but I pray that they will go forward and seek their own destinies.

They know that I love them, and that is all that I need in this world."

Yuki broke down and cried. She could hear his voice in those words. And more importantly, she could remember the love he had for her and her brothers. It was not fair. She wanted him to write more, to be here to hold her when she hurt and to tell her that he loved her. But, somehow, she could still feel him here, feel his love emanating from the pages of his journal.

Yoshi came over to lay his head on her back and said. " Sister, do not deny yourself this happiness. Father would not like it. If he were here, he would protect you and Joseph from Adel. Since he is not here, I shall do what he would. You are not alone, you have a family and friends. And now, you even have a love. Go to him, please."

Yuki continued to weep. She agonized over what to do. The complexity of her decision was just made harder. Now she was contending not only with herself, but with her brothers, Elsabethe, and her father.

" Yuki, Yuki." Oki ran in at that moment.

Both she and Yoshi looked up, her eyes still flooded with tears. " What is it?"

Oki caught his breath, " It's Joseph."

Yuki's eyes widened. " What happened? Is he hurt?"

" No, nothing like that. He is here. He just walked into the forest and sat down next to the old stream." Oki stood to the side of the entrance and looked back to where Joseph was.

Yoshi smiled. " Go to him, as you did the first day he was here. Even if he does not know you are a wolf, at least he might smile at you again. Take a long look at him and decide if this denial is worth it. Please."

Yuki felt defeated. Not only could she never turn down her brothers when they gave her the real puppy dog eyes, she yearned to see Joseph. " Alright. But stay behind. A wolf pack might frighten him." She stood, shook off the dust of the floor, and slowly made her way down to the little river.

༾

" Why haven't I been here before?" Joe said to himself while he sat on a large boulder and stitched.

In his hands was a small piece of mono canvas. He was using a large needle to stitch a nice little music note. It was a design he had done so often that he didn't need to see the pattern to stitch it.

He was sitting in a lower section of the forest, where the little creek had cut a path between the trees. During the late summer, the trees were still heavily foliaged, but not so much that they blocked the afternoon sunlight. The creek itself was crystal clear and had perfectly rounded stones that made it babble with the most soothing sounds.

Allison, as a wolf of course, walked up behind him. She was very hesitant to approach, as she was nervous about any human seeing her in this form. If he had not been so nice that first day, she might never approach him like this at all. But, she knew that his heart was kind and that he would not be terrified, or horrified, at the sight of this ugly dog.

Joseph planted the needle at the top of the small rectangle of fabric. He looked back at her after hearing her feet crumple leaves in the grasses. " Hello there. Been a long time."

She stopped and looked at him with frightened eyes. Somehow, she hadn't realized that he knew she was behind him.

He laughed, " It's alright, you should know that I won't harm you. Come on." he waved at her to move toward him.

She cautiously walked closer. He didn't move or even flinch when she came right next to him. Slowly sitting down, she looked directly at him. He put his hand on her head between her ears and scratched. She seemed to enjoy this sensation.

"You know. I have learned a lot about myself in the last few months. I was a selfish, shallow boy in high school. Then I met a girl who can only be described as homely, at best." The wolf frowned, though she still allowed him to pet her. He continued. " She warmed my heart and showed me that there was a whole lot to her other than what was on the outside. She was strong and she could flatten anyone who made fun of her. Yet she was weak. So much so that she could be brought to tears just hearing a sad story. I admired the strength, but I wanted to protect the weakness. She was in my arms and I never wanted to let go. Then, out of the blue, she left and I haven't seen her since. I thought that I would go on and that she was just another girl. But I could not tear my thoughts away from her. She fills my heart, and without her, there is a void that hurts. Yet what hurts most of all is that I might have hurt her, and that is a burden that is unbearable."

Allison looked down, feeling terrible. She didn't want to tell him she was a wolf right now, while he was pouring out his heart to her when he didn't even know it. So, she took a deep breath and stood up, then started walking away.

Joe turned on the rock to watch her leave. "Allison, what did I do that was so wrong?"

She stopped and looked back. Could he know?

He smiled, " You know, you have the most beautiful eyes I have ever seen."

Now she knew, " Joseph?"

He nodded. " Yeah, I figured it out. It took me a while to convince myself it was true."

She walked back to him, confounded, yet overjoyed. Her tail was even wagging with elation. "Joseph, you are not frightened?"

" A little wierded out, yeah. But I sort of knew it all along."

" How? Did Elsabethe tell you something?" She was so happy that she leaned her head against his leg.

He smiled and continued petting her. " No. I sort of figured this out on my own. The story helped. But who can believe a fable? The first day I met you, at Elsabethes home, I looked into your eyes and saw the same eyes as I had seen on that wolf I met. I didn't fully believe it, but something in me added the parts together. Then, I found this." He pulled out his phone and accessed the photo he took of the picture at the old store.

She looked into the screen. " Oh, that. Elsabethe took me there. She thought I might meet a nice boy there, or something like that. As it turned out, I was the freak show. In fact, if I had any of my magic, I would have made sure that picture never existed."

He closed the phone, " Well, I'm glad it exists. It is a beautiful picture of a beautiful person. And it helped me realize it."

Yuki rubbed her head against his hand, her ears twitching slightly. " I don't understand how you can accept this so easily? Every other human who has found out either tried to kill me or ran away in fear."

Joseph watched her tail wag against the leaves and grasses. The thought of what he was looking at was still a little overwhelming. " Me, no, I was as solid as a rock. Just don't ask Elsabethe about the whole panic attack scene in her place. So, what is your name? Allison or Yuki?"

" Yuki Kitsune. But, if you would, call me Allison."

With great relief in his heart, he nodded. "Allison it is then. So, if you are real, then I guess that dream was not a dream."

She looked up to him, " Dream? What dream?"

" Two wolves came to me, the night we last saw each other. They were concerned about my intentions toward you. They wanted to be sure that I would be an honorable gentleman around you."

She glared back in the general direction of her den and said under her breath, " I am going to kill them."

" Huh?"

" Oh, nothing." She smiled at him.

Joseph paused for a moment, listening to the gentle stream. Then he asked,

" What happened?"

Allison knew exactly what he was asking, " It is hard to explain. There is a reason, but you did nothing wrong. That night, when we hugged, it was the most wonderful night I have had in three centuries."

" I am glad. I would never want to hurt you. "

Allison rubbed her head into his hand, " I know. I never felt as secure as when I was in your arms."

" I have that kind of effect on women." He teased.

She rolled her eyes at his joke.

Joseph laughed, " This is going to be hard to explain to mom and dad. But you are going to love them. They are weird parents, but nothing can be weirder than this."

Allison stepped back, " Oh, I don't think that would be wise. Humans have a hard time accepting things like me. Besides, I....I am still not sure if we should be together."

He stood up from the small boulder and walked toward her, " Why? You will startle them at first, but they will come to like you as much as I do."

" No, it is hard to explain. But I cannot." She stepped further away from him.

Joseph held out a hand. " Whatever the problem is, let me help, please. At least go out with me again. One date is hardly enough." He pulled out the folded up flyer for the festival. "Come with me to the festival."

She stopped and looked at him. Amazingly enough, his eyes were the same puppy-dog eyes as her brother's. In his eyes she could see that he was hurting. " All right."

" Good. It opens in a week and I thought that we could go opening night. Mom and dad will be there selling stuff out of a booth. I will take you around with my VIP pass to all the attractions. And I promise that if anyone treats you like a freakshow, they will be dealt with."

She giggled at him. " You don't have to give a black eye to everyone who stares. Just hold my hand and let them know that the ugliest girl at the festival is with the most handsome man. That will show them."

Now Joe rolled his eyes. " You aren't ugly and I am not all that handsome."

" Sure, that is why you take your shirt off whenever you can." she gave him a sneaky smile.

He was about to respond with a proper retort, but the ground shook, and a loud rumbling sound could be heard echoing throughout this part of the mountains.

" What was that?" Joe looked around with a touch of fear in his eyes.

Allison knew exactly what it was, but she didn't explain. " Just the earth moving, don't worry. Get home and….I will be at Elsabethe's to see you in a week."

He smiled, " You know, for a wolf, you do have the most beautiful eyes and a pretty cute tail."

She grinned, then the grin faded away. " Uh, and, don't tell your parents about what I really am. Please keep that between you, me, and Elsabethe."

He nodded, " I give you my word."

" Thank you." She ran off back toward her den.

Joe started back home. He was excited and yet still slightly dazed. Who wouldn't be a little bewildered? It is not normal to find out that magic is real and that the girl you care for is a wolf by day. In fact, he was still waiting to wake up and find himself in bed. By force of will he pushed all the concerns, worries, and thoughts about all of this away. After all he had been through, the knowledge that she still cared for him and was going out with him again overshadowed all else. If this was what real love felt like, then he never wanted it to go away.

ೞ

Chapter 21: The Second Date

The week passed both quickly and slowly. Joseph was so excited to find that Allison still liked him that he was dancing on air most of the time. Even so, he really needed to see her again to be sure that everything was as it seemed. Could she really be that wolf? Was he dreaming? Was he a damned fool if he asked another stupid question? He didn't care anymore. Something about her made him happy, and it was a fantastic happy.

" Well, you certainly are out of that funk you were in." Marla noted how Joe was smiling while he chopped up vegetables for the beef stew.

He looked up at her with a goofy smile, then pulled a pair of ear plug head-phones out, "What?"

She laughed, " I guess you aren't all gloomy anymore? Get over that girl?"

At that moment, William came in with a bag of potatoes, " No, haven't you heard? Joe and his girlfriend made up."

" Oh, really?" Marla looked over at her son with a smile.

" No, well yes, but no. I mean, we weren't on the outs or anything. She was just not feeling well and now she knows that everything is okay." He chopped a carrot with a practiced hand.

Marla dumped a pile of chopped stew meat into the pot and began the process of making the roux. " I don't understand. Was she sick?"

" No." Joe didn't want to elaborate, but he knew his mother.

" Okay. So what was wrong? If she wasn't sick and you two didn't fight, what was making her not feel well?" Marla opened up two containers of chicken broth.

Joe looked at both of his parents, one at the sink peeling potatoes and the other standing over a pot, both with their eyes fixed on him. " Alright, if you must know, Allison isn't very confident about her appearance. She isn't exactly a beauty queen. But she didn't understand that I don't care."

William continued peeling spuds and nodded. "Oh, I see, you are helping her build her confidence by going out with her."

Joe stopped chopping and cleared his throat. "No. I never want to hear that from either of you again. I am not charity dating her, I am honestly interested in her. Her beauty is far deeper than anything on the surface. She has taught me a thing or two about that. I want it clear that I care for her and that I don't care what she looks like."

" Alright, alright. I'm sorry." William felt that burn from across the room.

Marla was a little more astute than her husband. " I see. That is a nice practiced speech. Planning on repeating it often?"

Joseph rolled his eyes, as he often did with his parents. " The night we first dated, she was picked on by some idiots at the ice creamery and was hurt by them, emotionally. I want to be sure that everyone knows that when I take her to the festival this evening it will be because I care for her, not because I pity her. "

Marla came over and took the bowl of vegetables from him. " That is very nice, honey. Have you told her this?"

"Yes. Not in so many words, but she knows it." He looked out the window next to him, remembering a rainy night where he and Allison hugged passionately.

"What about the word 'Love'?" William challenged his son.

Joseph paused for a moment. He didn't know how to respond. "Well, no I haven't said that yet. But we had only one date."

"Ha." Marla retorted. "You may have only taken her out once, but you spent practically a summer together, each night. You ran out of this place so fast that the guests thought there was a fire drill. I have never seen you so excited to go see a girl. Even now, you are acting the fool when you think about seeing her."

Joe was going to respond, but thought better of it. "I guess, maybe." The more he thought about it, the more it made sense. He had never told a girl before that he loved her, but he never felt for a girl as much as he felt for Allison. In fact, when she stopped seeing him, it hurt in a way that no other break-up had. The others were like business deals, they dated him to make themselves look better. And when they were done, it was simply over. Yet, when Allison was not with him, he felt terrible. He wanted to make her feel better, he wanted her to make him feel better. He wanted her, something he had never felt for another girl. With a growing smile, he looked at his father. "No, I haven't told her yet, but I just might."

"Oh, I should bring the camera." Marla was teasing him.

Joe rolled his eyes, again, "Shut up."

☙

"Stop shaking." Elsabethe stitched while a dog sat on her couch, looking like she was about to shake her fur off.

Allison looked at the front door, then to the back door. "He might come in."

Elsabethe picked up the little alarm clock next to her chair. "It's three. He said he wasn't coming over until six, which is when the sun starts to set. Now, don't worry. Besides, he knows what you are."

"I know, I know. But, I still don't like him to see me like this. The more I think about the festival, the more I cannot get the images out of my head of the last festival." She got off the sofa and paced around the room.

Elsabethe nodded. "That was unfortunate."

Allison stopped pacing for a moment and looked directly at the stitching witch. "Unfortunate? Cruel is the better word. They literally threw things at me and called me a freak show."

"You have to remember the time period. There were such things as traveling freak shows. They were cruel ways of making different looking people seem even crazier. Society has changed since then. People won't do that to you today."

"Did Joseph tell you what happened on our date?" Allison sat down in the middle of the living room floor.

Elsabethe nodded. "Sort of. He told me that you were tormented by some drunk kids and that you dealt them a pretty harsh blow."

Allison looked down, " He wasn't there for everything. They were hateful, at best. Their words were eerily similar to some of the horrible things said to me eighty years ago. I had to hold myself back from leaving that boy without the use of half of his body for the rest of his life. Not only did they hurt me, but they also brought me to a point that I never wanted to be."

Elsabethe smiled. " But you didn't, and you know full well that Joseph will be by your side, no matter what insults you hear. Please, don't give up on humanity for the bullies of society. Three thousand years and they have hardly changed. But there are good people, kind people who will see you like Joseph does." She laughed, " Okay, maybe not as romantically as Joseph, but they won't hurl mean words and objects at you."

Allison nodded. " I guess you're right. If anything, he has shown me that there are good people in this world. "

" Yes. So, calm down and don't worry. You both will be just fine. " She continued stitching.

Allison tried to calm herself, but she literally couldn't be still. She was practically wearing a circular path around the living room floor. Elsabethe decided not to mention the shedding which was always worse when Yuki was nervous.

Elsabethe, who was stitching on a small patch of fabric that was shaped like a heart, noticed Allison's anxiousness. " What is wrong? You aren't only worried about this date tonight."

Allison looked at the old witch. " Have you not felt the tremors? Do you not sense the power growing in the woods?"

"My dear sister is coming soon, you are right. But she isn't here now, and you should not worry about her. I will deal with her if she comes." Elsabethe set down her crystal needle and picked up a selection of lace she was going to attach to the outside of the heart.

Allison frowned. "Do you not worry about this? She is powerful. And when she comes, she will be quite angry with us."

"She will be furious, I am sure of that. But, she is not more powerful than I. Her needle is the same as mine, it is the yin to my yang." She smiled at that analogy.

"I know, but I am so scared for Joseph. I should not have accepted this date. I should not have let him see me again. I don't want to see him die, I don't want him to die." She was pacing again, becoming more and more panicked.

"My dear, be calm. Please have faith that love is the answer. Adel has power and control, but she does not have the power to control love. Don't let her fear mongering taunt you. Be at peace, and believe that I will do everything that I can to protect both of you. This night is not for worrying, it is for re-igniting what should never have been left to dwindle." She held up the heart-shaped fabric.

"Huh?" Allison was not sure what that meant.

"Come here, dear, I have something very special for you." She held the heart out for the wolf.

Allison came over, first sniffing in the general direction of the heart. "What is that, a spell?"

" Yes. One that I can cast only once per person, and I thought that this evening would be perfect. Now, let me see your chest." Elsabethe took the heart in one hand and the crystal needle in the other. Allison sat, sticking out her furry chest slightly. Elsabethe placed the heart right on the center. Then the old witch asked, " Tell me, do you love him?"

" Love? I...care for him. A lot." She had given this a lot of thought, but never said it aloud.

Elsabethe calmly asked again, " Look into your heart and ask yourself, do you love him."

The wolf looked down for a moment, then closed her eyes. She could feel his arms around her, then she heard the way he always complimented her eyes. Then she saw him standing among the trees when he finally realized what she was, with his hand held out in her direction, offering to be with her. A smile played across her thin lips and she opened her eyes.

" Yes....Yes I do. I love him."

All at once, the wolf transformed into the girl that she only was at night. Elsabethe stood as Allison transitioned, keeping the heart placed against her chest. She then pinned the heart to the dress she usually wore and appeared each time she transformed into a human, using the crystal needle to attach it. " There. Oh, one more thing. One night enchanted to dance and dream, beloved by one in this scene, now a lovely dress there will be, that all eyes will see the beauty in thee." The crystal needle flashed brightly and the drab dress that Allison normally wore magically changed into a lovely gown of emerald green with flecks of gold threaded throughout. A tatted lace collar appeared around the neckline, as well as around each cuff.

Elsabethe held out her hand and a floor length mirror appeared in front of Allison.

" Now, see the beautiful girl."

Allison looked into the mirror, completely amazed. " Oh, this is wonderful. But, how? I…"

" As I said, this will only last until sunset when the transformation normally occurs. I will be unable to cast this spell over you again. So, use it wisely."

Allison looked at herself with a giddy smile, then it melted when she noticed that the furry patches were still showing. " I guess this is permanent." she touched the patch on her face.

Elsabethe nodded. " I cannot completely undo Adel's magic, but I can bring you this far."

Allison let it go and smiled again. She was admiring the dress. " You are truly a fairy god-mother."

Elsabethe chuckled. " Oh, I told those Grimm boys that they should have written me in as the witch, not a fairy, but they were so worried about backlash. Oh well. So, now you must go and see your man. Take him to the festival early; get as much time in as you can."

Allison stopped and looked at the little heart that was still pinned to her with the crystal needle. "Should you not have this now? It would be dangerous to be without the needle. "

Elsabethe held up her hand. " No, please, wear it. That is what is keeping the spell active. Without it, you are a wolf."

" Are you sure about this?"

" Yes, dear. I trust that I shall be safe this one night. Three hundred years have passed without a dire need of that needle; one more night is not going to be a problem. Now, go, be with the man who has made your heart strong." Elsabethe was just about to push her out of the house.

Allison looked toward the door, seeing the sunny day outside, her excitement building. "Yes, I think I will go and surprise him."

ಌ

" Don't be so nervous. You don't have to see her until later, so calm yourself down." Marla set down some boxes of their products for the festival while her son re-combed his hair.

Joseph was dressed slightly less elaborately than he would to go to church on Sunday. This was only a second date and to an outdoor festival of all places. But he wanted to make a good impression. A part of him was still worried that he would offend his date, so he would put on his best for her. Besides, he was terribly nervous about dating a three hundred year old magical creature. More than once he would get a little lost in thought about what had happened in the last three hundred years. Then he would settle his mind and focus on the girl he knew today, not her age or what had happened to her.

William walked through with a money box in his hands. " Sport, your date isn't until later. Are you going to drive us nuts until then?"

Joe put his comb into his pocket. " No. I guess I am being a little foolish. I am just a touch nervous about all of this. You don't know her; she isn't like any other girl."

Marla laughed, " Honey, a girl is a girl. She will be pleased if you simply show her a good time."

Joe nodded. " Yeah, sure."

William frowned. " Are we going to get to meet her?"

Joseph shook his head, " Nope. I don't want to scare her that badly. She has been through a lot and I doubt that she could handle a blow like you guys yet."

"Thanks." Marla sneered at her son and walked to another part of the house to clean.

" I was just being funny." Joseph didn't realize that he might've gone too far.

Before anyone could say anything else, there came a small, timid knock on the front door.

" Who could that be? We don't have another booking until next Saturday." William stopped and looked at the front door.

Marla smiled, " Maybe it's Joe's date. ''

Joe shook his head, knowing that the sun was still up. " I can honestly say that it is not her."

" I guess we ought to find out before they decide we aren't home. " William set aside the money box, and then opened the door.

Allison was standing there, her eyes cast downward. " uh, is, uh…" her tongue refused to work, she expected Joseph to answer.

William's eyes bugged, but he simply smiled. "You must be this Allison our son has been fussing over. Come in, please."

" Allison. Why you just made a liar out of our son" Marla joked, which received a glare in response from Joseph.

" Huh?" Allison was confused and very nervous.

Joe came quickly to the door. " Allison? I didn't think that…you could be here this early?" he censored his words so as not to alarm his parents.

She looked up relieved to see him. " Elsabethe found a way." she patted the heart attached to her dress.

William looked at what she was pointing too, "That is a very nice pin. Joe says that you stitch, too. Did you make that?"

She shook her head and very softly answered, "No, Elsabethe made it for me this afternoon. It is a special item for me to wear to today's events."

William smiled at her with almost the same cute smile that Joe had. " It is very lovely on you."

She blushed, " Thank you, Mr. Henderson."

Joseph looked at her and smiled. " You look quite lovely. That dress is very nice on you, and the color is amazing against your eyes."

She turned around, letting him get the whole effect of the dress. " You should see me in green when I had red hair."

Just then a bright flash filled the room. A buzzing sound followed with Marla pulling a photo from the bottom of her antiquated camera. " Perfect."

" Mooom, what are you doing?" Joe rolled his eyes and groaned like a teenager.

Allison looked around like a deer about to leap across a road. " What was that?"

" My parents, doing their dead level best to make this an awkward moment. '' Joe blinked several times to get the green spots out of his vision, which did little good.

Marla came over, waving the picture around to help it develop. " So you are the girl that Joe has been dressing up for. I must say, that is a lovely dress."

Allison regained her composure after the sneak attack photography, and looked down again. " Thank you, it was a gift for this evening."

" Oh my, that is the most awful picture I have seen." Marla looked at what she had snapped.

" Mom!" Joe was already in his defensive attitude.

But she was right. In the image, Joe was looking at Allison, who was looking at the camera with wide eyes. William was covering the other half of the picture with his back.

" Come on, stand still so that I can get a good shot." Marla backed up to try to get a better picture.

" No, please, I don't like photos." Allison was about to run out of the house.

Joe stopped her with a gentle hold on her shoulders. " Please, it will be fine, just you and me. I want it, in case you disappear again. I would like to have at least this much of you."

She could not resist his charm. For the first time, she allowed herself to be photographed with a smile on her face. Joe stood next to her and put his arm around her back. She smiled and gazed at him affectionately. With that another flash bathed them and the picture was set.

" Perfect." Marla showed them the developed image. She looked at it, focusing hard on it, " That is interesting."

Joe looked at it too. " What?"

She pointed to the needle pinning the heart onto Allison, it was glowing, not just flickering from the camera flash. " How about that? I guess I caught that just right, or something."

Joe looked back at Allison. " Oh, Elsabethe's needle, it is very special." He walked back to the girl and quietly said, " She gave you her needle?"

Allison softly answered. " For the night only. It is keeping the spell working."

Joe shrugged. " I guess then we shouldn't waste any time. Let's get going to the festival."

Marla nodded. " That is a brilliant idea. You two go on ahead and I will be right behind you to set up the booth for this weekend."

" I thought dad was going to set up tonight?" Joe asked while walking Allison out.

" No, no, he will be here to watch the place. We have to have someone here to take calls in case of bookings. Besides, the booth we have is barely a table and three walls. Now, get going, I doubt you want your mother driving you on a date." She was ready to push him out, especially while he was escorting a girl.

Joe agreed and walked out with Allison. They started down the path which would lead to the park where he usually stopped during his jogs. The festival was around the lake, which meant that it was not all that far from the bed and breakfast. Joe didn't mind walking, more private time with Allison.

ଽଠ

Chapter 22: The Return

Oki and Yoshi walked around the forest, each more nervous than they had ever been. Something was stirring, something that had not stirred for centuries.

" Brother, do you feel this too?" Oki looked around in fear.

Yoshi sniffed the air, " I, I don't know what this is. But I fear that I have an idea, and it isn't good."

Both walked down to the little creek. Oki sat at its side and lowered his head to lap up some water. Yoshi looked around, " Could we be this nervous over our sister's absence?"

Oki lifted his head, water dripping from his face, " Perhaps. We may be too worried about what is to happen and not living in the moment."

" Since when did you become so wise?" Yoshi teased his brother.

Oki shrugged, " I am over three hundred years old. Wisdom does come with age. Look at Elsabethe."

" Yeah, you have the wisdom of a woman who must be over two thousand years old." Yoshi snickered.

" Actually, we are over three thousand years old." a new voice said this from apparently nowhere.

" Who..who is there?" Yoshi jumped up and looked around.

A faint laugh could be heard in the distance, echoing among the trees and coming closer. It was not an echo but a gust of wind, blasting through the trees at unnatural speeds. Leaves lifted from the ground and gathered force with the ensuing gale.

" What is happening?" Oki dug his claws into the ground to hold himself in place.

Yoshi was toppled over before he could answer. The winds twisted and contorted like a wicked dance of demons. Then, joining the menagerie of leaves and other debris was a cacophony of sounds, wailing winds howling through the trees, throbbing bells, all topped by an ominous wicked laughter.

" A TRIUMPHANT RETURN!" The voice called out among the devilish cackling.

Streaks of lightning arched between the trees and crawled along the ground. The storm was becoming a single force of twisted winds, carrying thousands of leaves into a spiral, converging on a single location in the midst of the forest, directly over the lone creek, tossing and churning its waters. The lightning became more intense, cracking the air and resounding with enormous booms, shaking the very earth with the power of the sound waves.

With the lightning dancing off of the trees, the electricity culminated into a single spot. The whipping winds also focused on this single location, forcing the leaves into what appeared to be an hourglass shape in the air.

Yoshi stood up, but was once again tossed aside by the amazing winds. No matter which way he tried to move, the fierce gales fought him.

Oki, still clinging to the ground, was pressed downward as he was even closer to the epicenter of this calamity of nature. He looked up at what was forming and then yelled to his brother. " IT IS ADEL! SHE HAS RETURNED! "

" OKI!" Yoshi tried to run to his brother, but was slammed back by the winds once again.

" YOSHI, HELP!" Oki tried to take a step but was held fast by the storms pressure.

Suddenly the winds died down and a figure formed in the air. Adel was finally coming back together. Oki broke into a run but was not too far into his mad dash before he was jerked backward by an unseen force.

" OKI!" Yoshi cried out and started to run to his brother's rescue.

" GET YUKI!" Oki yelled to his brother.

Yoshi stopped. He had to carefully consider his next move. Realizing they would need their sister's strength to fight Adel he followed his brother's words and ran out of the forest.

After he stopped being dragged across the ground Oki looked up and saw the woman who had haunted his dreams for the last three centuries.

" My dear little wolf, it is pointless to fight back." She held up her hand and the obsidian needle appeared in it. " My powers have fully returned."

" Wh…wha…what do you want?" Oki asked, his heart racing.

Adel grabbed him by the neck and lifted him up to her face. " The crystal needle, revenge against my sister,… oh, and the death of that brat Yuki."

Oki choked out, " I would sooner die." Then with every ounce of strength he had, he reached around with his head and sunk his teeth into her arm.

She screeched in pain and threw him across the forest floor.

Oki immediately came to his feet and growled in her general direction. He dashed at her with the intention of ripping the flesh from her body.

Adel pointed her needle at him, " Sleep!" the word echoed in the trees and a purple colored mist struck him in the face. He crashed into the ground chin first, sleeping quietly under this spell. She smiled at him, " Brave for a powerless mutt. Perhaps you will prove useful against my sister." Leaving him in his sleeping state, she began to prepare her plans for how she would deal with her sister. Luring a witch of Elsabethes power into a trap was something that would take serious consideration and proper tactical planning.

☯

" Two, please." Joe stood at the booth that sold the arm bands for the carnival attractions. He showed his VIP pass that allowed him free admittance.

Allison was right beside him pressing slightly against him. " This is so different than when I was here last." She hoped her nervousness didn't show.

Joe waited for the ticket boy to get him the two green paper arm bands. " Well, that was eighty years ago. Things have changed."

Allison grinned. " I know. Everything is so different than it was in the nineteen twenties."

" Even though eight decades have passed since you were last here, I will do my best to show you how to enjoy a carnival like this. " He looked up to see the bewildered expression on the teen in the booth, who had his hand out with the bands. " What?"

The boy didn't say anything; for he was sure what he heard wasn't true. Joe and Allison walked away, heading right into the heart of the festivities.

The festival was a standard local town event, with rides, booths, and shows. The center attraction was a spread of traditional carnival rides, spinning, dizzying rides for people to get ill on for their own pleasure. There was a large roller coaster to one side with a Ferris wheel dominating the silhouette of the whole festival. To either side of the carnival rides were lines of booths. To the east was every game a fair could offer from water guns and basketball hoops, to the ever present milk bottle ring toss. To the west of the center were the rows of booths selling local items. Here one could sample every delicacy that was made famous around these parts. They boasted the best chow chow this side of the Mississippi and handmade wooden items. There was even a place to buy hand cut walking sticks made from oddly shaped tree roots.

The first place, though, that every patron would make their way through was the food court. These booths filled the air with the smells of cooked sausages and onions, funnel cakes, and corn dogs. Ice cream vendors and soda fountains were dotted between the other unique items. It was a caloric disaster at any other time, but today it was a treat.

" Put this on." Joe showed her the green arm band, which he had already attached to his wrist.

She looked at his arm and then at hers, " How? It is but paper? "

He laughed and peeled the sticker off the back and held up her arm. Taking special care not to stick any of the strong glue to the fur on her arm, he put it on for her. " It is a way that the carnies can see that we have paid for our visit. This way we can ride all the rides we want."

"Rides?" She was still very new to this, as she had hidden herself well from the world these past three hundred years.

He chortled, "Oh, I have much to teach you. Yes, rides to scramble ones brains. It is an adventure that all teens love to accomplish at least once on a date."

Allison looked at him in horror, "You would do this for fun?"

"Just wait, we have time for you to understand. Why don't we start small? I smell something that I never pass up at a festival." He pulled her along to a colorful cart where a cotton candy machine was busy at work twisting some of the fuzzy confection onto cardboard funnels.

Joe got the vendor to make an especially large ball of the sweet cotton for him and even wrapped it with two sticks like a popsicle.

Allison took out a lump of the fluff and looked at it like it was made of sludge.

"What are we to do with this? Spin it into thread?"

Joe laughed, as he had done all afternoon with this curious girl. "No, we eat it." he pulled loose some for himself and put it into his mouth.

She waited for him to choke on it, but found that he rather enjoyed it. So, she hesitantly put what she had already pulled off into her mouth. Her eyes widened and she smiled. "Oh my, it vanished leaving the most wonderful flavor. What flavor is that?"

"Blue. I think it is supposed to be blueberry, but that has been remade so often by artificial means that the flavor is just as unique as the candy itself. Go ahead, have all you want." He held it out for her.

She took some with her left hand, and wrapped her right arm around his left and walked with him. "This is delicious. I have missed too much these last 300 years."

Joseph smiled, " You have missed a lot. I hope that I can bring just a little of that back to you. Now, let's go on some of the rides. I want to get your education started as soon as possible."

They ran off like the teens they were toward the smaller rides, so that she might get used to them slowly. Joe got her on the egg beater ride and sat so that she would slide up to him with the force of the spinning motion. At first, she was terrified seeing the others on the ride and what it did, but, upon seeing them laugh and enjoy every moment of it, she was more eager to give it a chance. Besides, she enjoyed the idea of being squished up against Joseph.

ଔ

Elsabethe had an uneasy feeling. She was unsure if this was due to the fact that she didn't have her needle, having not been separated from it like this for as long as she could remember. But there was more to it than that. It was a feeling like a warning deep in her bones.

She walked around the inside of her home more than once, finding nothing out of the ordinary. Now she decided she would explore the outside, just to be sure everything was alright with the world. But, the outside was not well at all. There was an uneasy feeling in the air, more intense than anything she had felt yet.

" ELSABETHE!!" Oki's voice carried on the wind and it was more than terrified.

" Oki?" she coughed out, her unease jumping straight to sheer terror.

" HELP!" the same voice cried out, the sound fading in the breeze, as if he were fading away.

Elsabethe snapped her fingers and a broom appeared next to her. Mounting it quickly, she flew into the trees. These hills were deep and the forest was thick. If she were to reach him in time, she would have to be faster than a walking pace.

She flew between the trees with the expertise of a military jet pilot. As she approached the center of the forest the uneasy feeling inside her grew. Upon reaching the place near the little river, she found the ground was unusually scattered with foliage and natural debris. " Oki?" she looked around. Then she noticed a strange pile of leaves on top of something. By the tail she knew it was one of the wolf brothers. "Oki." she ran to him.

He looked to her while she tried to dig him out from under the odd leaves. " It…it is a….trap." he mustered out while the sleep spell was still trying to keep him at bay.

" A trap?" Elsabethe stood up just in time to be thrown against a tree by a very strong slap of wind. The gale was blowing so hard that she could not pry herself away from the bark.

Then, out of the shadows and out of the nightmares of three hundred years, Adel walked toward Elsabethe. Her thin hand was pointed at Elsabethe, controlling the blast of wind.

Elsabethe's eyes widened and she gasped out. "Adel."

☙

Chapter 23: Fighting the Past

Joseph and Allison strolled through a little tent museum dedicated to the festival's eightieth year in operation. After a few of the smaller rides, Allison wished to regain her composure before allowing him to get her on something called a roller coaster.

Joe stopped and looked at a display of posters. They were the first twenty posters used to advertise for this event. " Wow, it sure has changed. No rides, just shows."

Allison nodded. " Yes, back when I first came, there was hardly anything other than big tent events. They paraded animals like elephants, lions, and tigers through a big top. Then they would have some kind of acrobat demonstration. "

" When did they change over to the carnival style rides and all?" He asked her.

She shrugged. " I don't know. I stopped reading about the festival after about ten years."

" 1947." A man answered from behind them.

Joe and Allison turned around to find a man in a classic red striped suit that ringmasters wore. He was smiling and had a name tag which announced his title as keeper of the museum. Joe smiled, " What about 1947?"

" You asked when the carnival rides and all started. It was 1947. The festival organizers wanted to change the event to bring in the crowds. After the war, people wanted more entertainment, and the old acts just weren't cutting it. So, they brought in a whole new event." He smiled brightly at Allison. " Say, that is an incredible costume."

Allison frowned. " What!?"

Joe held her hand and brought her closer to him, so to hopefully keep her cool. The curator nodded. "Yup, that is a fine costume of the mystery girl." He waved his hand at some men at one door. " Come over here, I found her."

A group of photographers came quickly and surrounded them. Several took pictures while others were writing something down.

Joe asked. " What is going on? "

A new photographer snapped another shot, though Allison blocked the camera with her hand. "That was terrible. " He held up his camera again.

Joe stepped in front of her and even put a hand on the first camera he could reach. " What are you doing?"

The curator answered, as kindly as he could. "You see, we were hoping some of the guests would come in costume, but we never imagined that we would have a girl who would dress up as the famous mystery girl."

" Mystery Girl? " Joe asked.

" You mean that she didn't tell you?" He walked Joe and Allison over to a small display about the first festival. " Here she is. " He pointed out a photo. Amazingly enough, there was a blown up picture of Allison. It was a part of the photo that Joe saw in the shop. If you didn't know what you were looking at, you might think that it was just a blotchy picture. " You see, this girl came and everyone thought that she was a prank from the traveling circus. It was quite the scandal. The town brought a formal lawsuit against the traveling circus, but when the trial came, they could not find the girl. Since then, she has simply been known as the mystery girl and among the historians of this event she is famous. "

The Crystal Needle

Allison was looking at the picture, wanting dearly to be able to burn it. That was one of the worst days of her life and now it was displayed for everyone to gawk at. " Joe, I want to leave. "

Joe held her hand. " Yes, I understand." He pushed aside the curator. " Please excuse us. "

" Wait, please, one shot for the paper." The newsman asked.

Allison turned around and yelled. " I didn't want my picture taken then, and I don't want it taken now!"

The people stopped, all confused about that statement. Joe quickly walked her away out toward the rides, getting as many rowdy teenagers between them and the press as possible. He didn't want to fight them, and he certainly didn't want to try and explain what she just said.

" Allison, are you okay?" Joe stopped her and looked at her.

She smiled, though she was still a little flushed. "Yes, I am. "

He held her closer to him. " We can go home if you are uncomfortable here. "

She shook her head. " No. I am still enjoying being here with you. I never wanted to be remembered for that event, but now that I have been confronted with it again, I guess....I'm okay. Now, can we try that big ride you were so enamored with? "

He nodded, and walked her onward toward the roller coaster. The press, fortunately, didn't pursue them. It was likely that they didn't even understand what she said. So they moved on to the other fluff stories during the event. The larger media only sent a helicopter to witness the festivities, as it was nothing more than a simple county fair to them. They never even worried about the odd girl who so closely resembled the famous 'Mystery Girl'.

༶

Meanwhile:

" Sister. It is nice to see you after all this time." Adel strolled toward the tree where she had pinned Elsabethe, her hand still casting a spell of wind to hold her sister at bay. Cocking her head to the side, she asked sarcastically, " Have you nothing to say to your dear sister?"

Elsabethe could hardly breathe under the tremendous pressure. She turned her face to her sister, and said a single word. " Flight. "

" What? " Adel did not understand.

Fortunately, Elsabethe's old broom understood for it flew right for its owner. Its path caused it to slam into Adel, sending her across the ground and breaking the spell.

Elsabethe caught the broom stick with her hand and stood for a moment to catch her breath.

" HOW DARE YOU! " Adel threw her hand out and a bolt of red energy shot at Elsabethe.

Elsabethe quickly held up her broom, which took the brunt of the energy and exploded. Then she pointed at the ground, " Earth. " The soil bubbled up and caused Adel to roll down an embankment toward the old river.

Elsabethe, still a little winded, held out a hand to the pile of leaves. " Dis-spell!" The mound scattered and the wolf was freed, but was still too injured to move.

Oki looked to Elsabethe. " Run." he wheezed out.

Just then Adel came flying through the trees, a mass of water surrounding her like a tidal wave. It gathered foliage and even some branches still attached to trees. She was screaming with fury, riding the wave right for her sister.

Elsabethe stood back with her arms up, "Shield!" She called out and a pocket of energy surrounded Oki, who could not protect himself.

It was not enough to stop the onslaught of the wave. Elsabethe was tossed into the wave and slammed around like flotsam in the ocean. Adel hovered over the new lake and moved her needle around like stirring a great soup. " Toss and turn, tumble and churn!"

Just then, the twisting whirlpool slowed down and nearly stopped. Elsabethe rose up too, her hands folded in front of her while she chanted an ancient Egyptian spell. Shooting her hands upward, the waters evaporated into a mist, harmlessly dispersing into the sky.

" Humans may not do well against such magic, Adel, but witches are a good deal more sturdy. Or have you forgotten whom you are dealing with. THUNDER!" Elsabethe thrust her hand forward and a bolt of lightning came directly out of her palm, flying toward Adel.

Adel sliced her needle in the air and the energy spell was dispersed against the ground. "Oh, I know how to deal with you, old sister. Let us see how you handle this! EDOLPLEX!" The ground under where Elsabethe was hovering exploded straight upward. It was not a single explosion but thousands of smaller ones, impossible to dodge and even harder to stop.

" Reflect." Elsabethe's spell was all but futile, merely sending one of the smaller explosions at her sister as she herself was tossed against a tree, and then slammed to the ground.

Adel laughed evilly at her sister, uncaring of the injuries she might have sustained.

" So weak? What has become of you, sister?"

Elsabethe sat up, not able to stand yet. " I am who I am, your sister and the protector of this world against the likes of you. SWARM!" she held out her palms and hundreds of magical bugs swarmed towards Adel, who swung her needle at them, dispersing them in small groups. Then she held her needle directly over her head. " ECHO!" A large shockwave of sound exploded around her and all the bugs were disintegrated by the ensuing force. After the last bug was gone, Adel slowly let her hand down, " Now I understand. Now I know why your power seems so insignificant to my own. Do you not have your needle? What have you done with it?"

Elsabethe smiled. Her legs were healing quickly and she needed to buy time, so she parlayed. " I have hidden it where you will not find it."

" You fool. Separating yourself from your needle has only ensured my eventual success, and the end of everything you hold dear." She looked up, holding out her arms in victory. "This world has been handed to me."

" So long as the crystal needle is out there, your power means nothing. You can even destroy me, but you cannot destroy it."

Adel frowned at her, " Oh, dear sister, I have no plans on destroying you, not this day. Yes, I will punish you. But your punishment should fit your crimes. It should be equal to what was done to me. I will bind you, here in this damned forest." She stepped back holding out her arms and began to chant a binding spell. It was not the same one used on her, but it would sufficiently bind Elsabethe.

Elsabethe smiled, " Don't think I am finished, not just yet." she slammed both of her hands in to the ground, burrowing her fingers into the soil. " Nature, help me." she whispered.

All around Adel, hundreds, and then thousands of vines shot out of the earth and started wrapping around her. She sliced through vines and disenchanted as much as she could, but they just kept coming.

Elsabethe was able to stand again, her body healed from the slight injuries. Her hands were out, controlling the vines covering her sister. " I may not have my needle, but I am still a witch, and I will not go down without a fight."

Adel was becoming so ensnared by the vines that her counter spells were not doing any good. Her face and her hand with the needle were all that could be seen. " I…will not…be stopped. I…." the vine covered her face and continued up her arm which was held straight up with the needle pointing towards the sky.

Elsabethe focused her mind and considered what to do next. Then, with the heat of a bonfire, a wave of blistering air blasted out from around the pile of vines. The natural twine was seared to cinders by the ball of fire emanating from inside. Adel burst upwards floating in the air covered in flames. " YOU ARE NOTHING COMPARED TO ME!" She screamed across the forest. Simply holding out her arm, the fire discharged from around her in a great wave slamming Elsabethe back to the ground. She was knocked senseless for only a moment, but it was long enough for her sister to complete her spell.

Adel twisted and embroidered a spell over Elsabethe. Just before the last stitch was completed, she leaned in to say a final word. " Pity, if you had just had your needle, I would not be able to do this. Fortunate for me, since I don't have a pack of magic foxes helping." with that and a single stitch in the air, the spell was completed.

Elsabethe opened her eyes and looked at her sister, then spread to the breeze as a pile of leaves.

" So, the crystal needle is gone. Perhaps that foolish boy and his ugly dog girl know where I should start looking. Goodbye, sister." She left the forest for the first time in three hundred years, with the same mission she had entered it all those centuries ago.

☙

" Wow, that was exciting!" Allison proclaimed for the seventh time after having finished her first ride on a roller coaster.

Joseph, who was trying to calm her down, pulled her along. " Yes, they are quite something. You should try one in a theme park because they are bigger, faster, and have more loops."

She smiled at him her eyes wide, " Surely they are dangerous with so much motion and turns?"

He laughed, " No, they are safe. Only a few have died while riding and those that have were doing something foolish. They are as safe as riding in a car, probably much safer. Now, why don't we....what?" he noticed her enthusiastic attitude was gone and she was again hiding beside him.

She pointed to another part of the area. " They are staring and laughing at me."

" They are n..." he was about to disagree, but he saw a group of teens pointing and mocking her. Several looked very familiar to him. " Oh, I see."

" Let's leave." Her first reaction was to just get away.

Joe smiled, " No. Let's give them something to stare at." He took her hand and kissed the back of it.

This only elicited barking and cat calls from the idiots. One even yelled out, " Why don't you hump her leg!"

Before Joseph could answer that absolutely disgusting comment, Allison looked at them. " I recognize that voice."

To Joe's great surprise, she stepped away from him and walked right toward the group of gawkers. Several of the boys simply laughed and stared unashamedly. One, the one who yelled at them, stopped having such a good time. He had a memory of this woman and what she could do to a fool. He even rubbed his shoulder where it still hurt.

" Oooh, Max, she likes you." one of the younger boys snickered.

She smiled at him, " Wanna dance?"

Max stepped back, " Uhhh."

" Boo!" she jolted her body in his direction, which caused him to flinch and turn to dash away. He twisted his feet and fell face first against the ground. Without looking back he scrambled to get up and finish his cowardly run.

" Ha, MAX! What's wrong?!" another kid yelled.

The group continued to laugh at their friend, which only displayed the true nature of these 'friends.'

Another said. " Max is scared, of a girl. Ha Ha Ha."

They all chortled about their own foolish comments, not exactly looking at Allison yet. She stood there, glowering at them and not budging an inch. Soon enough they all looked at her, realizing exactly how severe her gaze was. The laughter dwindled into snickers, then coughs. The whole group of people could hardly make eye contact with her.

" I would run if I were you." she growled at them.

Without another snicker, stumbling over each other in their haste, they ran off.

Joseph, who was watching this with great of curiosity, walked over to her. "That was impressive. You have changed."

She looked back at him with the same firm posture but a victorious smile. " You gave me a lot of courage." She didn't tell him that if that hadn't worked, she was ready to put herself in his arms, a win/win for her.

He took her hand, which was trembling, and walked her back toward their next destination. " You are something else."

" Can we do something that is in less of a crowd?" she asked, the butterflies in her stomach coming to the surface.

Joe held her closer, " Sure. Why don't we give the Ferris wheel a ride. We should be able to see the whole town from the top."

☙

Chapter 24: The Search Ends

William, having finished filing all the tax information he needed to file for July, walked around the house to lock the windows and back door. He was eager to get to the festival as he too was a carnival ride nut. His wife couldn't stand the rides, but he loved them and passed that along to his son.

" What on earth?" he was latching the back door shut when he saw what looked like lightning outside of the house. " I hope it isn't going to rain." He opened the door again and stepped out to check out the skies. To his surprise, the sky was as clear as it had ever been. There was not any lightning or thunder anywhere and the winds were as calm as the sky. " Strange," he muttered to himself and walked back in to lock the back door.

Pushing that oddness to the back of his mind, he went to lock the front door. He stopped just before actually latching the old style lock and picked up the photo of Joe and Allison that was still sitting on the bookcase next to the door. William looked at his son and the girl with him. He had absolutely no idea why his son really cared for this girl; that was something that only Joe could understand. He was proud of him, though he never said it before, but he found that Joes taste in girls was unfortunate, at best. Now, there was something sparking in his son that William had not seen before. Perhaps his son was growing up.

At that moment, the front door chimed.

"Now who could that be?" William set down the photo and turned on both the porch light and the lamp next to the door. Sure enough, there was the shadow of a woman standing in the doorway. He opened the door to find a woman dressed in a black dress that was very Victorian. Her hair was up in a tight bun streaked with dark and light grays. And her face could have been borrowed from a raven it was so severe and sharp. " May I help you?" he asked as nicely as he could.

She smiled to him. " May I enter?"

" Please do. If you are planning on booking, we have space available for next month, I am afraid this month is filled." He went over to get the book for registration.

" I have no intention on staying here. I was just curious as to what you have done with my house." She walked in, her pointed heels making a harsh sound against the wooden floor.

William set down the book. " Oh, so you must be Elsabethe's sister. It is nice to meet you. I hope you like what we have done with the old place." He approached her with a smile. He resisted saying 'but I thought you were dead' as that might sound rude. She didn't say anything, remaining silent while she looked around. So William filled the void by amiably telling her some of the work done on the house. " It took a lot of work to bring it up to code. I replaced all of the flooring with much newer wood and changed out the windows with weather proofed windows, to help with heating and cooling. And...."

" It is repugnant. Such a waste, but humans always do things that are unnecessary." She finally retorted.

"Excuse me?" He wasn't sure if he had heard that right.

Adel continued to look around, "Tell me, where is your son?"

"Joe? What do you want with him?" William was starting to not like the attitude of this woman.

She turned to him with her steely gaze, "Tell me, where is the boy who is called Joseph and the ugly girl with him?"

"I am sorry, but I am not telling you where he is until you tell me what you want with him." William's paternal instincts turned on and would not turn off.

Adel let out an annoyed sigh, "I want nothing with him. But he knows of something that I need, so does that girl. Now tell me where are they?"

"I am not telling you anything. Please leave." he pointed out the door.

She smiled at him, "Do not set yourself against me, foolish mortal, or I will do unkind things to you. Simply inform me of their whereabouts so that I might inquire as to where the crystal needle is."

"Fine, if you aren't going to leave I will contact the authorities." he pulled out his cell phone to call the police.

Adel turned with a shot, pulling out her obsidian needle in the motion. The end produced a black thread that flew about in the air. "Be stitched down." she said this and the thread encompassed him, tethering him to the couch. Then the thread penetrated his body and forced him against the fabric of the sofa. Soon, he was pressed into the material and became a piece of stitching, bound down like a quilted block, his body becoming two-dimensional. He wasn't dead for he was still able to see what was happening, but he was not human any more.

" You humans need to learn your place." She looked around freely for any evidence of how to find Joe and Allison.

To her great surprise and delight, she found a photo on the top of a book case near the front door. It was the picture that Marla had taken before they left on their date.

" Such a wonderful painting, surely this is a clear and recent image." she looked deeply into it. Her eyes fixed on the heart attached to Allison's dress. Only the magical eyes of a stitching witch could see the clear crystal needle in the image. " There it is."

Just then, the cell phone that had been in Williams hands began to ring and vibrate at the same time. It was now on the floor next to Adel's foot. She picked it up, curious as to what this device was. " An alarm system, or a way to communicate?" she turned it over and found the face of the phone was displaying the name of the caller, 'Marla'.

" Ah, the wife and mother of dear Joseph. Perhaps she will be more forthcoming with her information." She held out her needle toward the kitchen. A broom floated in from the nearest closet, a plastic model with yellow bristles. She held the broom between two fingers like one might hold a dirty diaper. " What have the humans done to the art of broom making?" Shrugging off the strange broom, she mounted it as she would any broom. She then held out her needle. " Take me to this Marla."

A red ball of energy shot out from her needle and blew apart the door of the house. She flew off in a gust with the obsidian needle guiding her, taking her directly to the festival.

ஐ

Chapter 25: Sweet Expectations

" Hey, Joe!" Marla called over to her son, who was walking down the shop row with his girl in hand.

Joseph strolled over to his family's booth. It was a simple tent with a sign for the bed and breakfast on display. A pile of brochures and pictures covered half the table, while jars of apple, pear, and peach butter were stacked to the other side. A festival patron picked up a flyer after buying a jar of the unique peach butter.

" How's business, mom?" Joe spread some apple butter on a cracker for Allison to try.

Marla let out an exhausted sigh, " Been doing fine. These locals have never heard of peach butter before and they are crazy for it. I guess southern comfort can be canned and sold up north."

Allison tried the apple butter with a bright smile, " Oh, this is wonderful. What do you call it?"

" Apple butter. An all-too-sweet treat for toast." Marla answered. " Have you never tried apple butter before?"

" No, I would remember something this nice. I have tried apples, since they first came to these shores and were planted in the forest where I live." She was so excited she forgot herself.

Joe's eyes widened. " Uh, what she means is that she has tried apples, but not apple butter."

" I got that. You don't have to translate." Marla stopped and smiled at her son,

" You know, you are a cute couple. I wish your father would hold my hand like that some days."

" What, dad isn't as romantic as you want him to be?" Joe stated in an obviously mocking tone.

The Crystal Needle

Marla rolled her eyes, " Your father wouldn't last five seconds before he was off to watch football, or to fix something on the house. Oh well, I guess romance is dead for us."

" I am sure that your husband still loves you." Allison took up another cracker to try the peach butter.

Marla laughed, " Oh, sweetie, I didn't mean it that way. Will loves me; he just doesn't show it like he used to back when we were your age." she looked around, " Where is that man anyway? He was supposed to be here half an hour ago."

Joe looked over the top of the crowd, trying to see if he could pick out his father. " I don't see him. Maybe he got some calls at the house."

" He had better get here, I am not running this all by myself tonight." Marla frowned at no one in particular.

" I can help for a while if you need me." Joe started to come around the table.

His mother stopped him, " Nope, I have something special planned for you two."

Allison looked up, " Us? What?"

Marla smiled with that sneaky face that always made Joseph worried. " They are having dancing contests all night. In about ten minutes there will be a ball-room dancing contest on the main floor just in front of the stage."

" Mom." Joseph whined like a child.

Marla ignored him, " I remember that my son was showing you some pretty nice dance moves that one night." She waited while Allison eagerly nodded. "Then he can certainly lead you to a victory in one of their dance contests."

Allison was eager, " Oh, that sounds wonderful."

The Crystal Needle

Joe slumped his shoulders. " You just love embarrassing me, don't you?"

Marla nodded, " It's a mother's job, honey. Besides, it will be romantic." she patted his pouting face.

Allison held onto his arm, " Is this like the dancing you showed me?"

" Yeah. Don't worry. You will be fine. Come on, or we will be late." Joe pulled her along with him.

Allison leaned into him and whispered, " We don't have to."

He smiled, " I would love to dance with you." He didn't say it, but he always pretended to be embarrassed at his moms actions. Besides, it would be romantic, as long as he didn't step on a toe.

ঔ

Yoshi ran as fast as his fur could handle. Soon enough, he was at the festival and had to slow down so that he could find his sister.

The festival was full of people and it would be hard for an untagged dog to get around without drawing too much attention. But he didn't have time to figure this out. He had to find Yuki. It was imperative. So, he did what he knew would give him space, he spoke.

" YUKI!" he called out as he walked into the thick of the people.

At first, people looked at one another to figure out who had called out this name. Yoshi pushed between people and did his best to sniff out his sister.

" Sister! Yuki!" He called out again and again.

The Crystal Needle

Soon enough, people's eyes widened and stood back from the talking dog. Gasps were followed by " is that dog talking" or " this must be a carnival stunt". Some even looked around for the person with the microphone.

Yoshi could care less, as long as they didn't get in his way. " Yuki! Adel is back!" he ran faster in the crowds, frantically looking for his sister. All the smells and the people were making it hard to track her.

" Hey, come back!" a security detail from the festival followed the dog, not wishing the beast to be loose at this event.

Yoshi saw them coming and started running faster. He wasn't paying close enough attention and one got right in his path. He skidded to a stop just before crashing into him. The man was going after him like a wrestler wanting to pin their opponent.

Yoshi growled while he announced. " Get out of my way."

The guard's eyes bugged out, but he was still trying to stop this creature. " I don't know what you are, but you have got to go."

Yoshi had enough. He made a perfect leap with his four paws bounding right at the guard. He head butted the man in the gut and toppled him over. Then Yoshi continued running through the thick crowds.

ಬಿ

Joseph and Allison walked toward the stage where they would, possibly, compete in a dance.

Allison looked up, " Oh, look, the sun has set. A shame really."

" Why?" Joe looked up to the orange and dark blue sky, with a few early stars beginning to peek out.

She stopped for a moment and pulled out the crystal needle from her dress. " It has been so long since I was able to see a blue sky as a human. After tonight, I shall forever be a dog by day. This spell can only be cast on me once."

" Oh, I sort of forgot about all of that. I guess I will have to get used to it." He knelt down and picked up a rose that had been dropped by someone. It was only the flower head, the stem had been cut off. "Here," he held it out for her.

She took it and smiled, " You're just too sweet. But something like this should be on a man." she held the rose against his breast pocket and pinned it with the crystal needle.

He looked down, " Thanks, but I don't usually wear flowers."

Allison put her hands on his chest then leaned in to smell the flower, " Perfect." she didn't say that she took a little pleasure in feeling his chest while she did this.

" What happened to that heart?" He looked around the ground.

Allison smiled, " When the spell was over, the heart vanished. "

Just then, they heard the sound of cloggers on a stage nearby. Joe took her hand, " Come on. Let's see if we really want to do this." They joined the large gathering and waited.

The crowds around the dance floor all applauded the group of professional dancers that had just finished a traditional Irish jig.

The announcer came over the mic, " Thank you. Now, for the second dance contest. Any brave souls out there for a good waltz." The man looked around at the people who were not jumping at the idea of a dance contest.

Joseph held onto Allison's hand firmly, so that she didn't slip away from him. He walked right out onto the dance floor.

" I see we have a brave pair here. I guess just one couple. What would you like to hear?" the announcer jokingly said.

Joseph turned about and surprised him. " 'Radetsky-Marsch number 228' please." He smiled while the man at the computer sound system searched his files for that particular piece of music. To his great surprise, he found that exact piece of music.

" Well, ladies and gentlemen, I see that we have a well-trained dancer in our midst. Why don't we see if they are worthy of winning the title as they are the only competitors." the announcer clapped his hands to encourage the crowd to do the same.

Joseph took up Allison's hand with his right hand and put his left on her waist. Immediately, he saw the panic in her eyes. " Don't worry, you will do fine." he softly said so that only she could hear.

" But they are watching." she said so softly that he hardly heard.

" It will be all right, just follow me." The music started at that very moment. It was a lively march with a full orchestra playing the old piece of music.

Together, they stepped to one side then the other, in short hops that fit the rhythm perfectly. Around the floor, as if they were following a group, they danced the waltz with the precision of years of training on his part and centuries of martial arts practice on hers. The humorous amusement of the crowd quickly turned to amazement. Joseph held out his arm and let Allison out in a half spin, then pulled her back in and held her closer to him.

She was so focused on her feet and watching his that she had not looked into his eyes. Joseph pulled her in closer to him, so that their bodies met and she could no longer look down.

She looked up into his eyes with fear still in hers. He continued dancing with her and gave her the most sincere smile he could. " You are doing fine, relax."

Allison began to follow him without looking and only stared into his eyes. The music didn't slow down, but they did as they were still watching each other closely.

" You know something." he said to her.

She smiled, " What?"

" You have the most beautiful eyes." he said again.

She blushed and continued to dance around the floor. " Thank you."

He held her out again and then spun her around with the music, finishing the music and the spin together.

The crowd applauded loudly and the announcer was saying something, but the couple didn't hear him. Joseph looked at her in his arms. " You know something."

" What?" she was never more enamored with him than she was at this moment.

" I love those eyes almost as much I love you." He said this with his heart racing.

She closed her eyes and let him kiss her. They didn't care that they had just won. It didn't matter. The prize they each wanted was something that now was given by the other. The crowds, music, everything of the festival faded away. It was a perfect moment when nothing could go wrong.

All of a sudden, the one sound that broke their perfect embrace also broke through the crowds. " YUKI!"

Allison looked down to find her brother flying toward her . " Yoshi? What on earth are you doing here?" She was angry and worried at the same time.

Yoshi stopped at the edge of the stage. Just then a whole pack of security guards met up with him and nearly dog-piled the dog. He grunted and gasped out. "Sister. Help me. "

Allison frowned and rushed over to them. "Please, he is with me. "

The guards started to remove themselves from the dog, the leader looking at her. " Is this thing you're doing?"

Allison took offense at that. " This 'thing' is my brother."

The guard didn't understand, or even try. " hope you know that wolves aren't pets around here. I am going to have to take you in."

Yoshi interrupted. " Sister, Adel, she has returned."

" What?" she was so confused that she wasn't sure if she heard him right.

The guard angrily approached her. " Young lady, are you listening to me?" He had his finger pointed in her face.

She grabbed his wrist and twisted it so that he could do nothing but come down to one knee and cringe in pain. His only response to this was " Ow ow ow ow."

Allison leaned over to him and calmly stated. " I am going to listen to what my brother has to say, then I am going to see what needs to be done. You are going to leave, or I will harm you further."

He nodded quickly and she let go. Allison then knelt down to her brother. " What is so important, Yoshi? "

Yoshi repeated himself. " It is Adel."

Allison became a pale white. Joe asked. " Adel? You mean that witch from the story?"

Yoshi nodded quickly, " She is back and is she ever mad."

" Oh, no. Joseph, Yoshi, we must get back to Elsabethe." Allisons deepest fears were coming true.

" I am afraid that would be futile." Adel's sinister voice came from over their heads.

With gasps from the humans, growling from the wolves, and panic from Joe, they all looked up to see the witch on her broom floating calmly over the festival.

Allison stepped up, " Adel, what have you done with your sister?"

" What had to be done. As with any traitor, she has been dealt with. Now, where is the crystal needle?" As she came down closer, the crowds parted and most ran.

" I will never give it to you." Allison stepped back, knowing what her brother was doing.

" Fine, you die first." Adel reared back to cast a bolt of dark energy at Allison.

Just then Yoshi jumped up and grabbed onto the end of the broom, using his weight to sling it around.

"OFF, DAMNED DOG!" Adel swung the broom around.

"This is for father!" Yoshi leapt onto the broom, jumped up, and bit down on Adel's right arm, aiming for the hand holding the obsidian needle.

Adel screamed and grabbed at the dog to get him off. Unfortunately, she retained her grasp on the needle.

Joe took the opportunity and ran, "Come on, we have to get out of here." He grabbed Allison's hand and pulled her along. She didn't resist and ran with him.

The crowds were scrambling and fleeing as fast as they could. Local security guards were coming in with guns ready. Unfortunately, they had no idea what they would be dealing with.

Adel lifted her shoulders and let a bolt of lightning run through her body and blast the dog off of her. Yoshi was thrown to the ground and then tumbled away with the residual energy crackling through his fur. He was on the ground as good as dead.

ೞ

"MOM!" Joseph ran with Allison to his family's booth.

People ran every direction frantically. Some were looking for their loved ones before fleeing; others were just trying to get away from the festival center. More than once, someone dashed into either Allison or Joseph.

"Mom! Where are you?" Joe got to his family's booth, only to find his mother wasn't standing there.

"Joe! What is going on?" Marla came out from hiding under the table.

"I don't have time to explain, just come with me." he put out his hand for her.

"Give me the crystal needle!" At that moment, Adel came flying over the tents, heading directly for them.

"OH DEAR GOD, WHAT IS THAT?!" Marla screamed and fell back out of shock.

Allison took a fighting stance, though it really didn't mean much against an onslaught of magic. Adel pointed her needle at them, "DIE!" she screamed and a blast of black shadowy magic shot out.

As if time stood still, Joseph watched the magic heading for Allison's heart and he knew exactly what he would do. "Allison!" Joe screamed as he leapt out to intercept it. The black energy hit him hard and threw him against Allison and they both were sent tumbling along the ground.

Five police officers, called in for backup, came running down the other end of the now empty tent row. They took up a position between where Allison and Joseph fell and the attacker. The officers produced their weapons and prepared to defend the citizens from this person.

"Stop... whatever you are!" the leader commanded.

Marla grabbed Joe's arm and pulled him under the table. Allison went under as well.

Adel smiled at the officers, "Humans and your pathetic weaponry. When will you learn to stop playing around?" She rose into the air and held out both arms, each hand filling with red magic.

"Fire." the commanding officer called out. They sprayed her with bullets, but it was no good. She had surrounded herself with a force field.

" Pathetic. NOW BEAR WITNESS TO REAL POWER!" her voice boomed over the landscape.

Both balls of red energy flew out and slammed into parts of the festival. One blew apart all of the food court in a single blast, while the other met the center of the large Ferris wheel and caused it to explode and fall over onto the roller coaster, both rides reduced to rubble.

" Now for you." she pointed her needle at the police officers, who were still trying to fire at her. With a slicing motion of her arm, the ground beneath them exploded upward, sending them flying through the air in all directions. She didn't want to kill all of them. She wanted some to run in fear and to spread that fear further and further. The reign of terror would begin here and now. When she ascended to power over all this land, they would have a healthy respect of her power.

༇

Chapter 26: Death

Joe's eyes were blurring and he could hardly breathe. He looked up to see an Allison he had never seen before. Her face was no longer covered in fur, and she had the most beautiful red hair with perfectly porcelain skin. Her hands against his face were soft and gentle, not rough as they had been. " Allison, you're so beautiful." He whispered as blackness filled his eyes and he no longer was with them.

Allison cried, the same way she had when she first realized that her father was gone.

" Oh, my son, no!" Marla cried too, putting her head on his chest.

Allison held her hand on her face, to wipe away the tears. To her great surprise, she was no longer furry. Opening her teary eyes, she looked at the back of her hand. It was as it had appeared over three hundred years ago. " What? This cannot be." she could not understand, but somehow, she was no longer cursed. She was once again a Kitsune.

Looking up with a shot, she sensed what was coming. With a quick motion of her hand, she created a force field around them. The tent was torn away in a fiery blast, but they were saved from any of the heat.

Adel sat on her broom, astonished at what she was seeing. " What is this?"

Allison stood up, cowering no longer. " You have lost, Adel. You lost the day you killed my father, and you will soon learn the fury of the Kitsune." With both hands out, she caused a great wind to carry her up into the air and knock back the witch on her broom.

Adel turned her broom into the prevailing winds and headed straight for Allison.

" Oh, little girl, I doubt you fully understand whom you are dealing with."

Allison took in a great breath, closing her eyes to chant an ancient spell of her people. With a monstrous blast, she let loose a stream of flame from her mouth and caught the witch by surprise. Adel was thrown clear across the festival grounds and landed with a crash in the burnt, bent remains of the amusement rides.

With a feeling of victory, Allison flew towards her enemy. Suddenly, the metal remains of the Ferris wheel and roller coaster lifted from the ground, carried by a torrent of wind and red energy. A support beam from the Ferris wheel slammed into Allison and knocked her to the ground.

Adel stood up on a flat sheet of metal from one of the destroyed carriages, riding it into the sky. " I do not die so easily, child. I am over three thousand years old, and I will not be taken down by a pup." She threw out her hands and shot a blast of electricity.

Allison, now standing, twisted and caught the energy like a great rope and held it at bay. " You may have age, but I have training the likes of which you have never known." She shoved her arms forward and the energy was thrust back at its creator. Adel was ready for this and was not shocked by the attack, letting it go into nothing.

" Let's see you fight all of this." Adel's eyes turned solid black. The remnants of the rides were joined by the rest of the debris, forming a funnel of refuse twisting around Allison.

Jumping from one flat surface to another, Allison dodged heavy chunks of metal with each leap. She could not seem to gain any ground on the witch, only managing to keep herself alive. Occasionally, she shot a blast of energy in the general direction of Adel, but these attacks did little good. Adel simply reflected them away with swipes of her needle.

༄

A news helicopter flew toward the massive funnel of metal. They were assigned to simply fly over the festival and take some footage for the news tonight, but they were getting the story of a lifetime.

Inside, the pilot worked furiously to keep the vehicle from being tossed out of the sky.

" Henry, are you getting this?"

The videographer tried his best to focus his camera on the people apparently in the middle of this mess. He had the entire side of the helicopter open so he could practically hang out of it to get the best shots. The image seemed to show a girl jumping from part to part in midair, all the while shooting some kind of lights at something else. But each time he tried to focus on the girl, the helicopter would jolt and he lost the shot. " Hold it steady, Jim. I have to get this. It's unbelievable! "

The helicopter was thrown around, but the pilot resettled it pretty well. " What is going on down there? All my electrical instruments are going crazy."

Henry stopped focusing the camera, " What? No!" he tried his link to the station, hoping to be getting this live on the air. It would be his best story yet. " Damnit, I lost contact."

"Oh, my god, what is that?!" The pilot saw Allison shooting magic bolts at Adel. Unfortunately, the helicopter was at the wrong place and definitely at the wrong time. Before the camera man could try another shot, a large part of the roller coaster slammed through the tail, sending the whole thing into a spiral that would crash in moments.

෴

Seeing this, Allison realized Adel's attention was diverted. She used this momentary lapse to her advantage. Jumping to a pair of cars from the coaster, she kicked off them with a magical leap, causing the cars to shoot away from her at accelerated speeds. The cars were heading right for Adel while Allison was headed right for the spiraling helicopter.

With a precisely timed motion, Allison flew through one side of the helicopter, grabbing both men with her hands and dragging them out the other side before it crashed into another section of the Ferris wheel. With a dramatic explosion, the helicopter was no more. Allison threw the men toward a lake, and then fell into a dive that was perfectly timed for her to land on another piece of flying debris.

Meanwhile, Adel was toppled out of the sky by the unexpected roller coaster cars. She barely rose in time to see the explosion from the helicopter.

"ENOUGH!" Adel was enraged. She pointed her needle at the sky and called out in a titanic roar, "RAIN OF THUNDER!" A brilliant white light shot out of her needle and spread around the spiraling debris causing electric sparks and explosions.

Allison could not escape this onslaught and was caught by the fury of the spell surrounding her as her world turned black.

෴

Marla leaned over her son, scared and horrified at his apparent death. She was so distraught that even the battle behind her was a distant thought. What could a mother do at a time like this but weep?

" Mother of Joseph." a strange and weakened voice called out.

Marla lifted her watery eyes, " Who…who is there?"

A wolf crawled over to her, dragging a hind leg that was broken. He was bloodied all over and one eye was swollen shut. " Please, listen to me. We have to get back to the forest."

" What..who?" she was stunned and still very distressed.

Yoshi took a hard breath and collected himself. His eyes fell upon Joseph, in particular the needle still pinned to his chest. " Take the needle, now."

Marla was confused. " What?"

" The needle on the rose, take it. It will help us." Yoshi finished crawling to Josephs side.

" Will you hurt me?" Marla was so terrified that it her chest ached.

He shook his head, " I am here to help. Just do what I say, please take the needle."

Marla looked at Joseph's chest where the rose was. The flower was dead and wilted from the magical blast. She pulled out the needle. " What do I do?"

Yoshi closed his eyes, " Take your sons hand and say exactly what I tell you."

Marla took Josephs lifeless hand, " All right."

" Home we go, in a flash as white as snow." He recalled this old spell that he had learned when he first came to the English world.

The Crystal Needle

She held tight, " Home we go, in a flash as white as snow." She had no idea what she was doing, but she did it exactly right.

In a marvelous white light, they were taken away from the festival and sent home.

※

Allison was lying on a flying piece of the debris, semi-conscious, and doing her best to think of a spell to save her, or at least stop Adel. She could hardly lift her arms, for the shock to her system was still too fresh.

" Joseph," she whispered.

※

Marla, Yoshi, and Joseph appeared at the first step up to their home. Yoshi was in so much pain that he could not lift himself and simply laid his head on Joseph.

Marla, still holding the crystal needle, was in shock. " What happened? Where are we?"

Yoshi took a raspy breath, coughed, and then answered. " We are at the place that is home to you. "

" But....how?" She was beginning to lose what little composure she had left.

Yoshi cleared his throat. " Take the needle to the trees."

" But…"

He became fierce. " NOW!"

Marla looked down at her son, then at the needle. Somehow, she wanted to believe that this would save him. So she stood and walked between the two ancient homes and held out the needle.

A pleasant laughter echoed in the trees and a great gale rushed the edge and twisted around Marla.

Yoshi closed his eyes with a smile on his face. He had done everything that he could. He may never see his sister or brother again, but at least he had tried his best.

☯

Adel was flying within the debris cloud, unafraid of its danger. " Now you understand what this all meant. Now you see that you never stood a chance against me. Where is the crystal needle?"

Allison turned to face her enemy one last time. She wanted to say so much, but all that came out was "Joseph."

" Joseph? Give me the needle and I may spare your life."

Allison smiled, her mouth working better now. "You have taken my father, and now my love; you cannot take anything else that would warrant that information. You cannot defeat me, even in death you won't defeat me." She actually laughed in the face of this woman.

Adel was furious, " Just like your father, so much ego, so many flaws. Now, you will die. Just-Like-Your-Father." Leaning back she poised herself to cast a final spell to destroy this girl.

At that moment, thousands of leaves streamed into the cloud of debris. There were so many leaves that they blocked out the sun and encompassed the two rivals, swarming like an angry hive of hornets. As quickly as they came, they left having got what they came for.

" MY NEEDLE!" Adel immediately realized her right hand was empty.

All at once, the debris began to rain down, the spell holding the tornado in motion was broken. Adel fell to the earth, surrounded by the damage she had caused.

Allison fell free of the last unidentifiable chunk of metal she had been lying on. But, unlike Adel, she was carried gently to the ground by the flood of leaves. Like thousands of gentle hands passing her along, she was moved toward the earth. Carefully, the leaves set Allison on her feet. Then, the leaves came together in a massive movement, turning into the kind form of Elsabethe, smiling and holding the obsidian needle in her hand.

Allison, who was slowly coming out of the shock of the electricity in her system, became aware of what had just happened. She ran to Elsabethe with her arms open.

" Ba-chan." she called out, which meant grandmother in the Kitsune's tongue.

Elsabethe hugged the girl, " Oh, my dear, it is finally over."

Allison, holding onto Elsabethe's shoulder, walked out of the mess.

Just then, Adel rose from the ground, angrier than ever and actually hurt this time. " I WILL KILL YOU YET GIRL! DEATH!" she held out her hand and another black ball of energy shot out at Allison.

With a swift motion, Allison instinctively turned and pointed her finger at Adel,

" Reflect."

The spell flashed off of the mirror of protection and returned to its creator. Adel was not expecting this turn of events and the death spell hit her dead in the chest. She stumbled back for a moment then looked at her sister in dismay. Her own hatred had finally taken her own life. Sighing her last breath, Adel turned into hundreds of thousands of pieces of thread and blew away in the wind.

Allison looked at Elsabethe, who was in a state of shock. " Now, Ba-chan, it is over."

∽

Chapter 27: What Love Brings

" This was the scene at the annual end of summer festival in Featherville county yesterday afternoon. Hundreds of guests and workers ran for their lives from an unidentified object that was causing damage." The newscaster showed the shaky image from a local cameraman who was at the festival to get some fun shots and was now running for his life. " Our camera crew in the sky was caught in some kind of tornadic winds that destroyed the amusement rides; News Channel 14's chopper in the sky was destroyed by flying debris. Fortunately, the two inside the helicopter were saved and landed safely in Lake Eureka. All footage from the event was destroyed when the helicopter crashed. The death toll has stopped at only 4, all officers who tried to apprehend a person causing trouble during the incident. Forty-five others were injured and seventeen of those hospitalized. We will have further information….."

Marla shut off the television, still shaken to see what had happened. " This cannot be happening." she said again.

" What was that, hon?" William came into the room, he was pulling another thread out of his shirt.

Marla looked up to him, " I want to wake up from this. My son should not be lying in a bed upstairs in this condition, magic isn't supposed to be real, and we are supposed to be a happy family."

" Listen, dear, we are a happy family. Nothing changed that. I know weird things have happened, but we are still together." William sat next to his wife.

Marla shuddered, " What will happen now? That girl isn't human, Elsabethe is some kind of witch. This is all so confusing."

Yoshi trotted in at that moment. He was sporting a splint on his hind leg that was broken which made him walk strange. He also had a bandage wrapped around his head which was mostly to cover the injured eye. " Do you have any dog biscuits?"

Marla jerked slightly, still startled by the sight of a talking dog. William, who was taking this in stride, answered. " No, but I can get some at the store later."

" Good." he looked at the woman staring at him, again. " Is she okay?"

Marla blinked, " I just can't seem to wrap my mind around all of this. "

Yoshi sat down, his back left leg sort of sticking out with the splint attached. " That is because you're smart."

" Huh?" William didn't understand, and neither did his wife.

" You see the world through the books and calculations that you've learned. Back when I was younger, before I was cursed, people who feared us the most were the most educated, yet they started inquisitions and witch hunts. It doesn't seem logical, but it is true. The more facts you learn, the more you have a hard time accepting something that defies those facts. But faith doesn't require copious amounts of facts. It is a child-like understanding that there are some things you will never fully understand. Do not worry, Mother of Joseph, in time you will accept my sister for what she is, even though you may never fully understand her. Goodness knows I still don't fully understand her and I have known her for over three hundred years."

Marla actually smiled. That made sense in a way. " Sure. But I am still waiting to wake up."

William laughed, " I cannot say that I haven't pinched myself once or twice thinking that I am not really talking to a dog."

" Wolf." Yoshi corrected him.

" Wolf, whatever."

Marla frowned at her husband. " Will, I know that you aren't foolish. Why are you so happy about all of this."

Yoshi was about to answer that, but William spoke first. " Honey. My son is upstairs in a bed, recovering from what I have been told should have killed him. This magical world may be odd, it might even frighten me at times. But it saved his life. My son is alive because of these strange wolves, their sister, and that witch. I am not smarter than you, I know that, but I know that I can accept almost anything that saves my son from death."

Marla was speechless, not having thought of it that way. " You're right. He is alive."

William's smiled at her like a new father, " Yes, he is." he hugged her. "Joe is alive and nothing compares to that feeling."

" I think I will find my brother." Yoshi hobbled out of the room, leaving the happy parents to each other.

☙

Joseph slowly opened his eyes; his left hand was on the top of a dog's head, which was lying next to him in the bed. His right hand was on his chest. He gingerly felt his chest to see if there was a hole in it. He was relieved not to find one.

" Who…what?" He looked around, very disoriented.

The dog lying next to him lifted its head and blinked a few times having just awoken. It was a wolf, one that he recognized immediately. The dog looked back toward another part of the room. " Hey, he's up."

Joe lifted his hand and sat up with a jolt, " What happened? Where am I?.....ALLISON?" His thoughts immediately returned to the moment before his eyes went black.

At that moment, Elsabethe came in with a tray of tea. She was happily surprised to find him awake. "Honey, wake up, " she tapped on a pile of red fur sleeping in a chair across the room. It was a beautiful fox, who got up and stretched out, then changed into a red headed girl.

She came straight over to him, " Joseph." she was very excited to see him up.

He paused and looked around, recognizing the old woman, the room, and even the dog next to him, but he didn't recognize the girl. Then he looked into her eyes. " Allison? Is that you?"

She nodded, " Yes, this is the real me." She took his right hand and held it, so happy that he was awake.

" What happened? Why am I here with a dog in my bed?" He looked at Elsabethe.

Allison shot a glare at her brother, " Oki, get out of that bed."

The dog jumped up so fast he nearly fell over the side to the floor. " But, but, it looked so comfortable."

" Oh, be kind, honey, he is recovering just as much as Joseph here. " Elsabethe poured a hot cup of tea for Joseph.

Joe looked at the girl next to him, " What happened? Is mom okay?"

The Crystal Needle

Allison patted his hand, " Your mother is fine, so is your father. After Elsabethe unstitched him, he was a little disoriented, but…"

" Unstitched? What?" Joe was completely lost.

Elsabethe handed him the tea. " You might want to let me explain. My sister used a twining spell on your father, but he was not actually harmed. I was able to undo her magic. Now that she is gone, her spells are a lot less powerful. Even Oki here was practically unharmed when I got to him. She was so focused on the crystal needle that she didn't really do much harm before finding you and Yuki." She rubbed the head of the unkempt dog next to her.

Joe held his head with his free hand, " All I remember was being hit by something horrible. It felt like a pile of rocks was dumped on me, and…the last thing I thought I would ever see was your face." He looked at Allison, which elicited blushing and a smile.

Elsabethe sat down in a chair near the bed. "You, my dear boy, tried to sacrifice yourself for Yuki here. An act that was amazing to behold. That is what broke her curse."

Allison, who had not be told the whole story yet, looked over to Elsabethe,

" What? How? He has no magic. "

" No, that he does not. But you see, there is a power that no magic can conquer, love. The old fables of a kiss breaking a spell have some merit, only it takes a love stronger than a kiss to truly accomplish anything significant. When Joseph here made the decision that his love for you was greater than his own life, that very moment cut the link between you and Adel and the spell over you was broken." Elsabethe sipped her tea.

Allison looked at Joseph for a moment. What does one say to a man who was willing to give his life for yours? " I…I don't know what to say."

Joe blushed and then joked it off, " Oh, it was nothing. …Wait, if that spell was supposed to kill her, why am I still alive?"

Elsabethe picked up the crystal needle, which was lying on the night stand next to his bed. " That which the obsidian needle does, can never fully destroy the bearer of the crystal needle, and so it is the other way around. The Crystal needle chose to protect you and therefore you became its bearer. The spell was harsh, and it seemed for a moment there that you would not make it, but the death magic wasn't completed because the crystal needle would not allow it."

Allison frowned, " How did Adel die then? She cast her own spell. Would her needle not protect her?"

Elsabethe looked at the obsidian needle, which was in her possession now, " Adel no longer had the obsidian needle. It is true that the needle both can cast its own spells and enhance others' magical abilities. But even without the needle, she still had magic, as did I. Her spell came from her own magic, not the needles. This is why you were able to deflect it so easily. She was foolish and did not believe she could be destroyed. That is why she didn't protect herself well enough."

" What about me?" Oki sat next to Elsabethe. Allison responded, " What about you?"

" Why are Yoshi and I still these ugly wolves?"

Elsabethe laughed, " Joseph here is deeply in love with Allison, not you. But do not fret, with Adel gone, the spell over you will weaken, and in time be broken."

" Or I could fall in love with someone." Oki added.

Elsabethe shook her head, " Well, son, you see every curse can be broken in one way or another, but it is never quite the same. You will have to discover that on your own if you do not wish to outwait the spell."

" Great." He huffed and then turned to leave.

Yuki looked at Elsabethe. " What happened to you? How is it you came to us as leaves?"

" Adel bound me much the same way that we bound her those three hundred years ago."

Joseph frowned, " But it took her three hundred years to leave the forest."

Elsabethe nodded. " When Oki, Yoshi and I crafted the plans on how to use their binding spell, I made sure that we focused on binding her needle first. Without it she was considerably less powerful. Then we bound her. She only bound me. The needle was with you, son. Your mother and Yoshi came back with you and she brought the needle to me. As I have said, the needles are extremely powerful. When I got my needle back it was only a small matter of a disenchantment to release myself. My sister being eager and overly confident was unwise and, fortunately for us, that was her ultimate downfall."

" What now?" Allison asked. " What do we do with the obsidian needle? It is far too dangerous to have around."

Elsabethe looked at it, then to them. " Do not blame the needle for what it crafts. Blame the stitcher. This needle is no more evil than mine, for mine could have been the tool of all this destruction and turmoil had fates been transposed. No, it is time that this needle finds a new host, a new person to carry on its noble mission. It needs to be in the hands of a good stitcher once again."

Allison was stunned. She had thought so disdainfully of that needle for so long that she could not feel anything other than animosity towards it. "Who then? "

" We should discuss this at a later time. Joseph needs his rest." Elsabethe took up the tea tray and walked out.

Allison stayed behind for a moment. She kissed him on the forehead and left with a smile. Joe watched her leave, still trying to understand everything.

༶

Days passed and the news began to tell the tales as though most of the event was just mass hysteria. As Elsabethe pointed out, humans have a way of explaining away the unknown. She didn't need to wipe memories or go explain anything to the authorities they did not need to know. More than once, the police came around to ask Marla questions, but they asked nothing more than what they asked any other registered vendor of the festival. Soon enough, life would move on for this little town and the world will not think of the odd incident that occurred here in Featherville.

The bed and breakfast would open again in a few weeks and they already were fully booked for the upcoming fall and Christmas seasons, so William and Marla were happy. Marla was coming to grips with everything now and she was beginning to like Allison. She could tell that her son was all the happier to have this beautiful girl around. William was sure that it would not be long before they held a nice wedding here in the mountains of Massachusetts.

Joseph spent a few days in bed, resting and recovering. Even when protected from a death spell, one cast with such malevolent intent will cause some injury. Fortunately for him, Elsabethe was good with healing charms and could help him recover. Joseph had spent this time pretty much alone. Once in a while Oki or Yoshi, or both, would come in and ask to sleep at the foot of his bed. They were a curious pair, human in ways, but more dog-like than Allison had been. They seemed more comfortable in their fur. Joe, on the other hand, was worried about Allison. She seemed distant from him, almost distracted when she did come to see him.

&

Allison slowly walked up to Elsabethe's house, enjoying the sunlight today. Each day she walked a little slower in the sun, remembering what it was like to not have this joy. Most people do not understand simple pleasures, those that one cannot buy but can receive any time they search for it. Yet when those pleasures are extracted from life, people soon learn how important and wonderful they are and yearn to have them when you cannot.

In time, she was at Elsabethe's front door. Without knocking, she entered, for she was like family to this old woman. To her surprise, Joe was sitting on the end of the couch, stitching on his long time project. It was an image that she had seen often over the summer.

" Oh! Hi!" she seemed startled.

Joe hardly looked up at her, while he continued stitching on his project. " Hello, Yuki."

" Yuki? You've always called me Allison." She stepped closer.

He continued to focus on his project. " I know. But, for some reason, you have changed."

She laughed, " Yeah, isn't it wonderful. I never thought I would look like this again." She ran her fingers through her long red hair.

" That is not what I mean. You have changed toward me. I wish I knew what I did wrong." He pulled out the last stitch and turned the piece over to bury the thread.

She let out a sigh, " I...I" she looked around in confusion. " Did you finish? I thought you finished that days ago."

He turned it over, the piece still held in the plastic frame. " I had something I wanted to change on it. I thought about this the night I first learned about your real identity. I was inspired, you might say."

" May I see it?" she slowly walked over to him.

He held it out for her. She could see that he had taken out all the stitches on the geisha style hair, and replaced it with a color that perfectly matched her red hair. " Oh." she was amazed, for he had only done this in the last few days.

Joe looked at it with a smile, " I wanted to make her as beautiful as you were to me, even as you were before. And after I thought that the last image I would see would be that beautiful face with that gorgeous red hair, I wanted to put it into the stitches of this piece. This way I would always have something that reminded me of you, even if you did not wish to be with me anymore."

Allison sat next to him. " I'm so sorry, I…I never wanted to hurt you. I just needed time to think."

" Think about what?" he had wanted to ask this for days.

She looked at the stitching, not willing to look into his eyes with so much pain in hers. "Being a full Kitsune again is wonderful, but it has brought back strong memories of my father. He died to protect me. Then, when Elsabethe told me that you were willing to die for me as well, I felt so horrible. I love you. More than I thought I could ever love another. Yet, the thought that you might end up like my father, is too much to bear."

" Allison, I love you. I may be willing to die for you, but I am also very willing to live for you. My life was spared and I intend to spend as much time with you as I can. If you would allow me."

She sniffed, " My life is so different than yours. You're human. Everything is so simple for humans. The magical world is hard and you may be put in harm's way again. And next time I might not be able to protect you."

He set aside the needle work and came closer to her, holding her by the shoulders. " I don't care. There is no tomorrow, no yesterday, only today. We can always worry about what may be and miss what is. I love you, that is enough for me to stay at your side no matter what problems we face. I am more frightened by marriage than dragons attacking, but we will face whatever comes. Do not push me out, please."

Allison looked up into his eyes, something she wanted to avoid for she knew what she would do if she were to see his face. Her heart melted and she could not resist him. Without a request, or another word, she kissed him. He finally did what he had wanted to do for days. Putting his arms around her, he pulled her in closer. The space between them was nonexistent and that was perfect.

She separated her lips from his, mostly to take a breath. With a lover's smile, she looked into his eyes again. " At least now you have a beautiful girl to have at your side."

He smiled back at her, " You were always beautiful to me." She giggled and pressed her forehead into his chest, trying hard not to cry again, this time with joy. He put his head on hers, "You know, being human isn't all that easy."

Just then, another person in the room sighed. Both looked to see Elsabethe standing in the doorway to the kitchen. She was smiling like a parent watching her child's first date. " Oh, you two are just too sweet. "

They slowly let go of each other, embarrassed like teenagers being caught necking on the front porch.

Allison cleared her throat, " Uh, yeah, well, uh, what did you need to see me for?"

Elsabethe, who was still grinning at them, came into the room. She sat in her chair right next to the couch. " My dear, I have a special request for you."

" For me?" Allison was a little nervous, Elsabethe had never asked for anything, other than for her to come and meet this boy.

" Yes. You see you have the heart of a stitcher, one that has transcended three hundred years and much strife. I believe that you are worthy of this task and I know that you will bring it honor and fulfill it at its best."

Allison looked at Joseph, who was just as dumbfounded as she was, then looked back to Elsabethe. " What could you want that is so important?"

Elsabethe picked up a silver needle case next to her chair. She opened it to reveal the obsidian needle. "I want you to carry the Obsidian needle. Be its guardian, stitcher, and keeper of its mission to continue the noble needle arts in all their glory."

Allison, who didn't reach out for the needle, looked shocked. " The obsidian needle? Me? I'm not worthy."

Elsabethe looked at the needle, motionless in the case. " I can think of no other who would be right for this mission. With it, you will be endowed with magic far beyond what you already know. Besides, there are tasks that need young blood to accomplish."

Joseph put his arm around her waist. " It would be an incredible honor. Will you do it? "

Allison felt so strong with his arm around her. She picked up the needle and looked at it. The glassy stone it was crafted from gave off a beautiful hue against the low light of the room. She sensed no evil from it, only calm power. At first she wanted time to think about this, but something started to creep into her mind. She looked into the needle and could sense its power resonating from the core. It was beautiful, like a perfectly crafted master piece of stitching, with every stitch carefully placed. In a strange way it was asking her to use it. The needle wanted to be used for good again and she knew it.

" Yes." She said quietly.

Elsabethe looked right at Allison. " Are you completely sure?"

The Kitsune nodded slowly. " Yes. I will do what Adel was supposed to. I will take this needle and be its host and crafter."

" Good. Now, my dear, you are the stitcher of the obsidian needle. May you always stitch in peace." Elsabethe was so proud of this girl, yet a part of her was very sad to be passing on her sister's needle, for it meant that Adel was truly gone forever.

Joseph looked at the needle, " That is incredible, awesome in the truest sense of the word." He thought for a moment, " Wait, what tasks need young blood?"

Elsabethe cleared her throat. " You see, there was a time when I began to suspect my sisters heart was hardening and becoming malevolent. Though I hoped that I was wrong, I knew that I should do what I must to protect this world from her power. We had crafted some unique and powerful items to help this land, in particular a map. These items could be used for great good, but they also could've easily been used for unspeakable evils. Even in the hands of a human, the map alone could be used to conquer this land without much trouble. Shortly after we met the Kitsune family, I sent these items away into the distant parts of the known land. Now that Adel no longer poses any threat, they must be returned. But finding them could prove to be difficult, for I have tried to locate them in the last few days and something is hiding them from me. You must go out there and retrieve them."

But that is another story.